FILE UNDER: ARSON

FILE UNDER: ARSON

Sarah Lacey

St. Martin's Press ☙ New York

Library of Congress Cataloging-in-Publication Data

Lacey, Sarah.
File under: arson / by Sarah Lacey.
p.   cm.
"A Thomas Dunne book."
ISBN 0-312-13972-1
1. Government investigators—England—Fiction.
2. Women detectives—England—Fiction.
I. Title.
PR6062.A29F54   1996
823'.914—dc20   95-42576   CIP

First published in Great Britain by
Hodder and Stoughton Ltd

First U.S. Edition: April 1996
10 9 8 7 6 5 4 3 2 1

For the old gang . . . this side and that.

1

Saying sorry to a newly buried corpse in a damp and windy graveyard
is not the most constructive way to offer an apology, but I'd left it a
little late for anything else. I'd never met Billy, and up until a week
ago I didn't know he existed, and then when I did, I'd told myself his
problems were none of my business. All of which goes to prove that
where conscience is concerned, things left undone are a lot more
troublesome than the things we poke into when we shouldn't. Billy
had taught me that the hard way, and I knew I was going to have to
put it right before Billy's ghost would go away and let me sleep nights
again.

Communion with the dead is not something I enjoy.

My name is Leah Hunter; I'm twenty-five, dark hair, dark eyes,
and I like my freedom too much to be anything but single . . . besides
which, living solo is an unbeatable way to keep down household
chores.

Solo and celibate are not necessarily synonymous, but the choice is
always mine.

By profession I'm a tax inspector, and I live and work in Bramfield,
the Yorkshire town I was born in, where pubs still sport dartboards
and beer-bellied males are a lot more commonplace than litter bins.

Over the last few months there'd been a spate of fires in and around
the town, all of them arson. Tuesday midnight, three weeks ago, the
cut-price carpet warehouse on the corner of Rutland Street burned
down. Nobody knew old Rosie had sneaked in there to sleep until late
next morning when the fire investigators found what was left of her.
And there wasn't much. I got to know just *how* much from Nicholls
when he brought round a takeaway, Wednesday night.

I'd expected him at eight and he didn't turn up until nine. I wasn't
best pleased but I could tell from both his face and the slightly
crumpled look that he'd had a hard day, and for once I was kind. I

looked at the brown-paper carrier bag dangling from his hand and forebore to ask why he was late. Instead I said sweetly, 'I, uh, thought we were eating out?'

His blue eyes looked at me sorrowfully. I stepped back and let him in.

'So,' I pursued, heading for the kitchen. 'What's the problem? Firebug been busy again?' He followed me with the droopy kind of air a lost dog gets, set the carrier bag on the table and didn't reply. I took that as a bad sign. Romancing a newly promoted detective inspector has its drawbacks.

I squinted at him and fed coffee into the filter machine. He shook his head, peeled off his police-issue waterproof jacket and started to wash his hands. For Nicholls to be that reticent it had to be something bad and I wasn't sure I wanted to hear it. I got out a couple of plates and plumbed the greasy depths of the brown bag. Chow mein with fried rice; banana fritters to follow. And I'm never going to be able to eat either of those things again without remembering Rosie.

Nicholls came and sat at the table and started to eat like he was hungry, which meant he'd been so busy he'd forgotten about feeding himself all day. I exercised a little tact and let him get on with it, which turned out to be very wise of me. It meant the fritters were just a pleasant memory and we'd near emptied the coffee jug before I got to hear about the fire. I was really glad not to have been the one who found Rosie.

Maybe it had been one of the days when she'd had money enough to buy so much booze she never got to feel what was happening to her. I fervently hoped that was so.

Rosie had been around Bramfield as long as I could remember, scavenging the market when the traders had gone home, picking through discarded cabbage leaves and mottled apples, vacantly wandering the streets with a junk-piled pram. Harmless and homeless. She deserved a lot better, like a roof over her head and a bed to sleep in, but the welfare state only works for those who know how to operate it and Rosie hadn't been one of the clever ones.

Catching the arsonist had been high on the police priority list for a while now, and Nicholls, on loan to CID from Regional Crime, had been named the man most likely to succeed. Up until then he hadn't been doing too well. Like he said, every town has its pet fire-raisers, most of them psychologically unstable individuals who get their kicks by watching the fire brigade work out. When arson occurs they're the first to be looked at, and according to Nicholls the Bramfield lot had been looked at very carefully and then some. It had really annoyed him the way they'd all been proved to be elsewhere when the fires started, especially since it meant they were getting to share in all the fun while some unknown did the torching. The success rate left a lot of insurance companies weeping.

Bonfires being a national pastime, arson isn't something that overworries the local citizenry. Until Rosie died no one had been hurt except in their pockets, and at least two local firms had cause to offer up a thank you to St Jude for liquidating stock and destroying account books at one and the same time. As a snoopy tax inspector I knew Inland Revenue had taken a different view. One of those two firms had been smelling decidedly dodgy.

I let Nicholls get on with unloading his angst and tried not to listen too hard to the grisly bits; it wasn't easy but at times like that it's the only thing to do.

When he'd finished I went round the table and gave him a sympathetic hug, after which one thing sort of naturally followed on from another and arson dropped out of mind for a while. He went home around midnight looking a whole lot perkier.

A couple of weeks after Rosie died a local teenager with a childhood liking for matches and a thick file with the child psychology service was charged with arson.

Funny how sometimes when you think a thing has ended it's only just begun.

Two days after the firebug had been locked in a secure unit to await trial, Charlie Fagan rang and said could I drop by his yard to chat about a family problem he thought I could maybe help with. I told him fine, I'd call around at his place on my way home. More confirmation in case I needed it that the road to hell is still paved with good intentions. You'd think by now I'd have learned to recognise the traps Providence sets for me.

I drove into Charlie's Car Repairs a little after five, turned in a neat circle and parked with the bonnet facing back the way I'd come. There was an old bronze-coloured Capri over the inspection pit with Charlie busy underneath it. When I got out of the car he slung a monkey wrench and two spanners up on to the concrete floor and hauled himself after them, short on height and porky, with a monk's fringe of hair grown long and tied in a ponytail to compensate for the baldness on top. He grinned the way he always does – Charlie's trademark – but this time there was something missing, a hint maybe that what was to come didn't sit easy on him. I wondered just what kind of family problems he had. He picked up a paraffin rag and gave his hands a quick rub. 'Kettle's boiled if you fancy a cuppa,' he said. 'Thought we'd have a chat in the office.'

'Uh-huh.'

It's hard to be anything more than noncommittal about Charlie's tea; sometimes it's good, other times I tend to get rid of it when he isn't looking. Right then I trailed after him into the lean-to glory hole, and thought about how 'office' was altogether too grand a word for a cramped space that smelled of grease, sweat and stale tobacco, the whole overhung with a subtle hint of mould. I wiped off a chair and sat.

'So what's the problem?' I said.

He messed with the kettle and got picky over the teabags.

I sighed. 'That bad, Charlie?'

'S'bout as bad as it can get. Sister's boy got himself in bother with the fuzz.'

I took a chipped mug from him gingerly and sniffed. Hygiene isn't exactly Charlie's strong point but today the brew smelled of tea more than paraffin.

'Not sure how I can help with that,' I said. 'Legal problems aren't exactly my province.'

He squinted sideways at me. 'Still cosy with that boyfriend of yours, are you?'

'What boyfriend?' I said cautiously. The caution didn't help.

He said brightly, 'That's good, 'cos it's him I want you to have a bit of a talk with.'

'Charlie . . . if your nephew has problems with the police I can't butt in on it.'

'Wouldn't be the first time.'

'That was different.'

'An' so's this; Billy's a good kid. Look, love, you owe me a favour or two. Don't like reminding you about that but a word in your fuzzy friend's ear won't cost.'

That's the thing about Charlie, when he's made his mind up he gets right to the point. I stalled a little.

'A word about what?'

'Them arson fires.'

'They've got somebody, Charlie. It's all over. It was some kid who liked to play with matches. No more fires.'

Sometimes I can be so dumb!

4

'Yeh, well,' he said. 'I know all about that, don't I? Who better? Only the kid they locked up didn't do it, an' that's what I want you to whisper.'

I blinked at him. Shit! Family problems! I shifted around and felt uncomfortable. 'Nicholls is no pushover. I'd need some good strong evidence to convince him he might be wrong. Have you got that, Charlie?'

'Come off it, love. If I'd got evidence like that, Billy wouldn't 'ave been locked up in the first place, would he?'

I took a long swallow of tea and thought about things. Talking to Nicholls might be easy, but trying to persuade him he could ever make an error of judgment is about equal to climbing the Eiger backwards. He has something of a blind spot when it comes to personal fallibility.

Charlie said, 'Look, he's a silly sod, our Billy, I admit that. No slates missing, not backward or nothing like that, just got a bend in his head about fire. Says he wants to join the fire service when he's done growing.' I looked at him, and he looked at me, and then he got round to telling me the rest of it.

Talking to Nicholls over a bar lunch next day wasn't as productive as I'd hoped. I'd thought good food would aid persuasion – how foolish of me. Suggesting Billy might not be the firebug after all didn't please him, he really hates anybody to suggest there's the incy-winciest chance the police might have got something wrong.

'Pyromania,' he said briskly. 'We know this kid has a morbid fascination for starting fires and you want me to let him off the hook? Come on, Leah, Billy started out with matches when he was five and burned down a shed. Went into psychiatric treatment at seven when he tried the same thing on his grandparents' house. A year after that he torched his school. I've read the file, Leah; he wouldn't have been charged if I'd any doubts.'

'Charlie Fagan doesn't have doubts either,' I said. 'And he already told me about that little catalogue of trouble. Billy is now fifteen and what you can't get out of is that he hasn't tried to burn down a damn thing since he was eight.'

'That we know about,' corrected Nicholls smugly. 'No doubt when we've poked around the files for unexplained fires a little while longer, we'll find he hasn't been the good boy his Uncle Charlie thinks.'

'Looking for something to fit him up with, are you?' I said nastily. His face closed up and looked disappointed. I quashed a sudden swell of conscience – Gran always said the truth hurt more than lies. He looked at his wristwatch then concentrated on the waitress's neat tray-balancing act. After that he developed an urge to read the back of the menu. I ignored both ploys and waited for him to get bored with reading where the firm's head office was and how many branches he could eat at. It took around two minutes.

He scowled in my direction.

'OK' I said. 'I give in. I won't ask you to dig around any more if that's the way you feel. Just remember, if you end up with egg on your face, don't blame me!'

'I haven't tried to fit Billy up; there wasn't any need,' he snapped. 'What'd be the point when he's admitted being at the fires.'

'And starting them? He admitted that too?'

'He will. In time.' He stuck his elbows on the table and gave me a hard look. 'Leah, we've got reliable witnesses who can put him in the vicinity of at least eight fires. How do you explain that?'

'How does Billy explain it?'

'Fairy stories. Says he got telephone messages telling him when and where to go. Not much different to a voices-in-the-head routine.'

'He's not a schizophrenic,' I snapped.

'Right. I don't believe he is. But it'd be a good cop-out if he could get away with it. Better than twenty years inside.'

'Billy's a juvenile.'

'So he is, Leah, thanks for reminding me.'

I took a peek at my watch and admired the waitress's skill in balancing her tray. When I picked up the menu and started to read the back of it Nicholls whipped it out of my hand and snarled. 'Fine! I'll look at it again, but there won't be anything new.'

'You made your mind up already? That's nice,' I said sweetly. 'I'll tell Charlie not to worry, you're not only good at your job, you're psychic!'

'Leah . . .'

'No problem,' I said as I got back into my coat. 'Just let me know if you come up with anything interesting, and by the way, proven pyromania is also a defence in law, so forget the twenty years' routine.' I gave him back the same smug look he'd been practising on me.

We halved the bill and went out on to the pavement where I turned up my collar against the wind and listened to Nicholls's little pep talk on how I shouldn't even think of digging around myself, and how Billy's family needed to get used to the idea of him being guilty. I didn't argue; illusions are such nice things to have. On top of which I wasn't filled with any great urge to do more than I had already. A word in Nicholls's ear was all Charlie had asked.

I put Billy and his problems on hold and got back to levying taxes, but around four thirty when I'd caught up on the paperwork he edged back into my thinking again.

Charlie had to be told that Nicholls had a watertight case and I didn't want to be the one to do that. I didn't want to have to tell him that maybe Billy's problem hadn't been cleared up when he was eight, that the truth was he'd just learned to be clever and his story of the telephone calls was evidence of that.

It wasn't something Charlie would want to hear.

And I didn't want him to ask me to do more.

Sleet pebbled the office windows, travelling sideways across the glass, cast to west, whitening the sills. April is the cruellest month, and I didn't see any lilacs around to mitigate that.

I knew Charlie would expect me to do more than just parrot Nicholls's verdict, but that would mean talking to Billy, hearing his side of it so I could make up my own mind about him. I'd have to get actively involved and my mind backed away from doing that. Better if for just this one time I left Nicholls to get on with it.

I stacked the files I'd been working on neatly in their rightful places, gathered up my belongings and headed home.

Walking into my attic nest usually cheers me, but that day was different; depression hovered over my head like a personal thundercloud. I turned on the lights and lit the gas fire, made a cheese sandwich spiced up with chutney, brewed fresh coffee and watched TV until ten.

The forebodings didn't go away.

At ten-o-one I went to bed, foolishly hoping that when I woke next morning all my problems would be solved.

They weren't of course. Life is never that simple.

7

2

Over the weekend the wind had shifted round from north-east to south-west, still frisky but a lot less cold. The fast change in temperature had got the local birds up early and singing loud enough to wake laggards. I stood out on the pavement and took in some good deep breaths.

Most mornings I go out for a run and that day was no exception. I'd gone home Friday with Billy and his problems entrenched in my mind and when I woke Monday morning they were still there. Pounding the streets seemed like a good way to shake them loose, but it didn't quite work out; solutions didn't come to mind and the only decision I made was that I couldn't put off talking to Charlie any longer. Maybe when I relayed what Nicholls had said I'd also find a way to convince myself it was just family affection that made Charlie so sure his nephew hadn't messed with matches again. That way I could let myself off the hook with an easy conscience.

I panted back home just before seven, took a fast shower and then breakfasted, walking briskly down to Dora's a little after seven thirty to pick up my car. Dora is a good friend of mine, a retired schoolteacher who lives a dozen houses away down Palmer's Run. She's pushing seventy but neither she nor her body have got around to admitting that yet. Dora gave up driving a car herself a couple of years ago on the grounds that motoring everywhere would make her fat and lazy. These days she cycles or walks, rents her empty garage space to me for extra pin money and stays beanpole slim.

The car I garage there is unique – one of Charlie Fagan's hybrids – a black Morris Minor shell that hides a BMW engine coupled with a close-ratio gearbox, and that adds up to a lot of speed and power.

Charlie always opens up for business before eight, so when the gates were still locked up tight at a quarter past I started to get edgy. By eight thirty the edginess turned to worry and kept on growing until just before nine when I had to give up and head for the office, taking the worry along with me. It was still hanging around in my head when Nicholls came visiting mid-morning. The cramped-up look on his face warned me he hadn't come with glad tidings, but that didn't make hearing what he had to tell me any easier.

What Billy had done wasn't unique. Half a dozen other young offenders locked up on remand had made the same choice over recent months, and all kinds of inquiries had been going on into the whys and wherefores. The tabloids had labelled it an epidemic of despair. I didn't know if they were right about that or not, but during Sunday night Billy had hanged himself. It didn't matter now whether I wanted to talk to him or not, he'd taken the decision away from me. Fifteen is too young to die. I felt sad, and I felt angry, and the anger spilled out.

I snapped, 'Shit, Nicholls, what goes on in these damn places? What happened to supervision? Do they hire some psycho to come and tuck them in at night with a rope for company? For God's sake, Billy was fifteen and there's a damn good chance he didn't commit the crime you put him inside for!'

He said stiffly, 'There'll be an inquiry.'

'Isn't there always! So what happens now? Case closed and everybody goes home?'

'Leah, be fair. The evidence we had pointed to Billy and it still does; his suicide doesn't change a thing. There won't be any more fires.'

How nice to have such certainty!

'I'd better get back to work,' I said, chilly as an ice chip. 'It's a busy month. Thanks for telling me about Billy.'

He shuffled his feet, shook his head and looked unhappy. Instead of letting it get to me I walked him to the door. Out in the corridor he turned round to face me and seemed on the point of saying something else. I closed the door quietly and didn't give him the chance.

'Nuthin' for you to feel bad about,' said Charlie, avoiding eye contact. 'Asked you to have a word in the boyfriend's ear, an' you did. You done what you could. It's Billy's ma what's got the problem now, knowing she could have got him out on bail 'stead of thinking it'd teach him a lesson.' He stared down at his hands, wiped his fingers on an oily rag and still didn't look at me. 'That's the trouble with kids, i'n'it? Never knowin' what they're going to come up with next except it'll be grief. If he walked in here now I'd half kill him.'

Things I wanted to say bunched up inside me. I'm no good in that kind of situation, I don't know how to deal with other people's misery. I shook my head, 'I just don't know what to tell you, Charlie.'

'Not your fault, told you that.' He gave his hands a final wipe and dumped the rag. 'Got to get on, love, got a bit behind an' all that.' I watched him wriggle back under the car he was working on and started walking away. 'See you, love,' he said.

'See you, Charlie.'

I went back to the hybrid and started up the engine, wondering how long it would be before I got Billy out of my head, and how it was I'd suddenly got so very good at minding my own business. Guilt is a burdensome thing to carry around. I couldn't stop thinking that maybe if I'd talked to Billy and let him know there was somebody on his side, things might have worked out differently.

Even so, if Providence hadn't nudged things along again I would probably still have let the whole sad business end right there.

The nudge came when I went into work next morning and Arnold's desk stayed empty. I didn't fret about that; I like him about as much as a thorn in the thumb, so times when he's absent just brighten the day. Around ten, Pete, my boss, came out of his glass-walled office, put a pink hand on my shoulder and dropped a key in front of me. When he bent his head I could tell he'd been at the peppermints again. He asked nicely if I'd take a look at the files Arnold had in his desk drawer and see if there was anything urgent.

'Sure thing,' I said brightly. 'Get right on to it. What's bitten the blue-eyed boy?'

'Chickenpox,' said Pete.

'Chickenpox?' My mouth stretched into an uncharitable grin, and when I squinted up I caught an echo of it in Pete's overhung eyes. 'Guess he'll be away for a while then?'

'Looks that way. More work all round but that can't be helped. He'll be glad to hear you were this upset about it.'

'I'm all broken up,' I said. 'Want me to start a collection, send him a get well card and flowers or something? A back scratcher maybe?'

Pete's fingers twitched. He shook his head, flattened his mouth and went back to his office.

I picked up the desk key and went to take a look in Arnold's drawers. There were a couple of assessment queries in there that he'd been dealing with, neither looked as if they'd be difficult to sort out, but a third file marked Hold looked a lot more interesting. I carried all three back to my own desk, thinking how it was really foolish to wonder if fate had smitten Arnold with chickenpox just so I'd get to see the Fast-Sell Carpet Company's accounts. I got myself a cup of coffee and started to browse.

Fast-Sell had been operating in Bramfield for only eighteen months although there'd been a cut-price carpet firm in the same premises before they came along. Trade had been so good it had gone into liquidation, which had been nice for the Fast-Sell incomers who'd picked up a lot of stock cheap. Nothing illegal about that; it's good, standard business practice. I checked how much stock the firm were carrying before the place burned down and blinked a little at the size of it. As insurance claims go, Fast-Sell were due to get a big payout.

That wouldn't have surprised me so much if I hadn't taken a walk round the place a couple of days before the fire.

Carpet shopping isn't something I make a habit of, but I'd finally got tired of looking at the green and brown strip in the hall that I'd inherited when I took over my attic three years ago. The expedition to Fast-Sell was a failure. All they had on show was tat, and my busy little brain told me cheap foam-backed acrylics coupled with imported low-price Axminster copies didn't add up to the kind of insurance loss I was looking at now.

I leaned on my elbows and stared at the certified accounts. Deciding exactly what stock had been in there was up to the insurance company's loss adjusters, it was none of my business. All I had to do was make sure Fast-Sell paid their taxes.

Perhaps I'd missed out on something when I went round the place. Like a whole floor maybe?

And maybe the moon was made of green cheese!

I went through the file again, read Arnold's notes, checked purchase and sales figures and came back to the stock figure. It tallied nicely with the stock that should have been in there. The discrepancy was in my own memory, and that bugged me.

I champed down on the end of my pen. The sense of things not quite right is hard to explain; like a lot of other things it comes with experience and right then it was working overtime. The whole thing was just one more bothersome detail I'd have done better to ignore, but, of course, I didn't.

3

I took a long lunch break, flexitime permitting that kind of thing, and went to check out what was left of the carpet warehouse. Most of the outer fabric was standing more or less complete, the thick stone walls three storeys high, windows blown out by the heat and blackened by smoke. Boarding up the lower windows seemed like a sensible precaution – easy access would have turned the place into an adventure playground. I moved on past the nailed-shut double doors and down the narrow back alley that separated Fast-Sell from the meat market. No windows there, just a sheer blank wall and a staff door I expected to find nailed shut like everything else – or maybe I just hoped it would be. Trying to outguess Providence is a big mistake.

The wood was heat-scorched but aside from an initial groan when I turned the handle the door swung open easily and let me see inside. Most of the stuff that had been in there was reduced to ashes, showing the intensity of heat. Fire had funnelled up through the floors burning a central vent. Part of the roof had gone and gaping timbers shone damp from all the April rain we'd been having. I went in cautiously, skirting rubble that had tumbled down from the upper storeys on to the concrete floor.

The smell of burnt wood and soot and the more acrid chemical smell from man-made fibres still hung in the air. Hardly anything recognisable was left in there except for surreal metal shapes that had once been carpet stands. I thought about Rosie and wondered if she'd sneaked in the same way I had, and then I wondered where she had made her bed. It wasn't something I'd intended to think about and the images conjured up weren't welcome. I kicked at a piece of detritus and watched it skitter over the floor to fetch up against a pile of rubble. What did I think I was doing in there for God's sake? What could a burned-out carpet store tell me? Did I expect Rosie's ghost to pop out of some rubbish pile and say who'd torched the place and why? Then I got around to wondering why the damn door had been left open so I could just walk right in.

I was still busy with that when my eye picked up movement. Quietly and without fuss a woman's shape came out of a dark hole on the right where the washroom had been. I jumped a foot, said, 'Shit!' then backed up and sweated a little until the light hit her and I saw she was as solid as me – thirtyish, red hair, freckles and a Burberry mac. She had one of those deep-pitched voices men find sexy. 'Damn,' she commented, 'I didn't lock the door.' We stood and eyed each other up. 'You shouldn't be in here you know,' she said. 'It's definitely not safe.'

'Hum ... yes,' I said. 'Right! Only I have a sort of personal interest in the place, and come to that what are you doing here?'

She fished out a plastic ID that said she was Bethany Mills ACILA of Saxby Associates, chartered loss adjusters, which meant she had every right to be there and I had none. I scrabbled in my shoulder-bag and flashed her an ID of my own.

'Uh-oh, Inland Revenue,' she said. 'So what's the interest? The firm didn't pay their taxes?'

'Haven't needed to; they only just filed returns. I'm poking around unofficially. How about you?'

She shrugged. 'Overkill,' she said. 'I've been around the place twice before, plus there's the fire chief's report. I should have known there wouldn't be anything different this time.'

'Why go to that much trouble?'

'The insurers might want a second opinion. I'd hate for another loss adjuster to find something I'd missed.' We did some more eyeing up. She said, 'Suppose you tell me just what unofficial concern brought you?'

'I got to wondering how and where the fire started,' I said. 'It made me want to take a look around – not that I know what I'm looking for,' I added, opting to be honest for once.

'Want a guided tour?'

'Sure thing.'

I trotted after her and learned a little, like how whoever torched the place had used turpentine and nitric acid to start the thing off, and then made sure of a good blaze by setting up three separate flash points, one near the front door, one in the office and the third just about dead centre.

I picked up a scrap of nylon carpet a couple of inches across, edges singed and melted, turning it over in my fingers and thinking about Billy.

'I don't know if the kid they arrested burned this place down or not,' she said, watching my fingers, 'but whoever did it knew what they were about. It's a thorough job; there's hardly anything left – a couple of dozen pieces of carpet no bigger than the one you're holding. Very professional. I'm told the boy's been fire-raising since he was five.'

'I heard that too. Shame they won't be able to prove things either way.'

'Why's that?'

'He hanged himself.'

'Hell!' she said. 'That's bad.'

'Yes, isn't it though?' I dumped the piece of carpet and dusted off my fingers. 'You said "very professional" – how professional is that? Something an average fifteen-year-old would have at his fingertips?'

'I dunno. What's average these days? You read the papers; you know the only crime juveniles don't get into is politics.' She hiked up her sleeve and took a look at her watch. 'This is the third visit I've made and I haven't come up with anything new, so unless there's something else you specifically want to look at . . . ?' She lifted her eyebrows inquiringly and I shook my head.

'Like I said, I wouldn't know where to start. I'm no fire investigator, I just wanted to get the feel of it.' I did a slow turn and took it all in one more time. 'This supposed juvenile firebug went into therapy at eight years old,' I said. 'Did you know that? Since that time he's been clean. No fires.'

'If that turned out to be true I'd be surprised. Maybe he played with matches and didn't get caught? Who can say? All I know is there's been a whole string of fires around here and from reports I've read there's good evidence to place the same juvenile at every one.'

'That's what I heard too.'

'Hard to explain.'

We headed for the door. I said, 'I also heard phone calls were made telling the kid where to go so he could see a good fire.' She stopped in her tracks, then started off a little bit faster. Bethany Mills was rattled by that piece of information, probably because no one else had bothered to pass it on. Asking her about that got me nothing but a business card with her name and extension number on it.

'Look,' she said, 'if you come up with anything else that might be helpful I'd like to hear about it. Lord knows I haven't picked up a lot of information from this place.'

'As far as information goes I'd appreciate anything you could put my way too.' I gave her a little white business card of my own – it seemed a fair exchange.

'I'll bear it in mind.' She locked up, gave the door a good shove to check some nosy parker like myself couldn't get in there while she wasn't looking, and headed down the alley at a fast pace. I followed on in no great hurry. At the bottom she turned and looked back. I waved nicely and she gave me a quick flick in return. By the time I reached the street she was out of sight.

I grabbed some lunch in the market snack bar and spent the rest of the afternoon righteously earning my salary. At five I went home, washed my hair, cooked a frozen pizza and dined alone.

By rights, it being Tuesday, I should have worked out at the health club and a part of my mind was jumping around screaming with rage that I hadn't. I swallowed down the extra guilt and put my feet up. OK, so I'd slacked off on too many things since a bullet put me in hospital. But it was only temporary. I'd be back into my stride in no time flat.

Of course I would.

I'd been telling myself that for a long time now, and no one knows better than I how good I am at telling lies.

4

According to Charlie, Billy's inquest was one of those cut-and-dried, in-and-out affairs that don't take up too much of the coroner's time. Which, since I hear he plays a lot of golf, is probably the kind he likes to get. The verdict handed down was that Billy had taken his own life while in a state of mental turmoil. An interesting conclusion since I didn't remember mention of anybody taking the trouble to actually ask Billy himself much about his mental state at the time.

The funeral was scheduled for Thursday morning and I felt honour bound to attend. I told Pete I'd be taking a day's leave so I could go along and he waxed fatherly and sympathetic, which didn't work since he's not old enough yet to play that role. I ordered a tribute from the florist on Market Street and geared myself up to cope with all the tears and angst I knew would be around.

Wednesday night, feeling uptight and jumpy, I stayed up into the small hours drinking coffee and watching a rubbishy late film on TV. It wasn't the best way to prepare for something I would rather have avoided, but crawling early under the duvet was never any guarantee of sleep either.

Around two I turned off the set, rinsed out the filter machine and flopped into bed. Then I had fun lying around for a couple of hours watching ifs and buts hop around my head like rabbits. All of which meant I woke up late in a fine old grump feeling like someone had dumped a load of sand in my head. I thought about climbing into my sweats and doing some running, exercise being a good way to shake off any kind of a hangover, but the grump in me turned up its nose and headed for the kitchen and a high-calorie breakfast instead.

At ten thirty I changed into a grey suit and low-heeled black courts despite its being an unseasonably warm and sticky day, collected the car from Dora's and drove out to St Adrian's Church. Close family

17

members were there already, but friends were still arriving. I took a seat at the back and tried not to think about my reason for being there.

Billy's coffin stood lonely in front of the altar. I stared at it, feeling invisible threads of responsibility wrapping themselves around me and knew I couldn't back away any longer. Maybe when you come right down to it that's what life's all about, getting shoved by some obscure fate from one thing to another without any real say in the matter.

We sang some hymns and prayed a little, Charlie read a lesson and the vicar gave a homily on how God gathers the fairest flowers before they come to full bloom. Then he gave that idea a little more thought and backtracked to tell us what a tragedy it was that Billy had taken his own life. And a sin too, of course, although it would be forgiven. I guess ambivalence is what it's all about these days.

I squinted sideways. One of Bramfield CID's finest was perched uneasily a pew ahead on the other side of the aisle. I wondered if he was there from guilt or nosiness. His eyes shifted around, flitting from mourner to mourner. Definitely nosiness. Gratified, I stashed the knowledge away to annoy Nicholls with.

By and by it ended.

The church emptied out after Billy's coffin. Charlie saw me standing by the freshly dug hole and gave a little nod. Billy's mother and her two younger children didn't look at anything except the wooden casket.

Shit!

My eyes heated up with sand and I looked away fast.

It was going to rain; the sky had that uneasy, funny kind of glow about it and the humidity was creeping up. I squinted up at patchy blue fast losing ground to flat grey and hoped it would hold off until the burial ended. The vicar seemed to have the same thought. He took a look at yellow-fringed dark grey cloud massing in from the west and speeded up. I was glad about that. Seeing a coffin awash in a grave isn't the most comforting memory for kith and kin to take home with them.

I guess the clergyman's good angel must have been on duty that day. He beat the rain by five minutes which let most of the mourners get back to their cars without a soaking. I told Billy's mother awkwardly how sorry I was and she nodded, having heard it all before, then I passed up on Charlie's invitation to eat with the funeral party, knowing I couldn't have swallowed a thing. The vicar had no such qualms. The sky growled. I made good time to my parking place.

Rain began to fall in shy drops, speeding up as I got into the car and slumped over the steering wheel, resting on crossed arms, tired and dispirited enough to crawl into a hole and sleep for a month, and watched the rest of the cars drive away. I didn't know why I let myself do this kind of thing. A deluge of water rattled on the roof and bounced on the road. Maybe someone would put a tarpaulin over the hole.

I turned on the ignition and drove home.

Sometimes the three flights of stairs to my attic home can be like toiling up a mountain, and it was one of those days. Guilt isn't a good companion to hang around with; for one thing it keeps me awake nights and for another it nudges me into doing things I've been trying to avoid. All through Billy's funeral it had sat on my shoulder and whispered unkindly, and now, despite all attempts at mental exorcism, the sense of things left undone still walked with me. I let myself in and headed for the shower, stripping off and letting the water wash away my sins, coming out wet-footed and padding to the kitchen to get some coffee started. Enough is enough.

I towelled dry and donned a loose-jacketed, olive-drab pants suit that matched my mood, lightening it a little with a white silk T-shirt. My hands were sweating. Damn it! What was wrong with me? I wasn't going out to pick a fight with anybody, I was just going out to ask questions!

I swallowed down two cups of caffeine and ate a banana, then I locked up and went back down the mountain.

Bramfield's fire station isn't the classiest of buildings, being built of brown brick and the same shape as a shoe box, but the fire crews have a response time that would be hard to better. When you come right down to it that's what counts. I tucked the hybrid into a line of cars at the side and went looking for the station officer, picking up appreciative looks from a couple of manly men busy coiling hoses. I eyed up the muscle on show and gave the appreciative looks right back again. Sometimes I think I'm in the wrong line of work.

By and by I found the man I wanted. Five eleven, mid-forties, slightly fleshy, and a name badge that said he was John Redding. I flashed my ID and told him who I was. He lifted his eyebrows up an inch and invited me into a cosily spartan office cleverly designed to discourage visitors. The hard plastic chair had a seat that dipped back neatly so the front acted like a tourniquet. I sat on it gingerly and asked about the Fast-Sell warehouse. He looked relieved that was all

I wanted to talk about. Anybody would think tax inspectors were thought police. It's a terrible burden to carry around.

'Arson burned the place down and there was one fatality,' he said. 'That's common knowledge, so what is it you're asking me?'

'Just feeling my way through a problem. Did anything mark the Fast-Sell fire out as different from the other recent arson attacks on commercial property, or did they all follow the same pattern?'

'Same method used every time? No. Same arsonist? Possibly.' He examined his pen intently. 'Have to hope now there's been an arrest it's finished, won't we?'

'You think there's a doubt about that?'

'There's always room for doubt.'

'The police don't seem to see it that way.'

He spread his hands and shrugged. 'Can't help that.'

'It'd be a help to have a list of local fires where arson was the cause.'

'What would you want that for?'

'There could be a question of tax evasion.' He looked sceptical. 'It happens,' I said. 'Arson isn't solely a concern of insurance companies, although I'm sure you've had their investigators round already. Bethany Mills, for example.' I tried the name out hopefully and got a positive response.

'Astute lady, knows as much about arson as I do. She's been here to talk a couple of times.'

I raised my eyebrows. 'Only a couple? I thought that as the only local firm of loss adjusters, the company she represents would be involved more than that?'

'A lot of insurance companies use Leeds firms as part of long-established practice. And I thought we were only talking about that one fire?'

'Initially maybe, but you know how it is; one thing leads to another, and that's why I need a complete list so I can check it against our files.'

'Off the top of my head or official?'

'The top of your head will do fine,' I said.

He got a sheet of paper and started writing. I watched the list grow.

'I guess you know quite a bit about the fifteen-year-old they arrested,' I said. 'I hear the fire crews had seen him around a lot?'

He stopped writing and set the pen down. 'Young Billy? Now what would there be about Billy to interest Inland Revenue. Explain.'

'I'm mixing business with personal concern. I know his family and his death has knocked them out. They don't believe he set the fires. How do you react to that idea?'

20

'A lot of people follow fire engines. That doesn't make them arsonists.'

'It doesn't answer the question either.'

'Off the record?'

'Between you, me and this nice comfy chair.'

'It surprised me he knew that much about accelerants.'

'Did you tell the police that?'

'I told them, but I couldn't explain how he'd know where the fires would be.' He picked up the pen again. 'Difficult to put that down to coincidence.'

That's what Nicholls had said.

'The way you speak about him it sounds like you knew Billy well?'

'We all did. He's been dropping in here for years, looking at engines, chatting up crews. It'd got so we let him help out; polishing, winding, bits and bobs like that. It kept him happy.'

'Did you know about his background?'

'The three fires when he was a kid? Yes, he told us up front, said he was over it; all he wanted now was to get old enough to help put fires out.'

'So none of the crews officially reported seeing him around at the call-outs?'

He thought a bit. 'It was noticed,' he admitted. 'Not the sort of thing that wouldn't be. But not officially. It was reported to me and I had him in here for a talk.'

'Did you tell the police?'

'I did not. And I'm hoping you won't; it'd be my job on the line.'

'You were that sure he wasn't involved?'

'We can all be wrong,' he said.

Isn't that a fact? I wondered which would be the worst to cope with, Billy guilty or Billy innocent.

'Did he mention getting telephone calls?'

'He thought one of the lads here was tipping him off. I gave them all a good talking to and told Billy to stay home. The next three call-outs no one saw him around, the one after that was Fast-Sell.'

'And he was there?'

'Crying like a kid.'

'Why would he . . . ?'

'Burning flesh has its own smell and Billy was downwind.' He added a final name to the arson list and handed it over. 'I think that's everybody.'

I pushed the vision I'd had of Rosie away, running my eyes down

21

the list of buildings. The fires were more random than I'd thought, business firms, derelict property, a YEB substation and a council equipment store were all represented. I looked up. 'A public lavatory?'

Redding shrugged. 'A fire is a fire to a match-happy arsonist,' he said. 'All he wants is to see the hoses come out.'

'Unless he's after insurance money,' I said.

'In which case,' Redding said carefully, 'I don't think we're talking about Billy.'

The list in my hand seemed to get heavy. I folded it up and put it away, shaking hands with Redding and going back to the car.

Hearing an idea said out loud doesn't make it any easier to handle, especially that one, because when I came right down to it, I didn't think we were talking abut Billy either.

5

I sat in the car skewed sideways, Redding's list flat on the passenger seat, checking off fire locations on the town map. Sometimes such exercises are futile. When I was done I had eighteen little crosses that looked like someone had shaken a pen at random. As far as I could see only a demented monkey would be able to make a pattern out of them.

I put a circle around Billy's home and tried to come up with some logical connection. Cycle paths, bus routes, short cuts. Nothing came to mind. Then I thought about him standing downwind of Rosie's charring corpse and crying, and knew that if he had set the fire, the guilt of her dying could just possibly be a good enough reason for him to want to take his own life.

If he'd set it?

Why else would he cry?

Damn it! I was going round in circles here. If he'd set it, it couldn't be insurance fraud; if it was insurance fraud he couldn't have set it; if he hadn't set it why would he kill himself?

He wouldn't . . . but he had.

Impatiently I started up the car and made a circuitous tour of arson sites. Halfway down the list it hit me that the fires had not been uniformly successful. Some smaller places like the kebab house on Pilkington Street were busy trading again, while in a couple of derelict houses the fire hardly seemed to have got a hold at all. The same pattern of hit and miss continued until I got to the end.

How interesting! Four biggies burned to the ground and the rest hovering somewhere between scorched and badly charred. OK, so a couple of smaller places had burned down too, that still didn't change the overall balance. I folded up the map and put it and the list neatly in the glove compartment, worrying a little about the way some things tend to get more instead of less confusing. The problem was, I didn't understand what I was looking at, but curiosity had begun to settle on me like an unwanted itch. I could feel my mind begin to gear itself, searching out shards of information to fit together into some kind of logical sense.

I sat in the car for a couple of minutes looking at the puddles in the road. The rain had stopped more than an hour ago and the sky was shredding itself, breaking up and letting bits of gold come through. The idea strengthened that something a lot more criminal than random fire-raising had been going on. Close behind came a chill certainty that if that was so, Billy's suicide suddenly became a lot harder to explain. And that idea took me into things I really didn't want to think about at all.

My hands started to sweat again. Damn! I didn't have to do anything I didn't want to do. What in pity's sake was matter with me?

Easy. I was scared.

Such amazing insight astonished me.

I slid the gear lever into first and moved away, took a wrong left turn a mile along the road and found myself back at St Adrian's. Gold hands on the church clock said four thirty, and the only car around was mine. I left it lonely at the kerb and went in through the main gates, crunching over gravel. The oaken doors were fast shut, the whole place deserted, a festive mound of wreaths the only sign of life. I moved towards it, zigzagging between headstones, and thought about how, guilty or not, Billy had to have been scared too.

Hunkered on clay-wet soil I straightened a couple of wreaths, smoothed some petals and rashly declared an intent to get to the truth of things. Such promises are fraught with tricksy problems. I knew that from past experience, but I felt a whole lot better for having made it, and when I went back to the car some of the guilt I'd been carrying around stayed behind in the graveyard.

I drove back home, changed into leggings and a baggy white T-shirt and took a look in the fridge. Mother Hubbard would have been right at home there. I dumped out a slice of ham that had curled up to die and settled for a meal of pasta and pesto. Around seven I went to the health club. Jeff, the hunk who owns the place, wasn't around and his deputy was busy putting a new girl through her paces.

I didn't have the easiest of work-outs. I'd been slacking for too long and as I worked my way round the Nautilus machines most of my muscle groups screamed in protest. I guess after six months of near idleness they'd forgotten why they were there. I cut down on repetitions, lightened the weights and still found it tough. But hey! So what? A couple of weeks and I'd be back to making the whole thing look a breeze!

At ten thirty, full of virtue, I snuggled under the duvet and slept soundly until morning. If I'd had dreams I didn't remember them, and that was fine, because just lately I'd been having too many of the wrong kind.

There are times when being a tax inspector is like having the Christmas Fairy along, especially when it comes to nosing around in other people's business. I put in a couple of hours' honest labour and then did some checking up on my own account. I didn't feel guilty about that. If certain people were indulging in fraudulent fire claims, then Inland Revenue had to be losing out somewhere along the line, and nobody was going to rap my knuckles for stopping a revenue leak. On the other hand, if the arson epidemic really had been random, I didn't plan on telling anyone I'd been wasting my time.

With the file stacks to myself I snooped into other people's affairs and thought how nice it was to be part of one big, happy family, all dedicated to stopping artful dodgers getting away with the loot. Except that for once the snooping didn't get me anywhere. There'd been four major fires, including Fast-Sell, and the lone fact that one firm had been looking dodgy enough to investigate didn't count for a thing when all the relevant accounts were just so much burnt paper. Of the other three, although I already had my doubts about Fast-Sell, the remaining two had filed impeccable sets of accounts, certified by reputable accountants. Of course, that didn't necessarily prove a thing. Accountants work on figures given them by clients, and clients can be good at massaging books. The truth is that where scams are concerned there's a way round every regulation. The hard part for Inland Revenue is keeping one step ahead.

Not that I had evidence of a scam; all I had was Charlie's insistence that the arsonist was still out there and the memory of an abortive carpet-shopping trip.

I went back to my desk and fished out the card Bethany Mills gave me. When I rang and told her who I was she sounded surprised. 'Is this to do with the insurance claim? I hope you're going to say no it isn't because the recommendations are about ready to go through.'

'No,' I said. 'It isn't about the claim, or at least not directly. There are a couple of things need tidying up in the tax file and I'm short on up-to-date information. Like I have Fast-Sell listed as a private limited liability company with just one director. Would that still be correct? The name I have is Mark Drury.'

'He picked the place up cheap around eighteen months ago and I hear he was making a go of it,' she said. 'Shame this had to happen.'

'If he was that good then he'll pick up the pieces. You sure he was on his own? I heard a whisper he was a front man.'

She took a little thinking time. 'That's new to me,' she came back finally. 'As far as insurance is concerned he's sole owner. Maybe I should talk to my boss and see if he can come up with anything?'

'It's only a whisper,' I said. 'You know how things are, rumours go around and eventually they settle somewhere.'

'I'll pass it along and get back to you. Want to give me your phone number and extension? It'll save me hunting up the card you gave me.'

I told her the numbers obligingly.

'Might not be today,' she said. 'Colin's not in the office right now. I don't know how long he'll be gone but I'll do my best.'

'Anything you can come up with,' I said. 'Just one thing more about Drury. Do you have an address on Lime Walk? I've got the street but no number.'

'Twenty B. It's that big sprawling Victorian dump some entrepreneur turned into flats. I hear the rents are inflated but they're nice roomy apartments.'

'You've been there?'

'I needed to talk about the fire. He's OK. Fortyish, thinning on top, looks like a carpet salesman.'

'You don't say.'

She laughed. 'Well, I suppose some people fit their jobs and he's one of them.'

'I'd have thought to turn that place around he'd have needed a little more than a sales pitch.'

'If you put it that way, yes. Maybe looks aren't everything after all. Is that the lot or did you want to check something else?'

'That's it,' I said. 'Thanks, Bethany.'

'No trouble. I'll let you know what Colin comes up with.' We said our goodbyes and I listened to tinny crackles on the line for a couple of seconds before I put the phone down. There was no way round it, I'd just have to pay a visit to Lime Walk for myself.

6

The Wilberforce place looked a lot better for its conversion. Around the turn of the century some local bigwig had let a similarity of names go to his head and in a spirit of philanthropy had built and endowed an orphanage. The idea itself was good but it was a shame he hadn't picked a better architect. A mix of Wuthering Heights and Edgar Allen Poe is not somewhere I would willingly opt to spend my childhood. I parked outside and decided that today it looked a little better, probably because sand-blasted stone has a certain advantage over grey-green grime.

I climbed five semicircular steps and found that the arched front entrance had a new security light and eight bell buttons. I pushed the one marked twenty B and waited hopefully. The speaker panel said, 'Yeah. Who is it?' I shoved my face up to the grid.

'Leah Hunter, tax inspector. I need to take up a few minutes of your time to sort out a couple of queries.' I waited a while and listened to the silence. Obviously he had to give such things a little consideration. Or maybe he thought I was superthief come up with a new way to get in. I put my finger on the button again.

'OK,' he snapped, 'let me get my pants on.'

'Take your time,' I said, and did a little speculating on why he had them off.

By and by the front door buzzed and clicked and I went on through. Halfway up the second flight of stairs I met a dark-haired female coming down, thirtyish, pale grey leggings and a loose lambswool sweater in baby blue that matched her eyes. We sussed each other out in a nosy kind of way. She looked a little flushed.

'Warm day,' I said brightly. She looked right through me and didn't break step. Drury's door was open so I could see through to the living room. I rapped politely and waited to be asked in. This time it didn't take more than a couple of seconds to get his attention. He came down the hall slicking back damp hair and gave me a salesman's smile, his face wide at the temples and set with eyes that could see a sucker coming from a mile away.

'Sorry about the wait. You know how it is, get in the shower and the world comes to call. Go on through and I'll get us a drink. Want coffee or something stronger?'

'Straight information will do me fine,' I said. 'I wouldn't want to take up too much of your time.'

'Right now time is something I have in excess, until the insurance claim pays out, that is. After that I'll be back in business. Mind you, can't say I'm not enjoying the break, gives me a chance to build up new ideas.'

'Uh-huh. You'll be opening up in Bramfield again?'

'Why not? It's a nice little town, business is good – *was* good I should have said – and no reason I can see why it wouldn't be again.'

I shrugged. 'Starting out from scratch in new premises has to be a bigger risk than picking up a firm that's already up and running.'

'Maybe, maybe. Not something I have to make a decision on until the money comes. Have a seat and tell me what Inland Revenue need to know that I haven't already told them.'

I looked around. His taste in furnishings ran to low MFI units round the walls, a tan leather suite, glass coffee table and a very dead goatskin on a striped cream and tan carpet. I lowered myself into one of the easy chairs and the leather gave off vaguely rude and squeaky noises. 'Nice,' I said kindly and untruthfully.

'Friend in the trade,' he said, keen to impress he hadn't been spending undeclared profits. 'Could maybe get you fixed up cheap if you were in the market?'

'That's real kind, but no, I'm not. The reason I'm here, Mr Drury, is I don't seem able to find a letter from you advising us about the fire?'

'Oh, right! *That's* what the problem is. Look, I'm sorry, it was an oversight, not something I thought about, you know, with all the stress and everything happening at that time.'

'Understandable,' I nodded. 'I thought that'd be the reason.'

'So if you still need me to make it official . . . ?'

I got out my notebook and scribbled busily. 'No, that'll be fine now, thanks. Both the insurance company and your accountants will have copies of the inventory I suppose?'

'That's right.'

I made another little memo.

'OK. And can we confirm the name of your insurers?'

He looked like he was going to give me a little argument there, but then he changed his mind and made do with a small gripe instead. 'Northern Alliance,' he said. 'But I don't see what that has to do with tax accounts.'

'We may need to confirm the payout figure to make a final assessment of taxes.' I eyed him sympathetically. 'It must have been a shock to get burnt out that way. Were you home the night of the fire?'

He shifted restlessly. 'No, I wasn't, I was with my girlfriend.'

'Is that the nice-looking brunette I passed on the way in?'

'Now that really does have nothing to do with taxes.'

'Sorry,' I said, 'that was just personal curiosity carrying me away. Have you heard anything about the claim yet? I take it it's going through OK?'

He waved his hands, palms up. 'These things take time. Anybody'd think I didn't have creditors. I talked with Alliance yesterday; payment ought to be through in another couple of days. It'll be nice to get it all done with; it's dragged on too long already.'

'I'll bet. Must have been a real worry, especially when everyone knew right from the start it was arson. That kind of thing can lead to a lot of delays.'

'Luckily Fast-Sell wasn't the only business to be hit that way or things could have been difficult. The good thing is they finally got the firebug, everybody can lock up shop and go home now, get a good night's sleep.'

'Right. Save us a lot of extra work too.' I flicked pages and read through an old shopping list worriedly. 'Mr Drury, I'm sure you know how rumours get around, and I'm equally sure you know a lot of them get to reach Inland Revenue. Now, most of them turn out to be wrong but they all have to be checked. You understand that?'

His face got a flat look. 'Keep going.'

'You were sole owner of Fast-Sell?'

'That's what it says on the accounts.'

'We have information that contradicts that, Mr Drury. Occasionally the information we're given is wrong, but it all has to be looked at. I hope you're going to be honest with me here?'

'I already have been. Sole owner. Check the records.'

'I did that a while ago. The point is, you might have close links with – say – another carpet company, without the two of you being financially involved with each other. Or openly at any rate.'

'It'd be unusual for anybody to be in business and not have any contact with traders in the same line.'

'We're not talking contact, we're talking links.'

'You'll have to explain the difference.'

'A link would mean another firm had influence on Fast-Sell's business affairs. It might also mean an exchange of stock between the two. Something doesn't sell with you, you move it on; something doesn't sell for them, Fast-Sell takes it on. Such business arrangements tread on very thin ground where Inland Revenue is concerned.'

'I'd like to know who's been trying to cause trouble.'

'If names weren't kept confidential we wouldn't get any information.'

'Well, it's wrong this time. I trade around, pick up something cheap here, something cheap there, it all goes through the books. A firm's not doing well it'll sell a few rolls off at a loss to get some cash flow going. Now don't tell me that's illegal.'

'I wouldn't try to. What would be illegal is to overstate purchases and maybe at the same time understate sales. That's something I'm sure you know almost as well as me. The fact is a lot of people think they can get away with it until they get caught. Although I'm sure you wouldn't be so silly.'

'I wouldn't and I haven't. If you're accusing me, I think I ought to get my solicitor and accountant round.'

'I'm not accusing. This is a friendly chat to sort things out. If you were being accused it would be a lot more formal than this, Mr Drury, so if there's one firm in particular you've had a lot of contact with, then tell me now and let's get it out of the way.' I held my breath.

His hair was beginning to dry out; running his hands over it made a few strands stick up on top. The surface calm he wore was cracking but he didn't realise it yet. He said, 'This is stupid.'

I sat quietly and didn't answer.

A crease between his eyes messed up his forehead. He tried to work out exactly what it was I thought I knew. The answer, of course, was nothing, but it's always best that some things however insignificant remain a mystery. He picked at his thumbnail. 'This other carpet firm I'm supposed to have cosied up with – did this friendly informer give it a name?'

'Yes.' If I kept this up heaven would surely close its gates. I gave him a sympathetic smile. 'Regulations prevent me from telling you what the name is.'

'But it's a local firm?'

'Is it?'

'I don't know, you tell me. What happens next then? If I still say I don't know what you're talking about, what then?'

'Then I and another officer have to pay a visit to the named firm and go through it all again. And we would look very closely at that firm's trading accounts.'

He strung a couple of rude words together, gave me a sideways look and decided I wasn't shocked enough for an apology. Then he went and got himself a whisky. I felt like I was still holding my breath. He lifted his glass. 'You sure you won't have one?'

I shook my head and watched his sudden indecisiveness.

'QTO Carpets,' he said. 'Belongs to a friend of mine. So all right, I like to go and talk things over with him, business affairs, where to buy. What's wrong with that?'

'Nothing if the only connection between you is talking. QTO is also a sole trader?'

'Yes.'

'Owned by?'

'Ed Bailey.' I made another note. 'Look,' he fretted, 'there's nothing dodgy. He finds a bargain lot that's too big for him to handle and we split it. I do the same for him. Works both ways.'

'Uh-huh. Carrying on a joint business.' I made some more notes.

'No. Straight buying and selling. Separate.'

'Transactions not shown in your accounts.'

'No need for it. We split the stuff on site, my half goes through my books, his half goes through his. Nothing illegal in that.'

I closed my notebook and put it away. 'You've been very open with me, Mr Drury, and I appreciate that. Thanks.' I got up and moved towards the door. He came with me.

'That's the end of it then?'

'Not quite. I'll need the other trader to confirm that type of dealing between the two firms, but there shouldn't be any trouble with that. Where do I find QTO?'

'Sheffield. Out of your area.' He was quick.

'Right,' I said. 'Point taken. So I either get someone from Sheffield IR office to go visiting with me or I call on him informally.' I turned round in the doorway and let him make the decision. It didn't take more than a blink.

'I'll let him know you're coming,' he said.

I set the date. 'Tomorrow morning.' His eyebrows went up. 'Hey,'

I told him. 'I've got a lot more files than Fast-Sell's need tidying up. Be glad I don't drag it out.'

He didn't look glad, but in this life you can't have everything.

I skipped back downstairs, picked up a sandwich on the way back to the office and ate it at my desk. For once in my life ferreting around in things which didn't concern me might just have unearthed something which did. I could smell a variation on long-firm fraud and if I was right, Pete would be really pleased with me. Of course, to prove it meant I'd probably have to catch a firebug Bramfield's finest said didn't exist.

When I thought about that my hands started sweating again.

7

I hadn't expected Drury to bite back, but I'd been wrong about that. Mid-afternoon Pete called me into his office. The expression on his face said megagrump and his tone of voice and evasive eyes said I'd better have a damn good explanation for whatever it was I'd done wrong.

He said, 'D'you want to fill me in on Arnold's files?'

'Arnold's stuff seems fine to me,' I said brightly. 'Up to date, no ink blots, just what you'd expect.' He did a couple more doodles on his blotter. 'What's the problem? Did I miss something?'

'I don't know, Leah. You tell me.'

'Look,' I said. 'I don't know what this is about but I'll go through them again. If there's something I didn't see first time round I'll come back to you.'

He doodled some more, 'Suppose you get me the Fast-Sell file and we'll go through it together.' A light flashed on and off in my head.

'OK, Pete, fine, I'll do that – but it's funny you should pick on that one file. It's a firm I've been thinking of taking a closer look at.' I moved over to the door. 'Has something new come up?'

'Just bring in the file, will you?' Chilly, unfriendly, not a bit like Pete. I could feel my face heat up. I went back to my desk and yanked out the folder, slamming it down and taking a fast flick through the contents. When I looked up Pete was watching me through the glass with stony fixation. I slapped cover shut, carried the file into Pete's office and dropped it on the desk.

'That's it,' I said. 'Just as Arnold left it. Now what?'

'Now tell me what makes this particular file different from the rest?'

'I don't know if I can do that. I mean, on the face of it everything tallies, the accounts are properly accredited, the returns complete, but there's something I can't put my finger on. It's a gut feeling, nothing more.'

'Which is why you've given it some extra special attention?' I regarded him consideringly, wondering where he'd picked up that idea. Not from me that was for sure. He lifted his eyes up off the doodles and turned them on me. What lurked inside them looked a lot like disappointment. He said, 'You took a long lunch hour today. Why was that?'

'I needed to see a client. Come on, Pete? What am I supposed to have done, for God's sake?'

'What's the name of this client?'

I could feel myself pink up with annoyance. I snapped, 'What is this, Pete? Am I under investigation?'

'The client?'

Pete as aggrieved and distant as this was a new phenomenon. Worry asserted itself. I said carefully, 'I dropped in on a man named Mark Drury; he owned Fast-Sell and I wanted to ask him a few questions.' I could tell from his face that Pete's next trustful contribution would be, 'What questions?' so I saved him the bother. 'Fact is, I'm not convinced the stock Fast-Sell was carrying at the time of the fire matches up with the inventory Drury gave the insurers.'

'You told him that did you?'

Shit! No, I hadn't told Drury that. I hadn't wanted to frighten him into thinking up something clever before I had a chance to come up with some good evidence.

'Not exactly,' I said.

'Instead you gave him a cock-and-bull story about having information that would stop his insurers paying out if you passed it on.' The way Pete said that made it a statement, not a question.

'No,' I said. 'I didn't do that at all.'

'An informant wasn't mentioned?'

'Yes, it was, but . . .'

'You told Drury that for a financial consideration you'd keep the information to yourself.'

'I *what?* Damn it, you know me better than that, Pete!'

'Drury lodged a formal complaint and I've had to pass it on.' He looked weary and the bottom started to fall out of my stomach. He said, 'There'll be an investigation into the way you've handled your work prior to this complaint; in the meantime you're suspended. I'd like you to empty your desk and go home.'

'You think I go around asking for backhanders, Pete? Why would I do that, huh? It'd take an idiot to be that stupid.'

'It has to be looked into.'

'Well, thanks for the vote of confidence,' I said bitterly. 'I'm a damn good tax officer and this whole thing is bullshit!'

He walked to the door, his hand just lightly on my shoulder in passing. For the first time ever the gesture was welcome.

I'm not a gatherer and there weren't that many personal items to collect. All in all, they made a pitiful little heap on the desk top. I stuffed the whole lot in a big brown envelope and folded over the top. The room was quiet, everyone trying to work out what was going on. I wondered what explanation Pete would hand out when I was gone. Having him escort me out of the building was really embarrassing, but the one thing you can always count on him for is strict adherence to regulations.

It's a truly bad feeling to be outflanked. I sat in the hybrid and thought about how Drury's neat little table-turning trick had bought him enough time to take the money and run. He must be feeling really pleased with himself, and officially at least I couldn't do a thing about it. I took a last look at my third-floor window and went home. It wasn't what I wanted to do, but breaking something hard over Drury's head wouldn't exactly impress my own state of innocence.

When I got back to my eyrie I did a fast change into cut-offs and a T-shirt and headed straight out again to run off some steam; there might be a better way of dealing with life's little brickbats but if there is I haven't heard about it yet. When I'd used up the adreneline surge I circled home. Sometimes, like then, standing in the shower under a cascade of water can be really soothing. I took my time, waiting until the tension I still had in me slackened off, then I towelled dry, got into clean underpants and a long T-shirt and went to fix myself a tomato sandwich and fresh coffee.

Around five I rang Nicholls and invited him out to dinner; I knew he'd be enthusiastic when I said I'd foot the bill. He did a little probing to find out why I wanted to do that but I'm really good at stonewalling.

At seven thirty he turned up nicely washed and brushed and I pirouetted and let him see the trouble I'd gone to on his behalf. That's the nice thing about Nicholls, he always looks appreciative. 'So,' he said, handing me a not-too-generous bunch of freesia, 'what're we celebrating?'

I dumped the freesia in a jug and watched them rattle around. 'Did I say we were celebrating? Let's just eat first and talk later.'

'You got a promotion?'

'Uh-uh.'

'A rise?'

'No! Just get down to the car, Nicholls, and stop asking.'

'Your sister had twins?'

'Move it!' I said, and gave him a shove.

'Fine!' he said. 'Just fine! Only next time I get any good news you'll need to prise it out of me.'

'That so? What makes you think the news is good?'

He stopped mid-step and I nearly fell over him. 'It's bad?'

'It sucks,' I said, and went on around him and out the front door. I just love the way he never believes me when he hears the truth.

8

I didn't tell Nicholls he'd been wined and dined by a reputedly corrupt tax inspector until we got back to my attic home, and when I did, it took a while to convince him he wasn't just being set up for some big leg pull. Such obtuseness can be really irritating. When the message finally got through it took along some implications that really got under his skin. Innocent men don't mess around making false charges and if I wasn't on the take Drury had to be buying time. I watched him weigh up the possibilities.

'Sort of blows your comfy arson theory right out of the water, doesn't it?' I said, smiling at him sweetly. 'Unless you're going to come up with the idea that Billy had turned pro?'

'It doesn't follow,' he snapped back.

'What doesn't?'

'Look, Drury being an opportunist and torching his own place wouldn't clear Billy for the rest of the fires.'

'Oh, come on!' I said. 'Let's hear it for common sense!'

'You just got it!'

We glared at each other a little.

'OK,' I said. 'So let's hear what you plan to do about it.'

'Where's the evidence?'

That's another thing I don't like about Nicholls. He always has to have evidence.

'Nicholls,' I said, 'I'm just a wronged citizen, and you're the detective. Maybe you should go out and find some for yourself.'

'What you mean is there isn't any,' he came back. 'Damn it, Leah, why can't you just stop poking around instead of bringing things down on your head.'

'Because you'd let half the criminals around here get away if I did,' I said nastily.

He took on an injured look and said, 'Thanks.'

'That's OK! Any time.' I turned on the television. He turned it off again. 'Look,' I said, 'how do you expect me to get evidence? Evidence is what I was looking for when I got suspended.'

He finished up his coffee and got rid of the mug, then slid arm first to my end of the settee and said how sorry he was Pete hadn't backed me up. I told him stiffly that Pete didn't have any choice in the matter, then I left the settee to him and sat on the rug. Soft soap I can do without.

I turned the television back on and watched *News at Ten*. After a while Nicholls came down and joined me. 'I really am sorry,' he said. 'He won't get away with it.'

'Who won't?'

'Drury.'

'Guaranteeing that are you?' He didn't answer. I said, 'You'd better be, because if one of us doesn't prove I'm squeaky clean I join the dole queue. Or maybe I could get a job waiting tables.'

'It won't come to that,' he said.

Too right it wouldn't!

A couple of minutes went by.

'You have to trust me on it,' he said.

I already did, but maybe it wouldn't hurt just for once to tell him so. It's foolish to withhold simple pleasures.

'I trust you,' I said.

He got on a self-satisfied look.

We sat there for a while in amicable silence, watching murder and mayhem in diverse places flicker across the screen, then I started to think how nice his aftershave was and shuffled in a little closer. He lifted his arm and let me get right in. It felt really cosy sitting there and my mind wandered from one thing to another. I sneaked my fingers across his shirt and undid a few buttons. 'Now what are you up to?' he said.

'Uh, how about I'm searching a suspect for concealed weapons?'

'You won't find any,' he said.

'That so?' I picked up a little speed and he jerked and gave a sort of grunt. 'Feels like a weapon to me,' I murmured down his ear. 'How about that?' After which neither of us said much at all for a good long time. But that's one of the few positive virtues Nicholls has – when he knows there's something to be done he puts his whole mind to it.

Saturday morning I woke bright and early and thought about how I should run on down to the park, do a couple of circuits and then run all the way home again. Instead of which I took a leisurely soak in the tub and listened to Nicholls make breakfast. Sometimes a certain amount of indolence is good for the soul – or at least, that's what my bad fairy whispered; its good counterpart was hopping mad but I've grown quite good at ignoring such things.

The smell of toast and coffee got me dried off and dressed fast. Sometimes I wonder why no one has snapped Nicholls up yet. I tell myself that when it happens I won't feel bad about it and I know damn well I'm lying, but even so I'm not willing to take that extra step. Maybe one day I will, but it's still too far ahead for me to see it. There are all kinds of relationships, some tight enough to strangle, others so loose they don't count. Nicholls and I were somewhere in the middle and we were still in funtime. No strings, no hassle, no promises that could end up broken the way they had with Will who I'd loved enough for it to hurt really bad when I found out he already had a wife. Such painful things are hard to leave behind, and I guess the truth is that however good I feel with Nicholls I just haven't got back into the habit of being trusting.

I complimented him on the good coffee and scrambled eggs, shared the morning paper, and then kindly let him exercise his tidy ways with the washing-up while I tried to feel virtuous about drying the damn things. Then I gave him a sisterly kiss and sent him on his way. Some things have to be done solo and that day was going to be full of them.

The only real opening I could see to finding out more about Drury and his lying ways was through Bethany Mills, and I hoped she'd believe what I told her and not just think I was trying to stir up trouble to get back at him. I fished out her card and dialled her office number, then realised she probably didn't work Saturdays. Great!

I counted the rings. When it got to six someone picked up and I asked for Bethany. 'Well,' said the voice. 'She's sort of here but not here if you know what I mean.'

I didn't. 'Explain,' I said.

'I mean, she's in the building writing out a report, but she's not officially at work this morning. I'm not sure if she'll accept any business calls.'

'This isn't business,' I said. 'It's personal, and I'd be really grateful if you could find her.'

'I'll try,' she said. 'Who shall I say is calling?'

'Tell her it's Leah Hunter, and if it wasn't urgent I wouldn't be calling her until Monday.'

'Can you hold please?' A little click and I was listening to a bit of Vivaldi; such gimmicks are a wonderful way to kill good music.

By and by Bethany came on the line. 'Leah? I'm told this is personal?'

'As personal as you can get. Can we meet and talk?'

'Now you mean?'

'Whenever you can make it.'

'I'll be through here in about an hour. There's a pub just around the corner, the Wheatsheaf, do you know it?'

'I know it,' I said. 'Meet you inside?'

'Fine. Hope I can help.' *So did I.*

We hung up and I started to think about the good turn I was going to ask of her. It was a lot to expect considering we were practically strangers, and I wouldn't blame her one little bit if she said no. Of course if that's the answer she did decide to come up with, I was going to be in real trouble, and for once in my life I couldn't see any clear way out of it.

Unless Nicholls came up trumps.

Bullshit! Who was I kidding? With nothing to go on except a suspect tax inspector's opinion on the quality of some long vanished carpet stock, it'd take a miracle.

I'd been sitting in the Wheatsheaf with a Pils for about ten minutes when Bethany walked in. I waved and she came on over. Politely I asked what I could get her to drink. She glanced at my glass and said just a coffee. I got the circulating waitress's attention and made her wants known. Bethany shrugged out of her mac, leaving it draped over the back of her chair, leaned both elbows on the table and said, 'So what's the problem? I tried to get back to you yesterday, but some person called Val said you were taking indefinite leave.'

'You could call it that,' I said. 'It sounds a whole lot better than being suspended, which is where I'm at right now.'

Her eyes flickered. 'Then maybe I shouldn't be here.'

'Maybe, but I think we're both on the same side. You don't want to let an insurance fraud slip by, and I don't want hustling out of Inland Revenue for something I didn't do.'

The coffee came. Bethany tipped in the little pot of cream, stirred and said warily, 'Hustled for what?'

I've learned that the best thing to do with a direct question is give it a direct answer. I told her all about yesterday's little chat with Drury and the mess it had got me in, and she didn't miss a word. When I was through she took a few minutes' thinking time, then asked what I wanted from her.

'Easy,' I said. 'Just try to get Drury's payout delayed so there's time to dig around. That can't hurt anybody, and especially not the insurance company.'

'That's all?' she said dryly.

'Unless maybe you could hassle him a little. Worried people tend to panic and it might be useful to see how he reacts.' I looked at her and went for broke. 'A photocopy of Fast-Sell's inventory and anything you can dig up on Drury's trading background would also be a big help.'

'I'll need to do some thinking about this,' she said, getting up and putting her mac on. 'And I'm not going to make any promises before I do that.' She put her head on one side and eyed me measuringly. 'The fact is, if I put myself out to help I could end up in as much trouble as you, and I don't fancy the dole queue either.'

'Drury wouldn't try the same trick twice,' I told her knowledgeably as I paid the bill. 'Nobody's that dumb.'

'Let's hope!' she said when we stepped back out on to the street together. 'Problem is, successful ideas do tend to get overworked.' With a quick handshake she swung off back towards her office building. I watched her go and thought how useful a little networking can be.

9

Saturday is never the best day of the week for finding people hard at work behind a desk, but I'd been lucky with Bethany and I hoped I'd be lucky again. I turned left on to Bank Street and took a short cut down the alley to Goodwin Street and the Probation Office, expecting to find a friendly face. I'd got to know the people there really well, both from mutual griping sessions over coffee in the Courts building when IR prosecuted tax evaders and from a bad time a year ago when one of their officers got mixed up in lethal dealings. Since then I'd had more or less free entry to the place. Today I hoped they'd be able to come up with some information.

It bugged me that a slime like Drury could have got me suspended so fast, but it could just turn out to be the most stupid thing he'd ever done since I now had nothing to do with my time except poke into his crooked ways. Of course, right then I didn't know what kind of scam he was into except for torching his own place, but from our one and only meeting I didn't think he'd have had either the bottle or the know-how to do that little job for himself. Which meant he'd hired somebody, and I didn't believe for one minute that the somebody had been Billy.

Which meant that the arsonist was still out there looking for more work. It wasn't a very comforting thought.

I pushed through Probation's heavy door into reception, hoping there'd be someone around who knew the score well enough to talk about the secure unit Billy had been held in. It isn't the kind of chit-chat probation officers normally indulge in, but since I was owed a couple of favours it seemed like a good time to collect.

I hit the first snag when instead of Beverley's ever friendly face behind the high reception desk, I found a frosted-hair female who eyed me like she'd really had it with all the riff-raff dropping in. I switched on some charm. 'Hi,' I said. 'I'd like to see Stuart Fraser?'

'Come back Monday.'

Just that. Tart flat and charmproof.

I said, 'Does that mean he isn't here?'

She looked me up, and she looked me down. 'Clients aren't seen Saturday mornings.'

'*Clients* aren't seen?' I fished around in my shoulder-bag and her finger hovered over the panic button like I could be the female half of Bonnie and Clyde. I slammed a business card down. 'Just tell him I'm here,' I said crisply, 'and let him decide for himself, huh?'

She looked it over. 'Mr Fraser isn't in this morning.'

Judas! Why couldn't she just have said that in the first place? Some people are put on earth to be an annoyance and that's the truth. I snapped out, 'If Fraser isn't here, then who is?'

'Andrew Baker.'

Just the man I needed. With a bad temper and a chip on his shoulder he was going to be a big help. *Shit.* She put on a self-satisfied smirk and it was really wise of Providence to have Fraser come in from the street right then. He took a look at both our faces and saw just how well we'd been getting on. I was glad he found it amusing.

Fraser is in his late forties, bony, sandy and still eminently fanciable. He's also head of department and when he shook hands like he meant it and said he hoped somebody had been looking after me, my friendly little helpmeet didn't seem any too happy.

'Oh, sure, somebody's been looking after me just fine,' I said shortly. 'It's been a truly interesting experience, but now I could use a little real help if you have the time?' He said twenty minutes was all he'd got and I told him that was plenty.

He reached over the high counter to pick a couple of letters off Frosty's desk and said cajolingly, 'Valerie, my lovely, two cups of coffee in my office would be much appreciated.' I watched a rosy hue spread over her face and admired his tactics.

We went up to his first-floor room and he hunted up a comfy chair so we could both relax while he listened to the trouble I was in. I'd just précised it all nicely when Valerie came in with the coffee cups, and it seemed like as good a place as any to stay quiet for a while and hear what he had to say. Fraser isn't exactly a fast mover. He spent a little time on dunking a digestive, then a little more fishing it out with a spoon when he lost it; meantime I sipped delicately and fought back an urge to push him along.

Finally he put his feet up on the desk and said mildly, 'It looks like a real problem, Leah, but Billy didn't have a probation order on him and I don't see there's much I can do except sympathise.'

'Fraser, if I didn't believe you could help I wouldn't be here. There are a couple of things I need to know about Billy and you have access to the right channels.'

'Which are no doubt meant to be confidential,' he said.

Such pedantries are best ignored.

'Who's going to complain? Not Billy, that's for sure. I went to his funeral a couple of days ago and he didn't have that option left. You know, it'd be really interesting to hear what goes on in that secure unit. I mean it really puzzles me that it's so easy for kids to hang themselves in there.' His face closed up.

He said, 'It puzzles a lot of people, Leah, and with an inquiry going on it isn't debatable, so don't ask me.'

'I wasn't going to, Fraser. What I wanted was for you to find out if Billy got to know anybody in there that he might have opened up to, because if he did I'd appreciate a chance to talk to that person.'

'It might not get you the answers you want.'

'Any answer is better than silence. If Billy came out and said he was the arsonist then it'll save me looking for someone else to put the blame on.'

'And what's the other thing you planned to charm out of me?'

'I hoped you might chat up Billy's psychologist and maybe ask if she or he had been expecting anything like this?'

He sat back up and his native Scots burr got more pronounced. 'Are you sure you don't want me to get you a look at the police file too?'

I grinned, scribbled down my home number and gave it to him. 'Thanks, Fraser. You know I wouldn't ask if there was any other way.' I finished up my coffee and left him to read his mail.

It's around twenty-five miles to Sheffield and parking isn't easy. Neither is the traffic system. By and by I found a place in a multistorey and went to find QTO Carpets. Sizing up their stock wouldn't do me any good – one carpet looks much like any other except for the price. What interested me was seeing the size of their operation.

The further I walked, the more obvious it became that recession had hit the town badly. Empty shops stared blankly through flyposted windows and whole streets showed tatty patches of neglect. Maybe the town just couldn't afford to pay enough street cleaners.

QTO was a contrast. It looked like it didn't even know what the word recession meant. Big, brash and sprawling, with a green and yellow neon sign flashing out its name and special-offer stickers starring the windows. The prices looked too good to miss and the place wasn't short of customers. I wandered in and took a good look around. This wasn't carpet-barn rubbish but the discounts were high. Maybe they had a special deal going with the manufacturers. Or maybe, said my suspicious soul, carpets came in through the back door. Either way it looked like they were getting a fast turnover.

I grabbed an eager-beaver salesman. 'Hey,' I said. 'These prices are good – you sure it's all perfect stuff?'

'Nothing else but. Seconds are down in the basement and all marked up as that. Which carpet are you interested in? This one? I could maybe do an even better price.'

'That sounds a good offer but I'll need to go around at least once more before I make my mind up,' I said. 'How do you manage this kind of discount?'

'Bankrupt stock mostly. Perfect, though.'

'One man's loss is another man's profit,' I said. 'Looks like QTO's coming through the recession nicely. This the only shop or is it part of a group?'

He shrugged and fixed his eyes on a couple who looked about ready to buy. 'I just sell carpets,' he said. 'If you want to know anything about the business you'd need to ask the boss.'

'Is he around?'

'Somewhere. Maybe downstairs in the office or – no he's not, that's him over there by the Chinese rugs. Grey suit.' I swivelled and saw him, bald, chunky and fiftyish with the same Flash Harry smile that Drury had.

'Well, thanks a lot,' I said. 'I'll take another look around and when I've made up my mind I'll come and find you.'

'Pleasure,' he said. 'The name's Eric, and delivery's free.' He gave me a clincher kind of grin and I trotted away hoping he wouldn't be too disappointed when I didn't find him again. I spent a little time watching Bailey charm the punters, and denied a foolish urge to go over there and ask if he had good fire insurance. I was sure he had. I was equally sure he was pulling in money and this would be the last place he'd want to torch.

I headed back to the car park, stopping on the way to feed the inner me on tuna salad and a wedge of lemon-cream pie, the whole washed down by a pot of coffee.

Sometimes weekends seem more like a curse than a bonus. Maybe Miss Marple could come up with good ways to sleuth around when everybody closed up for a rest, but I couldn't, and it irked, although when I came to think about it Miss Marple did have one big handicap. She was such a law-abiding little soul.

I drove back home and gave that some careful thought.

10

On the way home wickedness whispered how much fun it would be to look around Drury's flat when he wasn't home. I gave the notion some thought. It seemed logical to suppose his Saturday nights called for something a little more exciting than lazing around in front of the TV. So . . . ?

I'm ashamed that such unlawful ideas enter my head unasked.

I stopped off at the minimart and did a little grocery shopping, then lugged it up the stairs, putting aside all thoughts of housebreaking and other such illicit acts. The last thing I needed right then was to be caught with my little pocket burglary kit trying to get into Drury's place.

I stowed the shopping, took a long soak in the tub, fixed a salad and watched the early evening news. The four horsemen were still out there busily preparing for Armageddon; it's amazing what fun some people get from blowing each other to bits. I worried a little about the state of the world.

At seven thirty I slipped into a skinny plum-coloured dress, fixed my hair and went to hang out on the meat-rack with a couple of girlfriends. I danced a little, drank a little, slapped down a few gropers and ended up around midnight eating Chinese at the Golden Dragon. Three grown females giggling over the waiter's ass like we were still at school. Ho-hum, sometimes that kind of diversion can be fun. I flopped into bed around two feeling better than I had for months.

Sunday morning I ran a few miles to clear my head, going back over the conversation I'd had with Drury and trying to come up with something that could have triggered him dropping the word corruption in Pete's ear. Some little thing I said had really worried him. He'd thought I might be getting near the truth and had a panic response. I ran a little faster. *He hadn't liked the idea of me going through QTO's trading accounts, that was for sure.*

Maybe I should have a word with someone at IR Sheffield? As ideas go, that one didn't live very long.

The dole queue is long and growing longer. Nobody would actively dice with joining it by picking up a suspended colleague's dropped ball.

I jogged home, showered, pulled on an Amnesty T-shirt and stripy leggings then cooked up mushrooms and potato cakes, eating with the morning paper spread out before me like a real prole, and drinking enough coffee to get me hyped enough to deal with the washing-up and some other patiently needy chores. Such occasional virtue always annoys the slut in me, so I spent the rest of the day being slothful, turning in early and sleeping like a babe until rain the size of elephant's tears woke me around six thirty next morning.

The only good thing about having nothing to do is that there's no necessity to dash outdoors on a filthy day and get soaked.

At ten, I skipped downstairs to Marcie's for coffee and a gossip. It was nice to see her looking good again – she'd just come through a really bad patch and I was glad she hadn't uprooted herself and moved on. Marcie is a single parent with a three-year-old son and earns her living by freelance illustration, turning out beautifully delicate artwork that's much in demand. It's nice the way she strictly rations the time she spends earning so she can have fun with young Ben. Luxuries, she says, will just have to wait. We talked about this and that and played with Ben's Lego until around eleven when the rain stopped and I went back upstairs to replan my day. But laziness can be addictive and I still hadn't got around to doing that when Stuart Fraser rang at twelve thirty and told me about Jaz.

Jaz, christened Jason Duncombe, had been in the secure unit with Billy, and according to Fraser they'd hit it off right away. 'If Billy talked about what he'd done or not done, it would have been to Jaz,' said Fraser. 'Nobody else could get anything out of him.'

'The staff you mean?'

'And the social workers.'

'I thought all the staff *were* social workers,' I said.

'Wouldn't be cost-effective,' Fraser said dryly. 'The bulk of staff are hired hands, they come a lot cheaper. There's maybe three trained people on the premises by day and one on call at night.'

'On call?'

'Sleeps on the premises.'

'Uh-huh. Anybody call him up the night Billy died?'

'After it happened. And that's all I'm going to tell you.'

'OK,' I said. 'I wouldn't want you to break the confidentiality rule, but bending it a little wouldn't hurt. How do I get to see Jaz? Can you get me a pass?'

'He got bound over five days ago and he's back in the family home. Thirty-eight Coronation Close, Westwood.'

Great! Doberman City!

'That's real good thinking,' I said. 'Just the place to keep him out of trouble.'

'Tell it to the government,' Fraser advised. 'Social Security doesn't exist for sixteen-to-eighteen-year-olds.'

'How about a training scheme?'

'Not enough places.'

'Hostels?'

'Not without a job.'

'Back to Catch-22 again,' I said.

'Best one yet.'

I asked if he'd had a chance to talk with Billy's psychologist, and he said it was a woman called Amanda Crane. Ms Crane hadn't expected Billy to reoffend and still couldn't understand how she'd missed the signs. I filed that away as ammunition to shoot at Nicholls. I told Fraser how I really appreciated the way he was helping and he reminded me there were no free lunches; expended effort on his part just left him with a favour to call in. I told him anytime he needed it, then we finished with the pleasantries and hung up.

I lunched on a cheese sandwich washed down with a can of Purdey's, changed into jeans and a pair of Nikes and tugged on a navy sweatshirt. By half past one I'd collected the car from Dora's and was heading through town towards Westwood.

The place had been built by the council in the nineteen fifties and flagged as a dream estate. Neat semidetached houses on grass-edged streets, gardens big enough to grow all the vegetables a family would need, and for a long time that's the way it had been. Then about the mid-sixties it all began to break down, social policy changed and difficult families were moved in among the nice well-kept homes. The idea was that better housing and good example would fast rub off on the awkward squad. It didn't, of course. Since when did bureaucrats ever get anything right? What happened was that the neighbours moved out and rusting prams and fridges took over whole streets.

Coronation Close was one of them.

I found number thirty-eight and pulled in behind an aged purple

Capri. A sticker in its rear window said *IF YOU WANT TO BONK, HONK*. Such an invitation was easy to resist. I got out and locked up carefully. Half a dozen kids were out watching me do that, but I guessed since they were pre-school my wheels were safe.

I crossed the pavement and did a brisk rat-a-tat on the front door. A couple of minutes went by and nothing happened except I thought I heard some shuffling going on behind it. I squinted back at the pavement; the tiny terrorists had edged a little nearer. One of them was lugging a half-brick. I rapped on the door again and it jerked open. I eyed the purple singlet and black Chinos and decided this just had to be the stud who drove the Capri; about five-ten and a face that looked like he was going to the dentist, black hair, longish and gelled. Maybe without the slump in his shoulders he'd have looked taller.

'Hi,' I said politely. 'I'm looking for Jaz.'

'Have to look somewhere else then, won't you?' he said, ''cos he's gone.'

'Where to?'

He was really good at curling his lip. 'Who cares?' The door began to close. I put a hand out and stopped it.

'Can I talk to Mrs Duncombe then?'

'Who?'

'Jaz's mother.'

He turned his head and yelled, '*Julie.*'

I blinked a little. The woman who flat-footed it to the front door looked nothing like my idea of a teenager's mother, a hard-eyed mousy blonde, wearing black leggings and a black T-shirt with the logo *Elvis lives* emblazoned in fluorescent pink with yellow stars. She looked about thirty, thirty-two. 'Yeh?' she said, leaning on the purple singlet. 'What you after?'

'Maybe I got the wrong house,' I said. 'I'm looking for Jaz.'

'You got the right house. What you want him for?'

'It's to do with him being bound over,' I lied.

Her face twisted. 'Get the fuck out of it!' she yelled. I backed up a step and she came out of the door like a torpedo, pushing past me and heading for the road. 'You throw that I'll rip your fucking willie off!' she howled. I turned round. The under-fives had sneaked up level with the cars and the one with a half-brick had it hoisted to his shoulder. He blinked at her but he didn't waver. The brick made a minute arc and clanged on metal. *Shit!* The kids scattered like well-trained guerrillas. I never knew under-fives could run that fast. She came back up the path muttering about what she'd do to the sodding little bastard when she got hold of him, and I fought down the urge to go and see which of us needed a paint job.

She scowled back over her shoulder. 'Kids!' she said. 'They should all be bloody strangled at birth.'

'You're Jaz's mother?' I said.

'What if I am?'

'I just need to find him, that's all.'

'Eddie here tossed him out.' She cuddled up to the purple singlet again and looked up at him fondly. 'Don't take any backchat, do you love?'

'Not from him.'

'So where would he be likely to go?'

'I dunno,' she said. 'What's it to me?'

Eddie said, 'I seen him yesterday with that skinny little twat he's knocking round with.'

'You see what I mean?' said Julie, looking me right in the face and spreading her hands. 'Got no respect, has he?' I looked right back at her and after a couple of seconds her eyes shifted.

'Does that mean he's staying at his girlfriend's?' I said. 'If so, maybe you can tell me her address.'

Julie shrugged.

Eddie said, 'They got a squat on Turpin Street.'

Turpin Street? People moved out and vermin moved in down there close on a year ago. I eyed the pair in front of me and thought about it. Maybe Jaz found some things harder to live with than rats.

I looked at Julie. 'That whole street is scheduled for demolition.'

'Tough!' said Eddie. I ignored him and kept on looking at Jaz's mother.

'Doesn't it bother you? I mean he's your son and he's homeless. Why can't he just live here until he finds a job or gets on a training scheme?'

'Look,' she snapped, 'I've fed him sixteen years and that's his lot. I'm entitled to live a life of my own and I don't want him in it. All right?' She reddened up. 'And stop looking like that. It's not just me that doesn't want him around, is it, Eddie?' Looking up at him again.

Eddie ran his hand over her rump and gave a little squeeze. 'Piss off,' he said pleasantly. 'You can see you're upsetting her.'

'I'll remember to tell that to Jaz when I find him. Meantime, try not to worry that without housing benefit he won't be able to find a good place to stay.'

'He'll survive,' said Eddie, giving me another of his lip curls. 'His twat'll look after him, won't she?' He tightened his hold on Julie, swung her inside and slammed the door.

Filled with impotent rage, I stomped back down the path and took a walk around the hybrid. *Neat!* The kid's half-brick had dented the Capri's rear wing and taken off a good strip of paint. I walked back round to the pavement, unlocked my car, climbed in and started up the engine. Sometimes it seems there's some justice in the world after all.

11

I drove slowly along Turpin Street and back again. The old terrace houses were blackened, bricks crumbling, windows smashed, doors covered in graffiti. Half-arches at pavement level let minimal light into damp cellars. The whole street looked saddened, head hung in shame, and it rubbed off a little on me. It seemed impossible that any of the houses would be fit to live in, but then I realised that to a homeless person a roof and four walls were always better than a cardboard box and two newspapers.

I tucked into the bottom of a side street at the end of an unevenly parked line of cars, their owners eschewing high parking fees in favour of a longer walk. I wasn't too sure I'd gamble that way myself, but none of the cars seemed new enough to tempt thieves or fast enough to give joyriders a buzz. A couple of dogs came along, plumed tails high, noses busy sniffing interesting smells, nudging each other the way that lovers do. Just past my hideaway they stopped to frolic, then played Chase Me Charlie down an arched alley.

Turpin Street isn't all that long. Thirty narrow, boarded-up terraced houses forlornly facing mirror images across a mess of potholes. Midway along, Prospect Road where I had my stake-out cut the whole thing in half.

From my vantage point I could see from one end of Turpin Street to the other, which was really enthralling; so much so that after half an hour boredom set in. Empty and derelict buildings have a limited amount of entertainment value and that's for sure.

I hunkered down with my feet on the dash and wondered if Eddie had told the truth.

If he hadn't, there wasn't much I could do about it.

I stared gloomily through the windscreen and thought about what fun it was waiting around like Polly at her party. I always hated that stupid nursery rhyme.

At four I drove to the shopping centre for a pee, bought a can of Pepsi and a cheese sandwich, then headed back to my stake-out worrying I might have missed them. Five o'clock came and went. I turned Radio Four on low and listened to *PM*. Why is it that news roundups are so depressing? The street behind me emptied of cars. At six thirty two kids I hoped were Jaz and his girlfriend turned into Turpin Street from the town end and went into the fifth house down. I gave them a couple of minutes to settle in before I locked up the car and went visiting.

I tried the door, turning the grimy knob and pushing. When it opened I went on in; it seemed a mite silly to knock. The door led directly into the front room and there was still lino on the floor showing green in the few places where grime had settled less thickly. I could hear voices coming from the back kitchen and tippitoed in that direction. I'd got halfway there when the girl came out and proved what sharp ears she had.

We stared at each other. She said hostilely, 'What you after? You haven't got no business in here.'

'I'm looking for Jaz – Jason Duncombe,' I said, and pasted on what I hoped was a friendly and reassuring smile. 'Is he here?' She looked all of fourteen – fifteen at the most – and undernourished, immature boobs poking at the fabric of a too-thin T-shirt, pale hair lank and lifeless and a spattering of spots around her nose and mouth. When I said Jaz's name she leaned up against the wall and thrust out one hip aggressively.

'Depends what you want him for. He's not going home if you're from the Social – not after his ma threw him out he's not. Met her have you? Bloody old cow-slag.' I hoped she meant his mother and not me.

'I called around. She said she didn't much care where Jaz was and I didn't have a chance to say a lot after that. She and Eddie have a neat way of slamming doors.' A faint spark of something or other lit up her eyes and then died again. Judas, but how did a kid like her end up on the streets? We eyed each other silently. I said, 'Is he your boyfriend?'

'What's it matter either way? What matters is he don't need no more social workers, OK? Fucked him up real good so far, haven't they? Them and his ma. Go on. Piss off. He's not here.' She pushed up from the wall and gained an inch in height. Great! Now she could almost look me in the eye.

'Look,' I said. 'I really need to talk to Jaz and I'm not a social

58

worker. Promise. There's a fry-up place round the corner on the main road and I'm getting really peckish. How about I buy us all a snack and we can talk there?' The spark came back in her eyes and this time it stayed around.

'What'd you want to do that for?'

'I already told you. I need to talk to him. I also need to eat. It seems like a good idea to do both at the same time.' For once lacing the truth with a little lie didn't make me feel too bad. I said, 'It's about a kid called Billy; Jaz met up with him in the secure unit. I've heard the official version of what happened in there and now I'd like to hear the real thing.' Her brain snapped to attention at that and her feet got ready to run. She shook her head. I held up a hand. 'Hey, I'm a friend, not a threat. Honest.' We went back to eyeing each other up.

'I'll ask him,' she said. 'All right? Why'n't you go on down the caff and if he wants a talk we'll come on round. OK?'

It wasn't OK. I didn't think they'd turn up. I viewed the alternatives. I could push past her, in which case Jaz would be out the back door like *zip*, or I could trot around to the gourmet fry-up place and risk not seeing either of them again without a lot of hunting.

'Fifteen minutes,' I said, 'and then I'm gone.'

'Yeh. OK. I'll tell him.' She crossed her skinny arms and waited for me to go. I left her to the damp and the peeling plaster and the smell of dry rot that mingled so nicely with stale urine. Bramfield doesn't have that much of a problem with homelessness and from what I'd just seen that was something to be glad about.

Maybe.

The maybe came in because I just then realised it didn't have any hostels either, save for that run by the Salvation Army, and that was only for people like Rosie, not youngsters like Jaz and his girlfriend.

I moved the car from the side street to a new parking spot near the Rainbow Café. The smell of grease hit me as soon as I went in, smoky rich and overpowering. I got myself a cup of coffee and a corner table and sat down to wait. After a while the smell didn't seem so bad. Fifteen minutes went by. Five more and I got up to go. At which point Jaz and the girl came in through the door, poised there ready for flight while they inspected the clientèle; four youngsters eating burgers and beans gave them quick looks and then forgot about them. The counter hand offered a welcoming smile. I looked ostentatiously at my watch. They communicated silently with each other, closed the door and came on over.

I said, 'Nice to meet you, Jaz. I'm Leah Hunter,' and stuck out a hand. He stared at it as if I'd offered him a grenade, then gave it a quick squeeze and sat down. I sat back on my own seat and the girl still wary sat next to Jaz. 'I don't know your name yet,' I said.

'S'right,' she said. 'That's 'cos I haven't told it you.' Jaz nudged her. ''S Jude,' she muttered.

'OK, so now we all know each other what'll you have to eat?' Another exchanged look. 'I'm buying,' I said.

Jaz said, 'Burgers'd be nice.'

I got a coffee refill from the counter and paid in advance for the burgers, a management policy which seemed to have a lot of horse sense. When I sat back down the two kids had their heads together deciding how to play things. I hoped I could get the questions right. Jaz got in first.

'Jude says what you want to talk about is Billy. That right is it?' he said leaning over the table, trying his hand at mind-reading.

'That's it,' I said. The counterman came with a couple more coffees and I shoved the sugar across. 'I want to know if he talked to you about the fires. Some people don't believe he started them.'

'Like who?'

'Like his family. Like me.'

'Yeh, well, doesn't matter a lot now does it? He's out of it.'

'It matters,' I said. 'It matters if somebody else is getting away with it, and it matters to his family.' The burgers came, plain for me, French fries and beans for them. 'Jaz, I can't force you to tell me anything if you don't want to, but it's important for me to know why Billy did what he did. The police say because he was guilty and got a bad conscience. I don't believe that. Do you?'

He shrugged and got on with eating. After a bit he said, 'He told me about how he used to go down and watch 'em like, you know, the big fires. I don't know – sounded a bit creepy.' He went back to chewing.

'What sounded creepy? Billy?'

He swallowed too fast and nearly choked. Jude thumped on his back and his eyes watered. 'Daft,' she said, like they'd been together for years.

'Maybe we'd better eat first and talk later,' I said.

'Sing for his supper like,' said Jude, and I felt myself pink up. That wasn't the way I'd been looking at things.

'The creepy part was him getting phone calls,' Jaz said. 'I mean if he'd been a bit more streetwise he'd have known it was a setup, wouldn't he? But he was – not thick, but – I don't know. Anyway, he thought it was one of his mates at the fire station letting him know.'

60

'Letting him know what? Where the fires were?'

'Yeh.'

I didn't say anything for a bit after that, instead I thought about Billy, thinking he had a friend among the fire fighters tipping him off. Redding had told me the same thing. Jaz said Billy hadn't been streetwise, but did that mean he couldn't have made the whole story up? I looked at their empty plates, so clean they looked like they'd already been washed and waved a hopeful hand at the counterman. 'Coffee's really nice,' I said when he came over. 'How about three more, and apple pie to go with it?'

He did some quick calculating. 'Four pound eighty,' he said, and didn't move a muscle until he had it.

Jaz said, 'You don't have to . . .'

'Hey,' I cut in, 'I can't eat alone. OK?'

Jude frowned at the table. 'Still don't know why it matters to you,' she said. 'Not his sister or nothing.'

'No, I'm not,' I said. 'I never even knew him, but Billy's uncle is a good friend of mine and we help each other out. Like you and Jaz.'

'He's your bloke?' Disbelief there.

I recanted fast. 'Well, maybe not just like you and Jaz. Good friends. Nothing else.' The counterman came back and the kids' concentration switched. I tore a page out of my diary and scribbled down my home address and telephone number, putting it on the table before them. Jude picked it up. 'Just so you know where to find me,' I said. 'And try to think if Billy said anything else while you eat – tell yourself the person you're really helping is him and it might come easier.'

'Billy didn't tell me nothing else,' said Jaz. 'Look, we got on all right and I liked him, but I can't do nothing about what happened can I? Like I couldn't do nothing about it then.'

I sighed and took a fast look round the room. I was two cups of coffee ahead of them with a bladder fit to bust. I saw the door I wanted and shifted out of my seat. 'Just hang on two minutes, huh?' I said. 'I need to go somewhere.'

'Take your time,' said Jude.

I did, and when I came back from the loo they'd gone.

12

I stepped out from the café at a quarter past eight filled with irritation, peeved with the kids and peeved with myself for expecting them to sit around like a pair of angels and wait to be grilled. One thing was for sure; they wouldn't head back to Turpin Street until they thought I'd given up and gone home.

I scowled at the street and tried to come up with a good reason for the two of them to run off that way – or maybe they didn't need a reason. Up until now life hadn't exactly played them fair so what made me think I deserved better?

The whole area around Turpin Street and the Rainbow Café on the south side of town was run down and seedy. The few shops that were left – like the chemist and the newsagent – had windows thick with grime and pollution. At that time of night traffic was scant but come morning it would be nose to tail. A little further up the road punters were straggling into a local low-life dive with a flashing domino sign strung up above the door. The place was rough enough to earn a regular police presence outside on Saturday nights, and nobody with an IQ above eighty went near the place. I told myself that no two kids as obviously underage as Jaz and Jude could have sneaked in.

Or could they?

After a couple of seconds' thinking time I gave up on the idea of taking a peek – they wouldn't even have enough for the door charge.

I felt strung out and angry, like I really needed to unload some aggression, but short of beating up on the bouncer outside the Double-Six I'd no way of doing that. I eyed him speculatively. Five-eleven, thirteen stone and a face like a mean pit bull. Maybe I should go visit Nicholls instead.

The door-stop picked up he was being stared at and looked my way. His face transformed into a pit bull trying to smile. He winked and ducked his head in that cute way men have when they just know

63

they're irresistible. Then he jerked it sideways and gave me a come-on.

Whoo-ee! Did I really look that stupid?

I turned on my heel and stomped over to the hybrid. All that waiting around for two kids I'd managed to lose again really burned me up. Some days just seem like a waste of time.

I headed back to Palmer's Run and seethed some more about the way I'd set myself up to miss another Monday night's karate practice. I'd really let things slide there and I felt bad about it. No one knows better than I just how useful that kind of thing can be sometimes.

I garaged the car and jogged the short distance between Dora's place and mine, showing what good shape I was in by taking the stairs at the same fast pace. Such foolishness got me nothing but a stitch and I spent the rest of the night watching junk TV like a real couch potato.

I'd gone to bed expecting to wake up to a whole lot better day, but it didn't start off that way. When I came out from under the duvet there was enough rain coming down to bring out any latent Noah tendencies I might have harboured, and not a break in the sky. I took a hot shower and fixed breakfast, watching a mini-waterfall bypass the drainpipe while I ate. Little things like that can fill up a day. I shoved a couple more slices of bread in the toaster and dawdled over them, spreading each liberally with butter and then marmalade. Fat? Who cared! I did, of course, but that didn't stop me gobbling them down. Maybe such desire for comfort symbols came from the grey day; had to in fact because no way was I going to admit to depression.

I washed up my used pots like a good little house person and cleaned up the work surfaces. Happily such domesticity comes on me only rarely. I was looking around for some other equally entertaining activity to waste energy on when the telephone rang. I grabbed it up joyfully – right then even a heavy breather would have brightened my day – and said, 'Hi.' I waited. The voice was rich cream fondant and a notch below mid-range. A real smoothy. I didn't recognise either it or the name that went with it until he mentioned Bethany, then I remembered the Colin part belonged to her boss. Stanton was new to me.

'Bethany mentioned you,' I said, and added politely, 'What is it I can help you with, Mr Stanton?'

'Bethany passed on some doubts you seem to have about an arson claim where we've been acting as loss adjusters, Miss Hunter. I'd be interested to hear your ideas on it if you don't mind going through it all again?'

'Not a bit, do you want me to come down there?'

'I'm booked up on desk time until Thursday, but I can fit in a working lunch today. Unless you're busy?'

Was I busy? I was not.

'It sounds good to me,' I said. 'Where and when?'

'Same place you talked with Bethany?' he suggested. 'They do a good lunch. One o'clock suit?'

'Wheatsheaf at one sounds fine to me,' I said. 'It'll be nice to have some help in clearing this thing up.'

'I'm not sure that's exactly what I had in mind,' he came back, 'but we can talk about it.' Bet his boots he could I thought as we hung up.

I dragged out the Hoover and went on a dust-busting spree. Nothing too showy, mind; if Nicholls dropped in I'd hate him to think I was mending my ways.

At five to one I was sitting neat and businesslike in the Wheatsheaf and wondering what Bethany's boss looked like. Maybe we should have arranged to do something stupid like carry a copy of the *Sun*. I squinted around. Or maybe not. Such stupidity seemed more common than I'd thought. I sipped at a Pils and waited patiently. At ten past one he came in shaking rain off a Burberry mac and homed right in on me. I guessed Bethany's power of description had to be pretty good but I wasn't too sure about her choice of boss. His voice hadn't impressed me – I don't go much for verbal charm – and in the flesh Stanton looked altogether too sure of himself, like he'd spent his whole life being agreed with. I shook hands and checked him out. Middle forties, dark hair balded on top, brown eyes that didn't pick up the smile, wide forehead, narrow chin. The kind of man I'd warn my mother about. He looked at the Pils and said he hoped I hadn't been waiting too long and maybe we should go straight in to eat.

'Fine by me,' I said, 'but it looks a little crowded in there today. If you need to hurry maybe we'd be better with a bar snack.'

'I booked a table for one fifteen,' he said.

Uh-huh. How nice of him to get me there fifteen minutes early so I didn't keep him waiting! I picked up the Pils and took it with me, a little gesture intended to annoy. He pointed me to a window alcove with a two-seater table and gallantly pulled out a chair.

Such gentlemanly manners tend to make me suspicious; to begin with the whole thing is a kind of put-down. Just examine the implications inherent in all that stuff and they're saying you're nowhere near the same level of socioeconomic elevation as they are

65

and you're dumb to boot. In other words it's another part of the power game. I eyed the chair he was holding and sat myself opposite. His mouth tightened up a mite. I guess he felt a little irked I wasn't going to be as compliant as he'd hoped.

He sat down and the waiter brought over a couple of menus. I skimmed down mine and ordered omelette and green salad. Stanton went for steak pie. While we were waiting, he said, 'Bethany tells me you don't believe the Fast-Sell fire should be linked with the rest of the arson attacks. I'd be interested to hear why, especially when the police don't share the same doubts.'

'It isn't that straightforward,' I said. 'What solid evidence I have is confidential to Inland Revenue and I'm not free to discuss it. You can understand that?' He nodded. 'OK,' I said. 'What it boils down to is this. I'm pretty sure there's an insurance scam going on, and if that's so, I know you'll be as keen to stamp down on it as I am.'

'With verifiable proof I would be,' he agreed.

'Proof is what I hoped Bethany might help me get. I guess she told you that?'

'Miss Hunter, from what I hear you've been suspended, so why should I believe anything you tell me?'

'Drury made his complaint to keep me from digging any deeper into Fast-Sell's affairs. He wouldn't have done that if he didn't have something to hide.'

The waiter came back and we stopped talking while he set down his load. I reached for the pepper and Stanton said, 'How are you going to prove he wasn't telling the truth? It seems to be a case of your word against his.'

Shit! This man could really get under my skin.

'If you think I'm lying, why are we sitting here wasting time?' I said evenly. 'Go ahead and let the insurers finalise the claim, but if that's the way you see things I'd be really interested to know why I'm here.'

He took in a forkful of steak pie, munched on it a couple of times and swallowed, nodding all the while like his own mother had made it, then said vexatiously, 'Women like you tend to be less hysterical over a good meal than in an office.'

Wow!

I sat back and looked at him. It'd be real fun to tip that damn plate in his lap.

'Different planet altogether, huh?' I said. 'Just what kind of women give you trouble, Mr Stanton – the kind you forget to say thank you to before you put your pants back on? Let's get something straight. The subject we're here to talk about is insurance fraud, not your own personal prejudices! OK?'

He puced up prettily and took a fast look around to see who was listening; since I hadn't raised my voice the answer was nobody, but it did my heart good to see how it worried him. A little burst of perspiration had come out on his forehead. I got on with my omelette and left him to think things out; there's just no sense in letting good food go to waste. After a couple of seconds, he said, 'All right, Miss Hunter. I can allow you that little outburst. Now suppose we get down to exactly why you think that we as loss adjusters should try to hold up a claim.'

There are some people I just can't get fond of!

'Suppose we eat,' I said. 'And then if you approach it right, maybe we'll talk later.' He sat there and scowled for a while then fell to clearing his plate. I guess it had more to do with thrift than conviviality.

I finished up my food, waved at the waiter, and when he ambled over asked for Espresso coffee and my half of the bill. Stanton said he'd have a filter and put it all on his. I demurred, we argued, the waiter went away. I looked out the window and Stanton examined the intricacies of scrollwork on the cornice. By and by the waiter came back. When he'd delivered the coffees he set the bill in front of Stanton and fawningly hoped the meal had been satisfactory.

It's just one big boys' club out there!

'So,' I said. 'I suppose you're going to tell Bethany not to cooperate.'

'As things stand, yes I am, Miss Hunter. If you aren't willing to put what you know in front of me and be open, I don't see an alternative to that. I have to think of the reputation of Saxby Associates.'

'OK,' I said. 'Let's forget it, I'll just go straight to Northern Alliance. Bet they'll be interested to hear how keen you were to save them money.'

'Miss Hunter, I'm willing to listen to anything you have to say. It's you who refuse to share information. Give me facts and I'll see what I can do with them.'

'Well, it's nice to hear that, but I have a gut feeling you mean to do damn all. What do you want to know?'

I watched his urge to show indifference fight with a need to know. Mistakes in his line of work don't come cheap and there's a lot of unemployment about right now.

He swallowed down some sour hubris.

'Take it from the beginning, facts and not fairytales.'

I asked myself which was more important, cutting him down to size or getting some help in my corner. Help won. I went back to the beginning and set the whole thing in front of him, save for some little omissions I didn't see it could hurt him not to know. Like the way Nicholls didn't believe anything I'd told him except that Drury was lying through his teeth. In my experience such unimportant details are best not told.

'That's it?' he said when I'd finished.

'What did you expect?'

'Concrete evidence, not prejudiced supposition.' He shook his head at me and looked happy enough to bust. 'I'm sorry, Miss Hunter, I can sympathise with your position but all I'm prepared to do is look at the fire reports again. I'm reasonably sure they'll be in order.'

'That so?'

I checked the menu prices, grabbed up my purse and got out my share of the bill. 'Put it away,' he said, 'you could be a long time unemployed.'

I gritted my teeth and stepped out from the table.

'Tell you what,' I snapped. 'Let this scam slip through your fingers and you're going to be out there a lot longer than me, buddy boy!' I slammed the money hard down in front of him and got out of the place before I did something unladylike. Right then my sympathies were all with Bethany. With a boss like that she needed a real sweet lover to go home to. Which put me in mind of Nicholls.

Of course, when I went looking for him at the cop shop he wasn't around, but bet your life he would be the minute I didn't want him there.

13

I went home fuming with rage and shed the businesslike clothes in favour of black sweats. Two days of adrenaline overload had me feeling corked as a bottle, which in retrospect was good since it set me hunting up gym kit and heading straight back out again. Walking into the health club felt good until I got to the changing room and saw that somebody had had a busy weekend. I looked at the fresh pretty-pink walls. *Who'd picked on that colour?* I hoped the little boys' room had been done out in cute baby-blue to match. I changed fast, stuffed the sweats in a locker and wondered who'd been the busy bee with a paintbrush. The sight of all that girly-pink made me itch to join the graffiti set. When I padded out to the Nautilus machines Jeff was in there showing a petite blonde how to do a leg stretch. I said, 'Hi!' cheerily and selected the usual weights. Jeff left the blonde to her own devices and came over at a trot.

'Forget it, Leah,' he said, hauling me off the seat. 'Bodies need time to wind back up nice and slow; you can't just drop into the old fitness programme without risking some damage.'

I could feel the muscles in my shoulders bunch up in frustration. My, but I was sick of being pushed around and put down by males. I shook him off. 'Forget it yourself, Jeff. I managed fine when you weren't around Thursday, so don't butt in now. I need to work out.'

He stabbed out at me with a finger. 'Fine, do that, but not in this club. Not without a fitness check and a new programme. I mean it, Leah. I make the rules and you're not getting round them.'

'Great!' I yelled. 'Fine! Stuff the club!' The blonde was watching us with interest. I turned on my heel and walked out. Enough was enough. I sat around the changing room and thought about how easy it was to get antisocial tendencies. After a couple of minutes I went back out. Jeff was leaning up against the wall. 'OK,' I said snappily. 'So let's get on with it; just don't expect an apology is all.'

He shoved upright. 'Didn't even cross my mind,' he said, then gave me that slow, sexy smile of his that gets all the novitiate hearts aflutter. 'Tell you what though, it's good to have you back.'

We grinned at each other a little then I hooked up to the pulse monitor and set the treadmill for a good, brisk pace. 'Hang around,' I said. 'It'll be fun to see you eat your words.' Such confidence is seldom justified.

I got home around six thirty and went straight into a hot tub, soaking and topping up with fresh water for around forty minutes until I'd got good and waterlogged and my muscles had stopped jellifying, then I wolfed down a plate of spaghetti with Italian sauce and butter-fried mushrooms, stacked the pots and had me another lazy night. Early to bed and early to rise had never brought me wisdom so far but maybe there was still time.

In the dark depths of sleep I dreamed there was a fire alarm going off, then I opened up my eyes and found out it was only partly a dream. An edge of orange streetlight knifed through a gap in the bedroom curtains. The luminous hands on the clock said three thirty and someone was leaning on my doorbell. By now the entire house was probably awake. I pulled on a cotton wrap and staggered to the window. It didn't help. Whoever stood out there was just a dark blob. I cursed a little and went downstairs. Marcie stuck her head out of the middle flat as I went by. 'Know who it is?' I broke step and shook my head. 'I'll hang on here then,' she said. 'Just in case.' Marcie and I seem to have dropped into the habit of looking out for each other. I went on down and opened the locks. The waif from Turpin Street looked in at me like a lost child, shivering enough for me to hear her teeth chatter and giving off a faint, smoky smell. I took a quick glance up and down the street and pulled her inside before she passed out on the doorstep.

'It's three flights up,' I said. 'Think you can make it?' She nodded and moved at a loose lurch towards the bottom step. I put an arm around her shoulders and steadied her. Marcie watched us come, asked if I'd be OK, and went back inside when I said yes. We made it to the attic and I sat the girl down, poured half an inch of whisky in a glass and gave it to her. She swallowed it in one gulp, coughed a little and got some colour in her cheeks.

'I'd nowhere else to go,' she said, staring at her hands and the empty glass. 'The squat's burned up.'

'How about Jaz?'

She started to shake again.

70

'He was in there?'

'Yeh.' The word breathed out so quiet I hardly heard it. I put an arm around her, feeling tremors move through her body. She said dully, 'Can I flop here? Just tonight? Haven't got nowhere else.' For kids like Jude life can be a real gas.

I hunted out a cotton shift and showed her where the bathroom was. 'Try a hot tub,' I advised and added recklessly, 'use all the bubble bath and stuff you want.' She looked at the bottles and perked up a little. I left her alone. A couple of minutes later I heard the taps running and an overstrong scenty smell filled up the place.

I hauled out a sleeping bag and a couple of afghans inherited from Gran and made up a bed for her on the settee – what else could I do? Throw her out on the street? By rights I should call the police or else drive her down there. It was obvious they'd want to talk with her but I couldn't do that, not right then when she looked like a frazzled bird, tear-streaked and hurting. Her eyes were swollen dark Os in her face, reddened and grimed from all the rubbing and crying she'd been doing on her way across town.

While she was in the tub I heated up some milk and added a dollop of honey, and by and by when she came out looking like a scrubbed little girl I gave it to her to drink. Anybody would have thought she was starving. I watched it go down in a couple of gulps and went to make some sandwiches. Cheese and tomato were all I had on offer, but they went down with about the same speed as the hot milk, so I suppose she didn't really notice much about them except they were food.

Sometimes sadness creeps up so fast it can catch a person unawares, and it did that now. I jerked my mind back into logic mode and asked what had happened to Jaz and the house. She crawled into the nest I'd made her and looked at me. 'How do I know I can trust you?' she said.

'Look at it another way,' I said. 'What's the alternative?'

She sat back up and started to swing her legs out.

'Now what?' I said.

'Stupid, aren't I? Me and Jaz were all right before you come round. I shouldn't have listened, should I? It's me what told him he ought to talk to you, sold him out for a bleedin' cheeseburger. You snitched on us didn't you? Told 'em where me an' Jaz was squatting out.'

'Hey! I wouldn't do that. Think about it. Come on, wake up to what's happening. If I wanted you dead would I loan you my bubble bath?' The fist she'd bunched loosened itself and she slumped and shrugged. 'Get back in bed,' I said. 'You're safe, I promise that, but before you fall asleep tell me what happened.'

'I dunno, it . . . I mean . . . I'd been out to get some money so we could eat. Yeh . . . that's right,' she said, reading my mind. 'Tarting. Where else d'you expect me to get it? Down the Social? When I come back Jaz was acting jumpy – you know – shifting round, looking out the window every five minutes, and he wouldn't tell me what bugged him. Then these two fellas come down the street, an' he gets this scared look and shoves me out the back. "Go on," he says. "Get lost – you got to get out of sight." So I did what he said didn't I? I went over the back wall an' then went up the bus station for a bit. Then these two lads come and start taking the piss out of me so I went back to Jaz.' Her face screwed up and she started rocking. 'There isn't nobody lives round there any more is there? It's burning up, the squat an' everything, an' nobody knows, an' I've got to run up Tesco's to get in a phone what worked.'

'And you didn't see Jaz?'

She shook her head.

'What did the men look like?'

'Dunno, didn't see much. One of 'em had long hair.'

'How about the other?'

'I dunno. Shorter an' a belly.'

'What about clothes?'

'Belly had a leather jacket.' She closed her eyes and thought about it. 'Like a biker. Other one had a carrier bag.'

'What colour hair?'

'Brown.'

'Both of them?'

'Yeh.'

'What about pants – did they have blue jeans, or what?'

'Black. Wasn't nothing else. Just black. Everything.'

'It could be that Jaz got out too,' I said, trying to give her a hopeful thought to go to sleep on. She shook her head.

'He'd have waited around, he wouldn't have gone on and left me to worry. We was a real couple, not just mucking about.' She opened her eyes and looked up at me. 'You got a fella?' I nodded. 'Well, then. Would he? I mean, would he go off and leave you to think he was dead?'

'Depends if he had a choice. Maybe when they left he had to go with them.'

She gave the idea a little thought. A flicker of optimism came back.

'Yeh,' she said. 'They took him away someplace, so that's all right, I'll just have to find him, won't I?'

I said goodnight, turned off the light and went to bed with another slice of guilt. There was a better than even chance that Jaz's bones were nicely crisped than that he'd been kidnapped. There was no sense in admitting that to Jude though. A sleep would do her more good than being told the truth.

I set the alarm for seven thirty, planning to feed her before I worked on persuading her to go to the police about the men she'd seen down by the squat. Maybe if she looked through the mugshots she'd recognise one or both. It was a good thought but like most such things it didn't work out that way. When I went into the living room she'd folded up her bed and gone. A scrap of paper said, 'Thanks', and nothing else. Great! Now all I had to do was find her again.

I ate a solitary breakfast and then went to take a look at the house on Turpin Street. There's something about burned and gutted property, even if it was derelict to begin with, that seems inexplicably sad. Maybe it's because the windows look like empty eye sockets, or maybe it's thinking how many dreams have gone up in smoke along with the building.

I'd left the hybrid on the main road near the fry-up place and walked the rest of the way on foot. Sensible of me. Turpin Street was cordoned off with yellow tape and I guessed the council would need to speed up the demolition programme. Jaz's squat and a couple more houses had all gone the same way. Out front there wasn't much left but bare shells and scorched timbers. I stepped between cones and ducked under the tape. Maybe Jaz hadn't been in there after all; if he had, there'd have been two or three strong heroes in blue keeping sightseers away. I cheered up a little and went to take a closer look.

From the front there wasn't much to see, just blackened walls and collapsed ceilings. The front door, half burned away, hung drunkenly on one hinge. I moved down an arched passage between two intact houses and made my way to the back of number nine. I wasn't alone there. A man in a hard hat and yellow-banded donkey jacket was pacing around with a clipboard. He didn't look too glad to see me. He quit writing and gave me an unfriendly scowl. 'You looking for something?'

'Not exactly. I . . .'

'Then you've no business being here. The place is cordoned off. Don't you have eyes?'

I just love rude people.

'Yes, I've got eyes. I've also got reasons. Who's in charge around here?'

'Why?'

'Because he's the man I want to see.'

'Yeah, well, he's busy. Try me.'

'I just did,' I said politely, 'but it didn't inspire me.'

'That so? Talk or move on. It's all the same to me.' He gave his attention back to the clipboard. I moved past him to the back of the house. 'Hey,' he said. 'You can't do that.'

'I already have,' I said. 'It's always nice to talk to the guy in charge.' The back of the house was in slightly better shape than the front. I stuck my head through the gaping door and hollered: 'Anybody in there?' Somebody was. A piece of floorboard came down through a hole in the ceiling and cautious footsteps headed in the direction of the charred stairs. Just in case I wondered if they were together he wore an identical hard hat and banded jacket to the sweet-natured guy outside. He picked his way down to me sticking close to the wall. I gave him an encouraging smile. 'Are you the guy in charge?' Instead of answering he took my arm and started to hustle me away from the place. I dug my heels in and shook loose.

'OK,' he said. 'So what's the excuse? Your Auntie Mabel lived here twenty years ago or the local paper sent you?'

'Neither. I hoped I'd get some intelligent answers to a couple of questions. Guess it just shows how wrong I can be.'

He didn't like that but he backed off and took a better look. 'What questions?'

'How did the fire start?'

'What's your interest?'

'I know someone who was living here yesterday.'

'It's been empty two years.'

'Is that a fact? Take my word for it, it wasn't empty yesterday. Two kids were squatting and now one's missing.'

'Hell!' he said. 'You absolutely sure about that?'

'I wouldn't be here if I wasn't. Any chance someone died in there?'

'Have you been to the police?'

'Not yet. If the place is clear I don't want to involve them. These two kids have problems enough without me adding to them.'

'Yeah, well, it looks like arson. Maybe the kid you're looking for is lying low.'

'If you mean he might have started it the answer's no.'

He blinked a little and turned to stare up at the house. He looked a lot more worried than he had five minutes ago. I said, 'Are you with the fire service?' His chin ducked a fraction. 'Uh-huh. Well, I know you're pretty thorough, so I guess if you haven't found any bones in there I can stop worrying.' He shook his head and didn't say anything. 'Look,' I said. 'If you're still thinking the kids started it there's one good way to be sure. My guess is to get this much out of hand there'd have to have been an accelerant – the place was too damp to have caught hold without one – and if that's so I can tell you now they didn't even have money enough to buy food let alone something to burn this place up.'

'Lady,' he said, 'I don't know who you are but I think you just spoiled my day.' I was sorry about that but I wasn't exactly on a pleasure curve myself.

I left him to call up some help and went back to the car. He wasn't too happy to see me walk away but there wasn't anything he could do to stop me either. Time enough for me to talk to the boys in blue if the place yielded anything but rubble.

I tried to think where I would go if I were fourteen and homeless. I trawled the market and the shiny bright shopping mall, saw some look-alikes but not the real thing and remembered how she'd earned a little money. Where would I go to do that? There were terrible gaps in my knowledge and I regretted that. I cruised the streets like a kerb crawler and around two thirty when I was about to give up I saw her. Blue-and-white-striped socks and black lace-ups. Black leggings with a short, flowery flounced skirt. Denim jacket and pale blonde hair. And I was just a spit too late.

She climbed into a red Orion that took off fast.

I speeded up and stayed with it until the bypass roundabout, at which point the Orion cut in front of a funeral cavalcade and left me to wait and fume. By the time I zipped out behind the last car the red saloon was out of sight and fast driving didn't bring me up on it again. I went back to her pick-up point and parked where I could see it. Maybe she had her clients drop her off there. The thought of her having to do that kind of thing made me sick and sad and angry all at the same time. *Shit!* She was just a kid, she didn't know anything. Thoughts of psychos and perves jostled with the knowledge that she could pick up AIDS and be dead before she made it to grown-up.

At four I went home and fed myself stir-fry and hoped she'd come and ring my doorbell again. She didn't, of course.

14

The morning after I'd raised a little worry at the burned-out house on Turpin Street, I rang John Redding and asked if he'd heard any news about the place. There was a fairly long silence before he came back and said, 'You're the mystery female who thought someone might have died in there?'

'Was I right?'

'There's someone here who'd really like to talk to you about that. He's been wondering where to find you.'

'What someone?'

'One of our fire investigators. Martin Barlow. You met him yesterday.'

'He wants to talk on the phone or in person?'

A little debate went on before a voice I remembered took over from Redding. 'Miss Hunter, I'm glad you called. I think it would be a good idea if we talked.'

'That's fine by me,' I said. 'Do you want me to come down there?'

'Sooner the better. How long's it going to take you to get here?' I told him fifteen minutes and he grunted, said that would suit him nicely and hung up. I had a feeling the questions he wanted to ask centred around how I'd known about Jaz, which was tough because I didn't intend to tell him – not the whole truth anyway – not until I'd given a little more time to tracking down Jude. I changed into a less threadbare pair of jeans, pulled on a white T-shirt and navy blazer and gave a little more thought to which variation of the truth I should tell. I didn't expect to find one of Nicholls's colleagues sitting in on our little chat, but there he was, taking up a chair and looking just the way he had at Billy's funeral.

Without his hard hat on Barlow looked a couple of years younger than he had when he'd picked his way down the charred stairs yesterday, but still not less than forty, wiry hair near to being crew cut

77

and ears that bent over a little at the tops. Redding got me a chair, then hollered out of the door that he wanted four coffees up there fast before he came back and joined the rest of us.

Barlow said, 'Well, Miss Hunter, it's nice you could spare the time, so let's get right on with it. I'd be interested to hear why you thought there was a body in the Turpin Street house.'

'I'd be interested to know why CID are represented,' I said.

'That's something that worries you?'

'No,' I said, 'that's something that makes me feel curious.' I squinted round at the third man. 'DC Fry isn't it?' He nodded. 'Care to tell me why you're here?'

'Anything with the word arson in it tends to land on my desk,' he said.

'Uh-huh. That's why you were at Billy's funeral?'

He hitched around in his chair a little bit. 'That's it,' he said. Body language is great at picking out liars.

'So,' I said, 'let's get back to the fire. Was anybody in there?'

Barlow said, 'I'd rather you told us why you thought there was.'

I shrugged. 'If I'd been wrong you wouldn't be asking, so why not just come out and say so?' He cracked his fingers, lacing them together and then pulling back on the joints. I hate it when people do that. 'Come on,' I said. 'I didn't start the damn fire for pity's sake, so why not be up front about it?'

'All right. We found human remains; does that make you feel better?'

'Did it make *you* feel better?' I snapped. Idiot questions always get me riled.

Fry, CID's youngest if not brightest, began to make a few notes. I glowered at him, knowing where they'd end up.

Barlow opened up a brown manila file he had in front of him and flicked through it. He'd taken over Redding's desk, mainly I guessed because he thought it gave him more authority. He said, 'If it's all the same to you, Miss Hunter, I'd rather not waste more time on this than I have to. A few straight answers would help. You went to Turpin Street yesterday believing there was a body in the rubble, yes or no.'

I shook my head. 'I thought there might be, I hoped there wasn't. I'd talked to Jaz a couple of days earlier and he was worried he might have upset some bad people.'

'What people?'

'If I knew that I'd have already told my good friend, Inspector Nicholls.' I grinned at Fry. 'Causing death by fire isn't something I condone, Mr Barlow. Let's establish that right now so we know where we are, OK?'

'Then let's try a different approach. What was it that – Jaz did you say?' I nodded – 'had done to upset these people?'

'I'm not sure that would come under a fire officer's remit, but since the police are also represented here I'll let you share the knowledge. Jaz had been locked up in a secure unit at the same time as Billy Tyler. He's the kid who got picked up for all the arson fires we've been having lately. Unfortunately, having hanged himself, he can't prove his innocence.'

'Miss Hunter, I've heard a lot about your busybody nature and caustic wit, and I might as well tell you now, I'm not the kind of man to appreciate either. Investigating the cause of a fire is a job for experts. Stick with tax collecting and keep out from under my feet.'

This was a man it would be so easy to dislike. Would be? Hell. I already did. I shot an unkind look at Fry who was most likely to have been the blabbermouth. 'Look,' I told Barlow, 'since we're doing some straight talking here, my sense of humour is none of your damn business, and come to that neither is the investigation of a possibly unlawful death. So why don't you stick to sifting ashes and leave citizens' advice to the police?' We glared at each other for a while, both of us trying to come up with something that would shut the other up for good. Then I realised that in the not too distant future I might need him more than he would need me. I said, 'Look, we got off on the wrong foot and that's bad, but I want to find out about Jaz too. Believe it or not I liked the kid.' He sat back and looked a little mollified. The coffee came, better late than never, and we all nursed mugs for a while and thought about where we were at.

Fry said, 'We'll need to talk to you too since you seem to know who it is we're talking about. Maybe you could drop by later today and make a statement.' I sighed. I bet they'd be able to start a whole filing system down there with nothing in it but statements made by me.

'Sure,' I said agreeably. 'Soon as I get a minute I'll be right down there.' Luckily he didn't know me as well as Nicholls or he'd have pinned me down to a fixed time. I looked at Barlow. 'Is that it then?' I said. 'Nothing else you want to ask?'

'If I think of anything I'll know where to find you,' he said. I stood up and picked an imaginary fuzz-ball off my sleeve.

'It's been really nice,' I said, 'comparing notes like this. Maybe I'll drop by your office sometime and do it again.'

Barlow didn't smile. 'I'd guess I get to sit behind my desk for maybe a dozen hours a week,' he said. 'Most people give up on trying to pin me down; it's a waste of time.'

'You know it's a funny thing,' I said, 'but sometimes I get that way myself. It's a terrible thing to be pushed into being unhelpful.'

'I'll see you out,' said Redding kindly, and walked me downstairs. 'If you need anything don't be worried about coming back,' he said. 'There are ways of by-passing Barlow if it has to be done.'

'Thanks,' I said, 'I really appreciate that.'

'It's no problem. I know a little more of what goes on in Bramfield than he does that's all.' He squinted back at his office. 'He's not so bad when you get to know him. Good at his job. I guess you just wrong-footed him yesterday and he never did like having that kind of thing happen to him.'

We shook hands, then he turned around smartish and went to claim his desk back. I got into the hybrid and headed back into town, turning into Market Street and then swinging right.

When I pulled into his yard, Charlie was working on a red Escort, his legs and rump sticking out of the engine compartment like the back end of a panto horse. I parked by the side wall and climbed out. He straightened up and watched me come.

''Lo, love, wondered when you'd be round. Come for a bit of tea and sympathy?'

'A chat is all.'

'Don't need to bother with the kettle then. What's the problem?'

'No problem. I dropped by to see how your sister's doing.'

'Not good. Go to pieces if it weren't for the other two. How about you? Hear you got troubles too.'

'Can't think who told you that, Charlie,' I said.

'Never mind about who; bad news travels fast. I hear you're not tax inspecting no more. What's that about then? 'Cos of our Billy?'

'Asking the wrong questions got under somebody's tender skin. Don't worry about it; I haven't quit the job and I haven't got the sack. It's just that it and I are temporarily parted.'

'Want him sorting out then?'

'Who?'

'Whoever it is has the tender skin.'

'Nice of you to worry, Charlie, but it'll work out fine.'

He cleaned off a plug with a filthy paraffin rag and inspected it. 'Billy's gone an' that being so I don't want you to get into no more bother on his account. Like they told his ma, if he hadn't done it he wouldn't have topped himself, would he?'

80

'Who the hell told her that?'

'Some young CID feller what went round after Billy's funeral. Said how he was sorry and all that but they wasn't looking for nobody else.'

'That so?' I scuffed at the ground and picked up a washer, transferring grease from it to my hand. When I dumped it on the workbench Charlie offered me his rag. It seemed churlish not to accept, and rubbing the black stuff spread it around nicely. I gave the rag back, hunted up a tissue, and scrubbed some more. 'CID change their minds a lot,' I said. 'Especially when they make mistakes.'

I could see his ears prick.

'That's what you think then, is it?'

'The arson business didn't finish with Billy. There was a place on Turpin Street fired the night before last. Maybe they'll do a little rethink.'

'Thought it was kids mucking around did that lot. You saying it wasn't?'

'I'm saying I don't think it was kids,' I said.

'Well me money's on you then and stuff the fuzz.'

I got a rosy warm glow. How nice that someone had so much confidence in me. It made a real change from being tagged as a pain in the ass.

I said, 'Thanks for the vote of confidence, Charlie.'

'Only saying what I think, aren't I?' He started wiping his hands. 'Lucky it was empty.'

I said gently, 'A kid on remand the same time as Billy was in there – but that's between you and me, Charlie, and not for passing on.' The wiping picked up speed.

'That DI of yours know about it, does he?'

'If he's doing his job right.'

'Better leave it to him then; s'what he gets paid for. Don't want you in no bother, love.'

Feeling an absurd edge of irritation at such friendly concern, I took a step back and eyed him. He kept his eyes on the busy rag and worked on getting his hands a uniform shade of drab. I said, 'Come on, Charlie, I didn't come here to get a lecture.'

'Yeh, well, like me ma used to say, what you want you don't get, and what you get you don't want. Secret of life that, love. Wouldn't want to see you end up next to Billy 'cos you thought you was doing something for me.'

'I'm doing it for myself,' I snapped. 'I'm working at getting back my damn job. OK?'

'If you say so, love. Don't believe it like, but if you want any help doing it you only have to ask.' I hate it when people see through my lies. I told him I'd drop by again before Christmas and he grinned and stuck his head back under the bonnet. Getting back in the car I stiff-fingered him. A greasy hand came up from the Escort's innards and saluted me back in kind. That's the nice thing about friends – such rude gestures don't count.

15

Some things seem like sheer luck. I'd been cruising around looking for Jude and then suddenly there she was, wearing the same outfit and trying to pick up a punter. It made me sick to my stomach. There was no way the men so eager to get their rocks off could be unaware of her age. Her stick-thin, still childish body would give that away right from the start. Sometimes life gets too hurtful to think about. The time had ticked round to half past five and a fine drizzle of rain had damped down everything, including Jude's hair that clung to her face in fine tendrils and made her look even more like a waif.

When I pulled over to the kerb the car windows were steamed up a little and she didn't see who it was right away. I watched different things skitter over her face as I came to a stop. Hope that she'd earn a few pounds see-sawed with panic. *God!* She must go through that every time. I reached across and shoved open the door. 'Get in,' I said. 'I hate to eat alone.' She dithered and hopped around from one foot to the other. 'Come on, Jude, we need to talk, you owe me that much.'

She crossed the strip of pavement reluctantly. 'Where d'you want to go?'

'Someplace to eat for pity's sake. Now will you get in out of the rain before you end up with pneumonia?' She got in and closed the door. 'Seat belt,' I said.

She sat bolt upright and didn't look at me. 'You going to turn me in?'

'What for? You robbed a bank or cheeked a policeman?' She sat back and put her seat belt on. 'That's better,' I said and drove us to a Burger King. She put away a couple of double cheeseburgers while I played around with French fries and a coffee. If she got mad-cow disease it'd probably be all my fault. She swallowed the last bit and burped gently. Her face got a little colour back. 'Want anything else?'

I said. 'No? OK, where are you sleeping tonight?'

'Dunno. Around some place.'

'Another squat?'

Jude was feeling really communicative. She gave a shrug and sat back in her chair with her chin tucked down.

'OK,' I said. 'You don't want to talk that's fine. Let whoever torched the place on Turpin Street get away with it. Hell, what do I care?' She squinted up at me with old eyes and shrugged again. 'What's keeping you?' I said cruelly. 'You want to go looking for punters there's the door.' She stared at it like she was weighing up whether or not she could get out of it before I stopped her. Then she made her move. Anger got me up on my feet. I grabbed a scrawny arm and pointed back at the chair. 'Sit,' I snapped. 'And don't even think about leaving until we've talked.'

The pink fled out of her cheeks again. I became aware that everyone in the place was looking at us. Since when did I get to be school bully? I glared at her. Tears filled up her eyes and she sat down like a spanked pup. Shame filled me. I pulled my voice down to gentle. 'How about we have some more coffee, huh? Just don't run away while I fetch it, OK?' This time the nod came readily but I still kept an eye on her while I went and got it. The counter hand gave me a funny look but didn't say anything. When I got back to her the tears had gone.

'I don't have to tell you nothing. I don't have to talk, or get into your car, or nothing. Right?'

'Right.' I put a paper cup in front of her. 'When the house burned down there was someone still inside.' She opened up her eyes and the tears came back. I handed her a tissue.

'Told you, didn't I? Told you he wouldn't have just gone off without waiting for me.'

'Yes,' I said softly, 'you did. But I want to find out who did it, and you're the only one who can help me do that. I need to know who else knew about the squat. Jaz had told somebody where he'd be, hadn't he?'

'He said he wanted to get some money so we could get out of Bramfield and find a good place to live. We'd have been all right then, he could have got a job an' I could have kept house an'...'

'How did Jaz plan to get that kind of money?'

'Blackmail,' she said sadly. 'Feller called Gavin what works at that place Jaz got banged up in. Told him he wanted some money or he'd tell the fuzz what happened to Billy.' I sucked in a good long breath.

What happened to Billy? She stuck the heels of her hands in her eyes and rubbed hard. 'I told him he shouldn't have but he never would listen. Anyway, this Gavin said he'd have to talk to somebody else an' that's all Jaz'd tell me.'

'When did this happen?'

'After you come. Before we went down the caff.'

'Jude, this is really important. Do you know what Jaz meant about Billy?'

She shook her head. 'I asked him an' – he said to shut up about it.'

'The two men you saw on Turpin Street. Were they carrying anything?'

'Tesco bag. Thought I told you that.'

'How much did Jaz ask for?'

'I dunno.'

I drank off half the coffee and took some thinking time. Maybe Jaz had thought they were paying up fast, that the Tesco bag was full of money. 'When he told you to get out was he scared or excited?'

'I dunno, I just did what he said.'

'So why did you think he'd sent you away?'

''Cos he didn't want me to see what was going on, I suppose. An' he wouldn't want me to see it if he *was* scared, would he? Wasn't that much older than me you know, it's just he liked to think he could look after me.' She stuck her chin down again and I gave her another tissue.

'Just how much older was he?'

'A year or so.'

'Or two? Exactly how old are you, Jude? Thirteen? Fourteen?'

'What's it matter?' She clammed up again, drinking up her coffee and looking at the floor.

I said, 'Where are you sleeping tonight – you haven't told me yet.'

'Dunno.'

'I have a friend who might give you a bed if you're interested.'

'Why'd she do that?'

'Because she's a good person. Do you want me to call her?'

'I don't have to stay if I don't want to.'

'That's understood. It's that or the streets and I know which I'd choose.'

She sort of slumped like an old balloon. I didn't know a kid her age could look that weary. 'Suppose, if you want to then,' she said. I looked at the pay phone up a short flight of stairs near the washrooms. ''S'all right,' she said. 'Can't be bothered to run; it's not worth it.' I wanted to fold my arms around her and hug but I didn't do that. Some instinct told me it was about the last thing she'd want me to do. I climbed the eight steps and rang Dora, made my request and filled her in on the background. Just like I'd expected she said to bring Jude right round. I told her thanks, bundled the kid into my car and headed for Palmer's Run and a warm, safe night. That was about as far ahead as I could plan for her, because experience said she'd duck out come morning and make it twice as hard for me to find her again.

Sometimes I'm too pessimistic by half.

Dora had been watching out for us and had the front door wide open before we got in the gate. She came down the two stone steps and took a look at Jude's face, then she opened up her arms. I waited for the kid to back off like a startled rabbit, but no, she picked up Dora's magic in no time flat and went up the path like it was the yellow brick road. Dora is no plump mother figure; she's rangy-thin, bordering on boniness, and all those years as a headmistress, coupled with bringing up her own family have given her a no-nonsense approach to life. They've also given her a lot of insight into other people and I wish I had the half of it. She didn't say a word to Jude, just stood there hugging her while all the grief poured out. I swallowed hard and cleared my throat.

'Uh ... maybe I'll just head home and sort out a nightie and a change of outfit for Jude? I guess I'll have some things that'd fit.'

'You go ahead, we'll be fine,' said Dora. 'Supper's cooking and there's plenty for three. Shepherd's pie and blackberry crumble. Are you coming back to eat with us?'

I squinted at my watch – six forty-five – and thought about how good resolutions are hard to keep. Dammit, I needed to stick to a good exercise schedule and Thursday was work-out night. Then again I couldn't just dump Jude and run.

Dora said, 'Forty-five minutes to eating time.'

'Can't resist,' I said, then gave her a wave and sprinted for home. Halfway there I saw Nicholls's car and slowed right down. It didn't take much more than a pinch of sixth sense to know he wasn't just making a social call or to guess DC Fry had been spreading gossip.

He got out and waited for me.

'This is real nice,' I said brightly. 'But I can't go on the razzle. Tonight I'm eating at Dora's.'

He said waspily, 'Weren't you supposed to drop by the office?'

'Inland Revenue? No, don't think so.'

I trotted on up the front steps, let myself in, and started for the attic with Nicholls tagging along behind. He said, 'You agreed to come in and have a talk with CID. Remember?'

'Uh-huh. Fry did say something about that but he wasn't specific about it being today. Hope you haven't been sitting around waiting for me? I mean it'd be too bad if you'd had to let up on catching crooks just because of me.' I held the flat door for him politely. He made for the kitchen, emptied out the filter jug and gave it a rinse. 'Help yourself,' I told him politely.

'Don't be smart,' he snapped.

'Nicholls, you keep screwing your forehead up that way you'll get wrinkles and lose all that little-boy charisma you manage so well. Lighten up a bit.' He scowled a little harder. I shrugged. 'Suit yourself,' I said, 'but don't expect me to front for you at the beauty counter.'

He got a brew going, hooked out a kitchen chair, rocked back and looked at me. 'Tell me about it,' he invited. 'And make it good or so help me, I'm going to take you back down to headquarters and keep you there until you do.'

'Fine,' I said. 'All you had to do was ask. What do you want to know? About the fire? I didn't see it. About how nasty I was to the fire officers? There were two of them and one of me and they could have thrown me out any time they wanted.' He seemed to like that idea. I could see him thinking about it as he smiled. 'Anything else?' I asked sweetly.

'Start with how you knew there was somebody in there.'

Some things you just can't lie your way out of, and that was one of them. I told him I'd heard how friendly Billy and Jaz had been in the secure unit and how I'd tracked Jaz to the squat. He shook his head and said why wouldn't I let things rest. I asked what did it take to convince him there was an arsonist still out there, and he came right back and snapped that I was just grasping at straws because I still didn't want to accept it had been Billy all along.

'Fine,' I yelled. 'Just fine. Now explain how he gets up out of his grave and burns down a house. Tell me about it, why don't you.'

We scowled at each other for a while and then he said he had to go. I told him I was glad about that and now maybe I could go and eat. He stomped to the door and I stomped with him. When we got there I asked sarcastically if he was sure there was nothing else I could help him with. He growled something rude, clattered downstairs like there was two of him and banged the outside door. When he cooled down and got friendly again maybe I'd tell him the rest of it.

16

The nice thing about leggings is they fit anybody from Olive Oil to a lapsed Weightwatcher. I shoved two pairs, one black one stripy, into a carrier bag with a couple of oversized T-shirts and a new pack of bikini briefs, added pop socks and a shift nightie with Snoopy on its front, then took a quick shower, making it back to Dora's with a minute to spare. Jude was curled in an easy chair with Dora's fat tabby cat purring on top of her. It looked like love at first sight. When I dumped the carrier bag at the side of her, the plumy tail waved a little and told me to back off. I scratched a furry ear and a languid paw lifted and showed its claws. The cat and I get on fine but we're not overly sentimental. Dora dumped the moggie on the rug and told Jude there was just time for her to get the cat smell off her fingers before we ate, and maybe she could take the carrier bag upstairs at the same time? The kid took a look inside, said thanks like the word was really rusty and went off without a quibble. Dora said matter of factly, 'I like that child. It's time someone helped her straighten out.'

I grinned. Dora and I have a lot in common.

'Looks like you already started,' I said.

The tabby sneaked back up on the chair and started in pummelling the cushion. Dora eyed it. 'Depends how long I can hold on to her. She's talking about moving on tomorrow so this creature is the best hope we've got; it seems she can trust cats more than people.'

If Jude's home setup had been anything like Jaz's, I could see how she'd get that way. I squinted up the stairs and heard water running in the bathroom. I said quietly, 'She tell you anything about herself?'

'Not much more than I got from you on the phone. How long had she known the boy?'

'I don't know but from what I saw they really looked out for each other.' I moved towards the kitchen so Jude couldn't pick up what we said. She was bright enough to know we'd be talking about her but I

89

didn't want her to take fright and run. Neither did I want Dora to be unaware of what was involved. But Dora didn't need telling.

She said, 'Leah, you're going to tell me she's underage and should be turned over to Social Services, but you don't feel able to do it to her. I agree with you. It'll have to happen, by and by, but first there has to be some breathing space. I hope she can be talked into staying here for a while.'

'I hope that too. She's already dipped her toe into prostitution and it doesn't exactly excite me to think what might happen to her out there.'

Dora grabbed the oven cloth and took a peek in the oven. When she turned round her face was red.

'Victorian London had a thousand child brothels,' she said angrily, 'and I could scream when I hear glib talk about a return to Victorian standards. I'll think of some way to keep Jude here until we can figure out the best thing to do.' She cocked her head at me. 'How did you get to know her anyway?'

I heard Jude start down the stairs. 'It's too long a story to get into right now,' I said.

She stopped what she was doing and looked at me. 'Or something you don't want to talk about?'

'A bit of both maybe, but nothing to worry about. I'm not on anybody's hit list.'

'Things change,' she said cryptically. I was really glad she'd reminded me about that. Jude came in wearing stripy leggings and grey T-shirt and looked like she'd lost another two years off her age. I could see the same thought hit Dora. I said, 'Hey, they look good on you.' She looked an inch pleased but didn't say a thing.

Dora put supper on the table and Jude eyed cabbage greens like they might bite. 'Sit down and try it. If you don't like it I shan't throw a fit,' Dora said. She needn't have worried; Jude still ate food like tomorrow would be famine day.

I felt fat as a pig and she was still eating when I brought up Gavin again. It wasn't something I wanted to do but if she'd remembered anything else, then I needed to know it. 'Can't remember nothing else 'cos there isn't nothing,' she said.

'It's a pity Jaz let on where the squat was,' I said as much to myself as her, and she came right back at me, cheeks pinked up and ready to fight.

'Come off it! He wasn't that stupid! It wasn't him what said where we'd be.' Which was when the truth zapped me in all its ugliness.

Gavin didn't need to be told; all he had to do was look up the kid's home address and pay Jaz's mother and her delightful boyfriend a visit just the way I had. *Shit!* Jude read my face and said with simple intent. 'I'm going to get her for it. I've promised I will. Don't know how or when but I'm getting her. Bloody fucking cow!' Dora's eyebrows lifted but she didn't say a word. A couple of deep breaths went in, then Jude got out painfully, 'I want her in Hell, an' I want her to burn, an' burn, an' burn, an' burn, an' . . . an' . . . just like . . .' She overflowed and Dora grabbed a box of tissues and came round the table.

I began to clear pots, worrying all the while about how much effort the wrong people might put into finding Jude. It all depended on how much Gavin and his friends thought Jaz had told her. I folded the tablecloth neatly and put it away, looked at the pile of pots and ran hot water into the bowl, lacing it with a good squirt of detergent. No use hoping it wouldn't be known she'd shared the squat with Jaz, not when dear, sweet Eddie with his big mouth and purple Capri had been around to put them wise. Jaz's 'twat' – that's what he'd called her, which meant they also knew how she'd been making a little money.

I thought about them wanting her dead and cruising the streets the way I had.

Whoo! I wasn't going down that road. Some things are just too bad to think about.

Dora came to fill up the kettle. I squinted round and saw Jude heading out to the sitting room; after a minute the television came on. I went over and eased the door closed. Dora cocked her head. I said, 'Jude could be in a lot more trouble than I thought; there are probably people out looking for her and if so, they won't give up easily.'

She said briskly, 'What kind of people? Spell it out so I know what I'm supposed to protect her from.'

'Jaz's death was no accident,' I said. 'Whoever started the fire needs to make sure Jude can't give them any trouble. She may not have been there at the time, but if they got to know where Jaz was hanging out from his mother they also got to hear about Jude, and they don't know how much of their dirty business he told her.' We looked at each other for a few seconds, then she picked up a tea towel and dried some pots. I emptied the bowl and rinsed it round. Then the kettle boiled and Dora asked did I want tea or coffee. If a war had been going on around us I guess we'd have kept on doing the same

91

dumb things. She brewed up, put a cloth on a tray and got out cups and saucers.

'How much looking do you think they'll do?' she said.

'Enough to find her if she were out on the streets, and it won't be easy keeping her off them. I ought to let Nicholls talk to her but if I do that he'll want to hand her over to Social Services – he's a real prude when it comes to that kind of thing.' I picked up the tray and carried it through. Jude and the cat were back together looking cosy in the easy chair and Michael Ball was doing his usual stuff on the television. Should I tell her how much trouble running off again could get her in or would that scare her into doing it? What did I know about kids? Times like that I get to feel really helpless.

Curled up, sipping hot tea, it looked like running away was the last thing on Jude's mind. I hoped that wasn't just an illusion. At nine thirty I said goodnight and left her to Dora. Responsibility weighed heavy. I tucked hands into jacket pockets against the chill and scuffed along the pavement, sneaking sideways glances into lit windows like a regular Tom Peep and trying to make all the bits of information I had fit together into a whole. Maybe given a year or three I could do it.

17

I got home, kicked off my shoes and started a fresh brew of coffee. I drink a lot too much of the stuff but it helps me think. Occasionally ideas get thrown up that turn out to be not that good. I tend not to worry about such things until they've landed me in trouble but sometimes a crystal ball would come in handy. I put 'Midnight Soul' on the tape deck, then got cosy on the settee while I went back to looking where things might lead. I'd started out with just one question and it had generated a pile more. I didn't mind that . . . what bothered me was I couldn't come up with a fast way to get answers. Uncharitably I blamed the whole thing on Nicholls; if he weren't so pig-headed I wouldn't always end up having to do his job for him.

I kept trying to cram the facts I had into some logical kind of framework, but it just wasn't possible and after a while I could see why Nicholls couldn't get a tochold. Drury stood to get a quibble-free insurance payout because his losses had been blamed on a fifteen-year-old who was probably innocent. Jaz had probably died because of something he claimed to know about Billy's death. Billy had died because – because what? Because he was innocent of arson and when push came to shove he could have pointed out the real arsonist? That fitted into my scheme of things a lot better than Nicholls's theory that he'd killed himself from guilt. The problem was that when I stood my mind off to one side and looked at it, the idea grew in ugliness. The ramifications made me want to be wrong. If I wasn't, then some toerag had gone into Billy's room, tied the rope round his neck and made it look like a suicide.

Sod it! What kind of bastard did it take to do that?

Simple. *The kind who'd burned Jaz and the squat to a cinder because he'd tried to blackmail his way to a better life. That's who.* And if I was searching for likely candidates, Gavin had to top the list.

The idea grew on me.

Did someone pay him to look the other way – or did he tie the knot with his own fingers? While I was occupied with that thought a second notion crowded in; that Gavin himself might be the arsonist everyone had been looking for. A tingle chilly as a cold hand rubbed over my scalp. If that really was the answer then the process of law had delivered Billy neatly into the lion's mouth.

Except how could he have known enough about Gavin to pose a threat?

I paced over to the window and looked out at the darkness. If that had been the reason for Billy's death then Gavin had either been careless enough to give himself away or Billy had seen him at one or more of the fires and made the connection.

What other answer could there be?

I drew the curtains to close out the darkness and shivered, wondering exactly what Jaz had seen or heard that made his life forfeit too. It must have really spooked Gavin to know there was still someone who shared his secret. Spooked him enough to make him head down Turpin Street with another low-life and a can of petrol and set the squat ablaze. Which one had been Gavin? The long-haired or the fat-bellied?

Did they know Jude had seen them?

Worms crawled in the pit of my stomach.

So what did I do now? Have a talk with Gavin or leave him to Nicholls? If I was right about him he had three deaths on his conscience already and might not see a problem in having one more. The scar under my ribs twitched, reminding me how easy it is to make mistakes. I shied away from confrontation. One near-death experience was enough. I went out into the hall and told myself there were some things my lover could do better than me. Not that I'd ever admit it to his face, especially since most of the edge he has comes from carrying a warrant card. I lifted the phone and dialled his number.

Wouldn't you know it? He wasn't home.

I left a pithy little message on his answering machine and went to bed. It was a mistake. You'd think even a worrier like Nicholls would wait until morning before he got around to asking what I meant. But no, at a half after midnight when I was deep in fantasy land and having a real good time the doorbell got me up again. I staggered out of the bedroom with spiky hair and a temper to match and flip-flopped downstairs trailing remnants of sleep. He looked fresh as a daisy and I hated him.

'What's the matter?' I said. 'Your place burn down?' He looked at my state of dishabille and got a stupid grin on his face. I tidied up the wrap and yanked the belt good and tight. He brought his hand out from behind him and dangled a brown-paper carrier bag at nose level.

'Chow mein and wuntuns.'

'You want to sit out there and make a pig of yourself go right ahead, it's fine by me.' I started to close the door but not so fast he couldn't get his foot in. Wuntuns sounded good and I was waking up fast. I told him he was a pain in the ass and let him by. He got on his butter-wouldn't-melt look and made for the stairs. 'Don't get too comfortable,' I told him rattily, 'you won't be staying that long.'

Good neighbourliness forbade I slam the door.

I climbed back up to the attic and watched his neat little butt. I guess everybody gets to have some good points, even Nicholls.

He trotted straight through to the kitchen and I left him to it. I'm not good at things domestic at the best of times and after midnight I don't even try. I went off to comb out the spikes and scrub an hour's sleep off my teeth. When I got back he had the takeaway plated up in the microwave and coffee brewing. I bumped out a chair and sat. He sighed, his blue eyes giving me a sad teddy-bear stare.

'Don't look at me. This wasn't my idea and I'm not lifting a finger,' I said meanly, and put my feet up. I just never tire of watching other people do chores.

He poured out coffee, disinterred the takeaway and sat at the table, forking in bean sprouts like he hadn't eaten all day. I held back a couple of seconds but the rhythmic motion of fork from plate to mouth became so damned hypnotic I just had to join in. When he'd filled in some stomach space he eased up and said, 'How was I to know you wouldn't be up watching old movies?'

'Nicholls, give me some credit. You think all I do is watch old movies and wait for you to drop by?'

A look of injury crossed his face – he likes to pretend he's the hub of my life. He shifted around on his chair and went back to eating. I grinned a little and did the same. A minute or so later he said iffily, 'So what was the message about?'

'Finish up your food,' I told him, 'and accept that you won't have an appetite left when you find out the problem, OK?'

It took a little time for him to get the rhythm back, but I acted like I didn't notice and worked on which bits of truth I needed to be economical with.

Any mention of Jude was out. Keeping her safe had to be top priority and children's homes are notoriously easy to get both into and out of. Put her back into one of those and she'd be a sitting duck. The thought was unpleasant and I walked around it delicately. If I didn't turn her in, how was I going to keep her out of trouble? Suppose she skipped out of Dora's the way she'd skipped out of my place, wouldn't she be as vulnerable on the damn streets as in a home?

I eyed Nicholls's near empty plate and got ready to upset his neat ideas. He dumped his fork, put his elbows on the table and invited me to tell him what degree of incompetence he'd achieved. He's really good at getting the gist of messages. I patted his hand and explained to him sweetly and gently how the Bramfield murder rate had gone up by two. He got on a look that said an itsy-bit more provocation and he'd hike it up to three.

'I suppose,' he snapped back nastily, 'you've already stuck your nose in and talked to this Gavin What's-his-face?'

'Judas! Nicholls, what do you take me for? I'm not looking to mess with a murder hunt. All I want is to nail Drury and get my job back, the rest is up to you.'

'Why don't I believe you?'

'When did you ever? And look at the trouble it's caused,' I said smartly.

We spent a couple of minutes sulking at each other, then I looked at the clock and yawned. He got up and headed for the door. Halfway there he swung round and stabbed a finger. 'My office before ten or I send a squad car and have you hauled in.'

'You bet,' I said. 'On the button. Yessir.' He started walking again, stiff-necked. I cooed, 'And Nicholls?'

'*What!*'

I waved a hand. 'Look at the mess you made; aren't you going to clear it up?' He half shut his eyes and looked at me, then walked on out of the flat.

I did a quick rinse and stack with the plates, put some milk to heat and got out the cocoa tin, opened the flat door a half-inch, then put my feet up and played around with his car keys until he came back. He looked a mite peeved. I took the cocoa tin in one hand, the keys in the other and shimmied over to him. The clouds went out of his eyes and left them blue as a Bunsen flame. He put the keys in his pocket, dumped the cocoa tin on the table and turned off the milk ... and then we made love with a heat and energy that left the both of us trembling.

That's the best thing about Nicholls. When he really puts his mind to what he's doing he's *good*.

18

I woke at seven and eased out of bed. Nicholls twitched an eyelid and went back to sleep; hard work really knocks him out. I did all the necessary morning things in the bathroom, got into sweats and running shoes, drank a half-pint of milk and let myself out really quietly. It was one of those good late April mornings with the sky cerulean blue and a zip in the air like sparkling wine. I took a left, then a right, running down behind the houses to come back up Palmer's Run from the bottom. Dora is no sluggard and I needed to check on Jude. From the smell of toast, coffee and fried food, I guessed she was still around. Gastric juices started flowing and I got a stomach rumble. Dora let me in with a silent thumbs up. The kid's frou-frou skirt was flopping around in the washing machine, which would keep her runaway ways on hold for a while longer. She looked better already. It's just amazing what a little basic care can do for a person. We said 'Hi,' like two people who, with a little extra effort, could get to be good friends. She'd washed her hair and it fluffed out round her face, baby fine. Nobody could look less like a street kid – not until you got a good look at her eyes and saw all the things in there that most of us just don't want to see.

Dora loaded a third plate with eggs, tomatoes, mushrooms and fried bread, declaring matter of factly that she'd expected me to drop by. I thought, what the hell, who needs to run, and tucked in. With all the time I had on my hands right then I could pound the streets any time of day.

We talked about this and that and Jude cleaned up her plate and started on the toast. I still didn't know where she put the stuff.

Way back when I was little, Gran took in a stray dog and fed it up, a sweet-natured crossbreed that some manky person had grown tired of having around, although neither of us could think why. It followed Gran home from the market with bones near sticking out of its fur,

97

and for a time it was jumpy as a frog when there were other people around. By and by it got on a layer of fat and a glossy coat and ate like a trooper, and for maybe a year tucked biscuits away inside its soft mouth pouches, saving them in case life got hard again and it had to go back on the road. It stayed around for eight years, then went to sleep one night and never woke up and Gran and I couldn't stop crying. The memory pricked at my eyeballs and I near choked myself gulping coffee too fast. By the time I could breathe again I'd got a good excuse for looking frayed.

I guessed Jude and the dog had a lot in common.

Dora quit rubbing my back and said, 'Jude and I were just talking about my sister. It's been a while since I saw her and I think it's time I paid her a visit.' She went back to eating and I sat up straight and stared at her. Dammit, what was she thinking of? This wasn't exactly an ideal time to renew sisterly affections.

'Huh . . . I, er, that'd be nice,' I said. 'Really nice. In a month or so maybe, when the weather picks up.' I took a look at Jude's face but it didn't show anything much at all. She just kept on buttering a piece of toast like it had nothing to do with her.

Dora glanced over at the window. 'The weather looks good enough to me. I'll leave a key so you can feed Oscar and keep an eye on the place.'

Feed Oscar? Great! That cat's a really iffy feeder when Dora's not there. I pushed a mushroom around. This wasn't like Dora. 'Sure,' I said. 'Why not? Maybe I can give you a lift to the station.'

'That'd be a real help,' she said brightly. 'Drop by around one and we'll be through packing.'

We?

I said, 'Which sister?'

'The scatty one. Liza.'

Jude lifted up her head and grinned – obviously Dora had been letting her in on family secrets. I ate up the mushroom, relaxed a mite and waited to hear more.

'I had a talk with her just before you arrived,' Dora said, 'which means that by now she'll be baking for an army. I told her it was about time this child got to dip a toe in the sea. Can you believe she's never seen it yet?'

'Yes I 'ave seen it then, told you that,' Jude came in fast. 'On the telly. Lots of times. I know all about it.'

'No, you don't. You might think you do, but you don't,' Dora said. 'To know the sea you have to smell it and touch it, you have to see the spumy white horses on a stormy day and watch it change in colour from grey to blue when the sun comes out, and when you've done all that you still won't know it.' I saw Jude's eyes grow dreamy. Dora had spent her life teaching kids, and if that was a sample of the way she'd done it she must have been a wow.

'Sounds real fun,' I said. 'You sure you're not going to duck out again, Jude?'

'I promised, didn't I? Anyway, said it yourself, sounds real fun. An' what with Dora's back not being so good any more she needs me along to pick up seashells an' stuff.'

Dora's back not being so good?

She'd really been spinning the kid a line, but, hey, what did I care? Jude out of town was Jude in a safe place. We chit-chatted a little while longer, then I told the two of them I'd be back by one and headed home. It was close on nine o'clock and I didn't expect to find Nicholls still around, but since when did he ever behave the way I expected? I opened up the flat door and knew right away what he'd been up to. He looked really pleased with himself and I didn't have the heart to knock him down. I looked at tomatoes and mushrooms sizzling gently on the back burner and his neat pile of toast and told my first lie of the day. 'Mmm, that looks really good, Nicholls. Let me just take a shower and I'll be right with you.' He beamed like he'd just won the pools and cracked a couple of eggs. I dumped my clothes on the bedroom floor and got under the shower. Sometimes life leaves me so few options I could weep.

It was easy getting down to Nicholls's office by ten. How could I miss when he was around to drive me? I meekly made the statement Fry had asked for, and then repeated the whole process again so Nicholls had something white and tangible to put in the nice new file he opened up for Jaz and Gavin. After that I declined a coffee – where would I put it? – and got up to go. Nicholls cleared his throat a couple of times, shuffled a few papers around and looked uncomfortable. I waited patiently. He said, 'Look, I don't know where you heard this but it wasn't here.'

'Heard what?'

'That Drury had a wife.'

'Drury *had* a wife? You mean she walked out on him?'

'I didn't tell you that.'

'And she's still living in Bramfield and not feeling too well-disposed towards her ex maybe?'

'I don't know where you pick these things up, Leah.'

'And she might be inclined to dig the dirt on hubby if I knew where to find her. I wonder where that would be?'

He opened up a brown manila file, set it neatly on his blotter, and went out of the room. At times he can be every bit as devious as me. I scooted around the desk and copied down the stuff I needed before he had a change of mind. A couple of minutes later he came back and asked why I was still hanging around. It's nice we understand each other so well.

I walked home, shed a few calories and felt about a half a ton lighter, then with ninety minutes to go before I took Dora and Jude to the station, I flopped out on the bed and used up two thirds of them thinking up some good questions to put to Susan Elizabeth Drury. At half past twelve I dug around in the wardrobe and got out a padded jacket for Jude. The east-coast wind cuts through denim like it isn't there and I didn't want the kid to get pneumonia.

I got to Dora's ten minutes early and they were all packed up and ready to go. I could hear Oscar mewling at the back of the house and hoped he hadn't picked up any of Jude's wandering ways. I'd hate to have to explain to Dora why she had a missing cat; I'd also hate to have to spend a week looking for him. I loaded the boot, gave the parka to Jude and drove sedately to the station. Then I hung around for twenty minutes until their train came in so I could wave goodbye. I hoped Dora knew what she was doing.

I'd intended to go looking for Drury's ex-wife right after I left the station, but I couldn't stand the thought of Oscar caterwauling away in the kitchen and headed back to Palmer's Run instead. He gave me a look that said the whole thing was my fault and walked stiff-backed into the front room where he arched his back and spat at me. 'I love you too, Oscar,' I said kindly and left him to it.

Ladbrook Grove was at the other end of town, on a newish estate populated mainly by middle management and wannabees. Number forty-five was semidetached with white paint and a yellow front door with a brass knocker. It also had a bell. I tried that first and listened to the ding-dong chimes echo behind the door. Then it opened and Susan Elizabeth and I stared at each other. She had on white jeans and a pink gingham shirt, her face was lightly made up, her hair shaggy short, and I knew her. She said, 'Leah?' and I said, 'Susie?' in unison. Then she held the door wide open, and I walked in and wondered if knowing her would make asking nosy questions better or worse.

She said, 'I don't believe this; how did you find me? It must be, what – eight years?'

'That's about right,' I said. 'What happened after A-levels? I heard you'd moved away.'

She shrugged, 'What happened was I went to Loughborough, flunked out and got married. Really exciting stuff. How about you?'

'I stuck it out,' I said. 'Got a degree, joined Inland Revenue and I'm still there. Regular stick-in-the-mud.'

'Married?'

I shook my head. 'Uh-uh.'

'You always did have more sense than me,' she said. 'Come on through and we'll catch up. How'd you find me?' She moved along the hall to the kitchen and I followed on and wondered how she'd feel when she learned I wasn't there to renew an old friendship. There are a lot of women around called Susan Elizabeth and I hadn't expected this one to be Susie Knox from Bramfield Girls' Academy. I wondered how she'd let herself get taken in by a gumboil like Drury. I guess neither of us had turned into the perfect specimens of femininity our mothers had hoped for. 'Come on,' she said. 'Tell! How'd you find me?'

'Truth? I didn't know it was you until you opened the door.'

She filled up the kettle and put it on the hob. 'Don't tell me you came collecting taxes.'

'Not exactly; I came to talk about your husband.'

'Ex!'

'That makes it better.'

'What's he done now?' She dumped three tea bags in a blue-and-white ceramic pot and looked fed up.

'Got me suspended.'

'What for? Refusing to go to bed with him?'

'I didn't get to know him that well,' I said.

'You wouldn't need to; getting in a lift with him would be enough.'

'Sounds like he gave you some problems.'

'He's a shit. You want to drop him down a hole, I'll help you dig it. How'd you manage to get on the wrong side of him?'

'Asking too many questions about Fast-Sell's business affairs. I think there's been a little creative accounting going on.'

'Huh! Surprise me!' she said bitterly. 'He's as straight as a corkscrew. I tell you, Leah, if I'd known what he was like I'd have run a mile and kept on going.' The kettle clicked off, she filled the pot and stirred it around. 'Catch up first, hang him later. How's that?'

'Sounds great,' I said convincingly, and settled down to do some girl-talk. It would have been really unfriendly to tell her I'd just as soon get straight on with the hanging.

It took close on an hour for the conversation to move from memory lane to Drury; meantime we had some fun lazing around exchanging gossip the way we used to. But it wasn't easy. Other things weighed heavily on my mind and I was impatient to find out what she knew about her ex-husband's business affairs. I listened to what a nice guy he'd been when she first met him, and how she couldn't believe he'd cheat on her – until the tally count got to three she knew about and God knew how many she didn't.

'So you dumped him,' I approved. 'I can see how you were taken in, he's got a nice line in lies.'

'He tried to get it on with you?'

'Uh-uh. He knew I was a tax inspector – not even your ex would be that dumb. Look, Susie, I hate to ask you this, but how much do you know about his business affairs?'

She laughed out loud. 'They were all business affairs; secretaries, customers, colleagues, you name it and he's been there.' I opened my mouth but she held up a hand and shook her head. 'I know that's not what you meant. Tell me what it is you want and if I can help, I will.'

'When did you split up?'

'Six months back when he started spending more time with his latest than with me. Does that make a difference?'

Six months. The fires had already started then. I said, 'Did he know many people in the local business community? I'm thinking specially about the other firms that were hit by fire.'

'He must have done. He was in the Chamber of Commerce so it would have been hard not to. It wasn't something he talked about though.'

'He never brought home titbits about firms having recessionary problems? Things like that?'

103

She shook her head and looked fed up. 'Look, believe me, six months ago I was on the point of walking out. I wouldn't have wanted to listen much if he *had* talked business.'

'How about earlier than that – say the middle of last year?'

'Leah, I want to help but I can't remember.' She got up, looked out of the window, came back, folded her arms and looked depressed. 'The truth is I never got interested in talking business. *Any* kind of business. I don't even read the financial pages – they'd send me to sleep. Maybe if we'd had a good marriage it would have been different, but as it is, it'd got so I didn't care much what he did or who he slept with.'

I said, 'I'm truly sorry, I feel lousy about this; if there was another way I could do it, I would.' I looked at her. 'Maybe I should just go beat the truth out of him and make it easy on us both?'

She waved her hands in front of her. 'Pulling him apart's good fun. Keep the questions coming and maybe we'll get to something I know.'

'When you said he was straight as a corkscrew, what did you mean?'

'I mean put him in bed with the truth and they'd wake up strangers. Fast-Sell was supposed to be a get-rich-quick discount store, he said, and now look at it; all he gets is an insurance payment.'

'He doesn't seem to do badly for money,' I said. 'I mean there's this place and . . .'

'This is mine,' she came in quickly. 'Nothing to do with him. I'm not living grace and favour and I haven't had a penny maintenance.'

'You work?' I said.

'Damned hard. I'm a night-stacker. You know what that is? Restocking supermarket shelves. Lousy pay but it lets me do a day course in computing. As far as this goes –' she waved a hand – 'twenty thousand is inherited and the rest on a straight mortgage. And if the louse could have got his hands on it he would. You know what he said when I wouldn't put it in a joint account? Didn't I trust him!'

I sympathised a little and got back to Drury's finances. I said, 'You know he's living in a pricey conversion on Lime Walk? Nice place, built-in security system. It doesn't look as if he walked away from Fast-Sell empty-handed.'

'He wasn't empty-handed when he moved to Bramfield. He could have gone into something else if he'd wanted.' She shrugged. 'Don't ask me why he picked carpets.'

'Maybe he knew somebody in the trade.'

'You mean Ed Bailey? The first time I saw him – Mark brought him home for a drink soon after we came here and he stayed to eat – I didn't see any resemblance, but under those thick little skins they're identical twins, charming enough to knock your socks off and every bargain a dud. I bet they were hustling before they got out of kindergarten.' She shook her head and looked me in the eyes. 'I told myself I wouldn't get bitter but I didn't know it'd be this hard not to. When we left Loughborough he said he'd cut the old ties and change his ways, and you know what? *I believed* him. And then it all begins again.'

'So he's a lousy two-timer and a pushy salesman, but is he honest?'

'Mark? No way! That's one big reason I never let myself get interested in what he did. It's like eating meat and never visiting an abattoir. You can live with yourself so long as you don't see where the food comes from. When I first got to know him he said he worked for a finance company and I thought, mmm, brains and a good salary – can't be bad. Then he took me to look round the offices and they looked – you know – good. Black ash and chrome, nice carpets, pretty typists. Impressed the customers like mad; impressed me too, that and the rest of the package. Like I said, he's a charmer. So we got married and then I learned the *finance company* made loans to the kind of people who can't repay. You know the sort of thing? After a couple of months the interest amounts to as much as the loan and they end up crucified with debt. The whole thing stank and I told him so.'

'How did he take it?'

'Shrugged it off, then a month or so later came home and said he'd quit to start up on his own.'

'Same business?'

'He called it a financial consultancy. I guess I had mixed feelings. Mark said he'd be giving investment advice, broking cheap loans and mortgages, selling car insurance, that kind of thing. It sounded like something that'd need a lot of money up front and I'd never got round to asking how much he'd accumulated. I don't think I'd even cared that much; he was generous, we had a good social life and at that point I still trusted him.'

'He dug deep and had enough?'

She gestured impatiently. 'I don't know where he got it – maybe it was his own money, maybe it wasn't.'

My, but this got better by the minute. Drury works with a loan shark and ends up with enough to start up his own business. Unless, of course, he'd just been put in as a front man to drag in new punters. Or maybe he *had* owned the consultancy and did the same thing for a percentage. I looked at that idea and asked myself how he'd ended up selling carpets.

I shook my head. 'I don't get it, Susie. Why would a financial consultant want to act like a carpet salesman?'

'Look,' she said, 'I'm the last person to ask. When he left the loan sharks and went out on his own I felt proud of him – for the first and only time in our unblissful married life! Hard work and long hours, that's what he said it'd be. Well – I don't know if the work part was true but he wasn't wrong about the hours.' She threaded her fingers back through her hair then shook it out slowly. 'I was so *bloody dumb.*'

'He was playing around already?'

'The first in a ragged line of pussies.' She shrugged. 'I kind of lost interest in his *business* affairs after that. I should have left him to it, but he kept coming back and swearing it wouldn't happen again, and I kept falling for it.' She grinned lopsidedly. 'Lesson in life, Leah. Keep away from charmers.'

'So why give it up to come to Bramfield?'

'I think he'd been treading on some unsafe ground financially.' She put a hand up before I could get out another question. 'Don't ask it, Leah, because I don't know what he'd been up to, but he said the move would be a new start for us. No more women. Just stay with him this one more time and it would all come right.'

'What happened to the consultancy?'

'He sold out to the finance company he'd worked for. I need another cuppa, how about you?'

I shook my head and watched her boil up the kettle again. It might have been imagination but her shoulders seemed to sag a little more than they had when I came. I felt bad about that. Raking over old hurts can be a real bitch. She came back to the table, sat down, put her elbows on it and rested her chin on her cupped hands. We looked at each other a couple of seconds without speaking, then she said, 'Don't feel bad about asking questions, it does me good to unload and I don't have many people I can do that with. Bad-mouthing my ex is real good fun!'

I said, 'I guess he lied again.'

She sat back in her chair looking vexed enough to kill. 'You don't know the half of it,' she flared. 'You know what the bastard did? After all his smooth talk about a new start he has his old girlfriend follow him up here from Loughborough. I saw them driving together in his car cosy as two fleas. Isn't that just *sweet*?'

Times like that it's real easy to be lost for words.

20

Susie walked me to the door and said she felt bad about not being more help. I told her not to worry, just call me if she came up with anything new, then I left.

Driving fast and having your mind on other things is a lethal combination, so I took it slow, going over the things I'd talked about with Susie as I headed back into town. One thing was for sure – Drury was a natural when it came to telling lies. Still thinking about that, I cut along a couple of minor roads and came out behind the glass-and-concrete monster where I once had desk space, nudging into a parking slot without thinking. Glory be – I was nostalgic for the place! I sat for a couple of minutes with the engine ticking over, then decided that since I was there anyway I might as well do some tail-tweaking.

When I rode the lift up to the fourth floor and pushed innocently into Inland Revenue, Pete was taking a drink of tea and near choked himself. I hurried into his little glass office and thumped his back solicitously.

'Pete, you need to be more careful,' I said. 'Lucky I dropped by or you could have been in real trouble there.'

He swivelled his chair round and got his breath back. 'Leah! What the hell are you doing here?'

'Is that a nice way to greet a friend?'

He took a quick look at the big office. I did the same. My desk had a new occupant, a crew-cut, red-headed male with fat cheeks and freckles. He had his head down and a pile of files, and he looked real busy.

'It's OK,' I told Pete reassuringly. 'He doesn't know me from Mata Hari, so relax.' I got some tissues out from his Kleenex box and mopped around the desk top. 'Good thing there's nothing important lying around on here like Fast-Sell's file,' I chided. 'Spraying all this tea around could have got you suspended for tampering with evidence.'

He snatched the tissues off me and dumped them in the waste basket. '*Out!*' he said. I sat down in his visitor's chair and smiled at him nicely. He took another look at the redhead. Val looked up, saw me, and waggled her fingers. I waggled mine in return. Pete said, 'For God's sake!' and lowered his privacy blind.

'That's better,' I said. 'Makes me feel less like throwing him out the window. Did anyone remember to water my areca palm?'

'To hell with your areca palm,' he snapped. 'You know you're not supposed to be on the premises.'

My, but he was in a peeve. The only times I ever knew Pete to swear that way was on the occasions when his car went bullish and made him walk.

'You mean you haven't cleared my good name yet?'

He softened a little. 'Things take time.'

'That they do.' I dipped my head towards the blind. 'If he's permanent I'll take my plant home.' He looked embarrassed. I said, 'Hey, don't worry about it. Who needs a job when there's unemployment?'

He said gruffly, 'Bridges is an internal investigator and I'm sorry you had to see him.' Then he played around with his blotter and looked like he was having a struggle. Without looking at me, he said, 'If it's any help, they haven't turned up anything incriminating yet and I don't expect them to.'

I said, 'That's really nice of you, Pete, I appreciate it,' and got up to go. Maybe this hadn't been such a good idea after all. I'd forgotten that when push came to shove Pete usually came down on my side. He came out from behind his desk, opened the door and walked me to the lift.

I went back out to the hybrid and felt a little sad. Mud sticks and negative findings don't necessarily mean innocence; the truth was, unless I found a way to drop Drury into deep shit I could still end up jobless. It wasn't the most soothing thought I'd ever had. I backed out of the slot and went to look for Redding. It was a quarter to five, I didn't know when shifts began or ended, but I hoped he'd be there. He wasn't, of course. I got halfway to his office when I heard myself hailed, not by name but by, 'Hey, if you're looking for Redding he won't be back on watch until Sunday.'

I turned round.

The hunky-looking male with his eyes on me had a grease rag that looked a lot less messy than Charlie's. I started back down the steps and tried to remember something positive I'd done that day. He wiped the palm of his hand down over his backside and looked at it critically before he stuck it out. 'Dan Bush,' he said. I shook hands politely.

'Leah Hunter.'

'I've seen you here before,' he said. 'You were asking about young Billy?'

'That's right. I heard he'd been seen around at most of the arson fires and I wanted to know if that was the truth.'

He flattened out his lips and shook his head. 'He was a nice kid. Related to you was he?'

'Nephew of a friend. It's knocked his family out.'

He nodded. 'If you want to talk I'm finished here in ten minutes – we can go and eat some place where you can bend my ear.'

'That's nice of you but I don't think . . .'

'Billy and me got on well; I knew him better than Redding if that's what you want to talk about. Up to you. I'm not trying for a date.' He eyed me up and grinned. 'Not yet, anyway.'

I said, 'That's good because I'm not in the market, but a chat about Billy could be a real help. Where do you usually eat?'

'The pub on the corner does a good pie and peas.'

Nice directions except there were two corners and two pubs. I tossed a mental coin. 'Prince of Wales?'

'Feathers,' he said.

No one gets to be right every time.

I told him I'd see him inside and wandered on down to warm up a barstool. Maybe Providence had taken pity on me. I guess deep down I'm just a born optimist.

The Feathers wasn't overcrowded at that time of day; just eight people were in there enjoying the quaint old-fashioned atmosphere of spilled beer and cigarette smoke – four of them men in crumpled suits having a quiet argument. Over at the back under a yellow light a couple of long-haired and bejeaned males played darts. From what I could see of their wrist action they weren't going to make the league. There were no barstools. I put a foot up on the brass rail and asked for a Pils – it was warm. I asked for a chilled can.

''S'that or draught, take your pick,' the barman said, like he found customers a real drag.

'So shove it in the ice bucket a couple of minutes,' I suggested.

'What ice bucket?' he came back unhelpfully.

I fought back an urge to ask the name of his charm school. If the pie and peas were as good as the service, I'd be ruining my health for nothing.

I counted out the Pils money in small change, slowly and carefully so an extra penny didn't slip by. He slammed it in the till and went back to chatting up a blonde. She had boobs like a couple of hot-air balloons and a low-cut T-shirt about ready to burst at the seams. The way she was leaning towards him I guessed he could see her navel. I took the warm beer to a corner table and sat down to wait.

A couple of minutes later Dan Bush came in and got a half of bitter from the bar. I watched him bring it over. He sat down on the shabby red moquette next to me and I inched over a little. Thigh contact I can do without.

'So what do you think of the place?' he said with a froth on his top lip.

'One of a kind,' I said. 'You sure this is where you eat? I don't smell any cooking.'

He grinned. Shouted, 'Hey, Les! Two pie and peas, sharpish.' The barman broke off from his tête-à-tête and went out the back of the bar.

'I'm impressed,' I said. 'I didn't think he could move that fast.'

'He's got a lot of hidden talents,' said Dan, eyeing up the blonde. 'Surprises me sometimes.' Then he moved his eyes back to me. 'What did you want to know about Billy?'

I shrugged. 'Anything you can tell me, I guess, like how many fires he was seen at and what reason he gave for being there. If you knew him better than Redding, maybe he opened up to you more about that?'

'Opened up more? I don't know if he did. I know when we talked about it I tried to tell him it wasn't a good idea to show up at that many fires. Billy said he liked to see the appliances turn out. Fire-engine mad I suppose.'

'Did you ever get to suspect Billy might be the arsonist behind it all?'

'That's an unfair question considering I already said I liked the kid, but yes, I suppose the idea did go through my mind a couple of times. I mean he was open about having set fires in the past and it could have started up again. I don't know.' He raised his hands, then let them drop. 'The police never had doubts but you know all that yourself. I expect Redding told you how Billy'd been coming around the station helping out and messing with equipment?' I nodded. He said, 'We'd all got used to him; a couple of times we let him ride on the engines and it made his day.'

Les came back with a couple of plates stacked one on the other and separated by an aluminium ring. I still couldn't smell cooking. I started to worry it might be cold pie and peas, but no, when he got it over to us the stuff on the plates looked amazingly good and steamed gently. I hadn't had onion sauce in years. Gastric juices started flowing so fast I near grabbed the cutlery from his fat little paw. Dan drained off his glass and said he'd have another. Les looked at me and asked did I want another Pils? I told him no thanks I was still waiting for the one I had to cool down. He gave me a scowl that said we never were going to be friends.

I attacked the food with gusto and found it every bit as good as it looked. We ate for a while in amicable silence and I gave some thought to what other things Dan Bush might know about Billy. Had Billy told him about the telephone calls for example? I took a break from chomping to ask about that.

He took some thinking time, his plate getting emptier all the while. 'Yeah,' he said finally. 'I knew about that, but it sounded – you know – unlikely. I mean these calls would have had to come from the arsonist, right? And what reason would a firebug have had to ring up a kid like Billy?'

'Depends. If he was someone clever enough to set someone up as a fall guy, then Billy would have been perfect. Of course, whoever did the setting up would need to have had access to the information that Billy had deliberately committed arson when he was young.'

'Like I already said, Billy didn't keep that a secret so you could be looking at a lot of people. Family, family friends, kids he went to school with, the kids' parents and *their* friends, neighbours, professionals . . . You could go on for ever.'

'Plus all the crews at the fire station,' I said.

'You mean one of them set Billy up? That's insulting.'

'Billy's family think it's insulting to blame him,' I said sharply. 'And what makes you so sure some motor-mouth at the station couldn't have gossiped in a pub or someplace else about the kid who couldn't keep away from fires, and big red engines?'

'OK,' he said, putting his hands up. 'If you put it like that you could be right, it's the sort of thing you do without thinking.'

'Isn't it though?' I finished up my food and pushed the plate away. 'Look, let's not get at cross purposes here – we both liked Billy. If he didn't start the fires, I'm sure you'd like to see that proven as much as me.'

He put his plate on mine, skewed across the knife and fork and asked how I planned to do that. I told him I didn't know, that the kid I'd hoped could help me do that had died in an arson fire on Turpin Street. That seemed to rock him a little, his face shut down and I couldn't tell what he was thinking.

'The fact is,' I said, 'unless you've got ideas of your own, I'll just have to keep asking questions until I find someone with the right answers.'

'You've told the police all this?'

'Some of it.'

'How much?'

'Not much.'

'Seems you're in a bind.'

'I've been in binds before,' I said. 'I usually find a way out of them but I'm open to all the help I can get.'

'I'll ask around,' he said slowly. 'You've given me some things to think about. You'll be coming back to see Redding?'

'Probably. There are a few more things I'd like to ask him about the fires.'

'Ask me. Maybe I can save you time.'

'I don't think so. The things I want are probably stored at Birkenshaw Headquarters, but I appreciate the offer.' I reached for my purse. 'How much are the pies?'

He shook his head. 'On me.'

'Where do men pick up this hang-up about paying for things?' I said. 'We've all got principles and one of mine is to buy my own fodder.'

He shrugged. ' Two fifty.'

'Great,' I said, 'we're still friends. Thanks for your help, maybe I'll see you next time I talk to Redding.' I gave him my half of the bill and got up to go. He offered to walk back with me. I told him I'd be fine. He said maybe if I wasn't doing anything Saturday night we could go to Rockerfellas. Like I said, he was real hunky and the offer was tempting but I declined it nicely.

Sometimes principles can get in the way of fun, but the way I see it, romancing one man at a time is enough, and I really hoped Nicholls appreciated that.

21

I garaged the car and fed the cat. It wound around my ankles in a neat display of cupboard love. I felt a little mean locking up again and leaving it to its own devices, but short of moving into Dora's place there wasn't much I could do about that. When I got home, wouldn't you know it, Nicholls was back, sitting in his car and looking bored. All this hanging around was getting to be a habit. He got out stiffly, like he'd been there for hours.

I said tartly, 'In my next life I'm going to be a policeman; they do nothing but sit around all day.'

'They also get to look at dead bodies,' he snapped back. 'If you want to share that with me I'll run you down to the morgue.'

How sweet! There are some things I don't mind sharing with Nicholls, including my duvet, but I'd seen cadavers enough already. Perversity kept me from telling him that.

'Fine!' I crossed the hall fast and started up the stairs. 'You want to do that before or after you get fed?'

He grunted and shoved the front door shut. I guess maybe he wasn't too keen on the idea after all.

We made it to the attic without exchanging small talk and he beat me to the coffee machine again. I took a look in the freezer. All that empty space gave me a real guilt complex. I said, 'What do you want to eat, spaghetti and Italian sauce or Italian sauce and spaghetti?'

He said, 'You choose, I don't mind either way.'

'Or there's a couple of cans of poached frogs in swamp water. How's that grab you?'

'Sounds fine, whatever you've got.'

Judas! It must have been a really bad day!

I put a pan of water to boil, poured some olive oil in the frying pan, chopped a couple of onions and added some garlic. They sizzled nicely. I hunted up a can of tomatoes and some basil, added salt, sugar and plenty of black pepper, tossed in some olives and hoped it came out right. If it didn't, the mood Nicholls was in he'd never notice.

Halfway through eating he perked up enough to note that he was doing that. I poured him a caffeine refill and he perked up some more. I said, 'Nicholls, I wish you'd get round to telling me what's going on.' He kept on shovelling spaghetti and gave me a shifty look.

I turned the word *bodies* around in my mind and didn't like the pictures. *Whose* body, for Pete's sake? Worry settled.

He cleaned up his plate. 'You're not going to like hearing it,' he said. 'You want to know who the body belongs to? It belongs to a white male by the name of Gavin Liddell.'

'Shit!' I said.

'A straightforward road traffic accident.'

'That so? I take it Gavin Liddell is also Gavin from the secure unit?' He nodded.

'And getting himself killed was just coincidental?'

'I already told you. It was a straightforward RTA. Don't try making it into more.'

'Would I do that?' I said. 'What earthly reason would anybody have to shut him up?' The sigh came up from his boots. I refused to be swayed into sympathy.

'Look,' he complained, 'it's been a bad day, a post-mortem isn't exactly a trip to Disneyland.'

'Got it done already, huh? Why'd you do that when it's just a plain, simple accident?'

'To make sure it was just a plain, simple accident,' he snapped. 'I also asked for a preliminary mechanical report. You'll be interested to know the Suzuki's fifth gear seized up.'

'Just like that.'

'Leah, I can't turn every road accident into a murder inquiry.'

'Of course not,' I soothed. 'Why'd it seize up?'

'A faulty sprocket.'

'Uh-huh. Guess there's a lot of them about? A bad fault like that I'm surprised Suzuki haven't done a recall.' He looked a mite uncomfortable. 'Or have you checked on that already and found that that's the only faulty machine? How many coincidences does it take before Bramfield's ace detectives get their heads out of the sand?'

'Maybe I should send for Sam Spade,' he said huffily.

'Good idea, you might pick up some pointers.' I got up and went to the freezer, reaching inside for its sole occupant. 'You want some toffee pecan ice cream?' He had a lip on a mile long; he also had a fondness for toffee pecan. I watched the lip subside. It's so nice to know another person's weaknesses.

We pigged in mutual silence until he said aggrievedly, 'Did I say I was giving up? Did I?'

'You didn't have to,' I said disagreeably, 'I can go on past experience.'

He started ticking off on his fingers. 'Suzuki are sending out one of their top inspectors to check the cogwheel, the bike's been dusted for fingerprints, I've had a forensic team out checking around where he parked his bike, his room's been searched. Damn it, Leah, what more do you expect me to do?'

'Nothing. You're doing fine, I'm ashamed of myself.' He looked mollified. I let him eat the rest of his ice cream; when he'd done licking the spoon I said, 'Let's suppose I was wrong last night and Gavin wasn't the arsonist – that doesn't mean he didn't kill Billy, and if someone paid him to do that he might have become a liability. What did you find when you checked his bank account?'

'What makes you think I'd check his bank account?'

'Uh, no reason, I mean, I never saw him but I bet he didn't *look* like a paid assassin.' Nicholls's forehead creased up and he rubbed at it wearily. I swallowed down a morsel of sympathy. 'What *did* he look like?' I said. 'Tall, short, fat, thin . . .'

'Five seven, mousy hair, sharp nose, well-built . . .'

'Beer belly?' I interrupted.

'Thought you'd never seen him.'

'It was a lucky guess.'

He eyed me carefully. 'Why don't I believe that?'

'How would I know?' I dumped the dirty pots in the sink. 'Do you want more coffee?' I said. He shook his head, put his jacket on and said he felt like an early night. 'Good idea,' I agreed. 'Better not forget your car keys.' I plucked them off the work surface and dropped them on the table. He looked at them like they might bite then put them in his pocket. 'You going to reopen the arson enquiry?'

'There's no evidence to warrant it.'

'Not enough bodies yet?'

'I'll be in touch,' he said stiffly.

'Do that,' I agreed, 'and meantime I'll just keep on trying to find out who done what to whom.' I did a little ticking off of my own. 'Rosie, Billy, Jaz, Gavin. If you're not careful, Nicholls, Bramfield's going to end up as murder city.'

'And if *you're* not careful,' he snapped back, without regard for my tender sensibilities, 'you'll be next on the slab.'

I leered at him. 'I'll leave you my duvet!'

He just looked at me. There were all kinds of things in his eyes but I pretended I didn't see any of them. It was mean of me but he wasn't the only one with problems.

I took a leaf out of Nicholls's book and turned in early, falling almost immediately into a deep, dreamless sleep from which I woke feeling energetic and eager to get on with the day. I didn't stop to question why that was so, afraid that if I did, apprehension might creep back and sticky my palms; enough for then just to go with the flow.

I got into my running kit, did a few stretches and let myself quietly out of the house. The sky was pale blue streaked with pinky gold, the air smelled clean and fresh, and my feet felt like they wanted to go. I dropped back pleasurably into the old Saturday routine of a steady run to the park, two circuits of the perimeter path and home again. Optimism ran with me; I'd find a way to sort things out; didn't I always? Drury might think he was on a winning streak but I knew better; somebody was already panicking. Jaz and Gavin were proof of that, and if Drury put a foot wrong and started to look like a weak link, he could be next. I slowed right down there. He'd conspired to burn down his own business, of that I was sure, but could he also have been involved in the rest of the fires ... helped in the *planning* of them?

The thought stayed with me as I speeded up again.

A fire is a useful way to stave off bankruptcy when a firm is in trouble. Books can be cooked, stocks can be overstated, good stock can be moved out quietly before the arsonist gets busy – which is what I believed happened in Drury's case. But he could have been in more deeply – as a member of the Chamber of Commerce he'd get to hear which firms were having cash-flow problems and which owners might not be averse to an unlawful way of solving them.

It was an interesting scenario but did I really believe he had the brains to plan that kind of operation?

I took the idea home with me, pushed it to the back of my mind and left it to germinate. Maybe when it grew a little I'd share it with Nicholls.

I showered, changed into jeans and a sweatshirt, then breakfasted on orange juice and Weetabix, which was about all I had left in the place. Nicholls's early-morning fry-up the day before had really depleted the fridge. Depleted? Who was I kidding? Empty was a better word. I'd really have to get down to some supermarket shopping today. Whoo! – but I really hate pushing a trolley round the shelves.

At half past eight Dora rang to say she and Jude were doing fine and how was Oscar? I told her the tabby was doing fine too, then guiltily remembered I should have been down there giving him his breakfast milk instead of sitting around with the morning paper. That's the problem with enforced idleness; laziness tends to creep in. I told her to have fun and let me know if Jude caused any problems, then fast-footed it back to the kitchen to dump the breakfast pots in with last night's supper dishes, after which I snatched up bag and jacket and got halfway out the door when the phone rang again.

This time it was Bethany wanting to know how things were. I told her fine but I'd do better if I could pick up some information about Drury. She said she was sorry about that but Colin had given her a definite no. Colin was a pain in the bum. I told her that too and she said maybe I'd just got the wrong impression. One of us had, that was for sure! When she asked if anything else had happened on my personal arsonist hunt I told her about Jaz and Gavin. She went quiet for a while, then said that was just terrible and maybe I should play safe and wait for the Inland Revenue investigation to prove me innocent. That way I wouldn't put myself in any danger.

I said, 'I don't plan to put myself in any danger, Bethany, but if you're that worried maybe you could sneak out the information I asked for without Colin knowing?'

'I can't do that,' she said. 'He's taken the file.'

'Why'd he do that?'

'I suppose he thought I might do a little photocopying on your account. You do seem to have rubbed each other up the wrong way.'

'Uh-huh.'

'What happens next then?' she said. 'Any plans?'

'Right now I have to go feed a cat. After that I plan to catch up on some grocery shopping, and when I've had my fill of excitement I also plan to find out who else might have tracked Jaz to Turpin Street.'

'How are you going to do that?'

'I'll let you know when I've done it,' I said. She gave me some more advice on how I should take care, then we said goodbye and hung up. This time I made it out of the flat without having to turn back.

The moggie did a little dance to show how glad he was to see me and lapped up his milk in double-quick time. I tipped out his litter tray and put in some fresh lining. When Dora was home he got to play out in the garden but I didn't dare do that in case he took off on a cat odyssey. Spending the next week looking for him wasn't something I cared to think about.

He went over to the catflap and asked me prettily to take off the bolt. Riddled with guilt I topped up his saucer and added a little cream. He looked up at me knowingly.

On the way out I plumped up his damn cushion.

22

Supermarkets are money traps and that's a fact. It took three trips to haul the groceries upstairs and after that I had to find someplace to stow the damn things. I turfed two bits of mouldy cheese out of the fridge and restocked its shelves, then sat back on my heels to admire it. Such orderliness appears only rarely and an undomesticated slut like myself needs to savour it.

Some days start off good and then slowly deteriorate. When I stacked the last can it was close on half past eleven and I was feeling tetchy, the day seemed to have slipped out of my hands already and I didn't like that. I'd planned to fit in a morning visit to Eddie and Julie so I could find out who else they'd told about Jaz's hideaway; now I'd have to put the expedition off until I'd cleaned myself up and grabbed a quick snack.

I took a shower, dressed in black jeans and a rosy silk shirt, shoved some laundry in the washing machine, and heated up a can of beans. The back of my mind was filled with urgency and I didn't know why. Maybe I was developing a latent psychic ability. If I was, it'd be a big help; I could stay home with a crystal ball and leave all the running around to Nicholls.

I'd dumped the bean plate in the sink with the rest of the pile and was having a farewell pee when Marcie knocked on the door. I buttoned up my flies and went to see what she wanted. She looked flustered enough to throw a fit.

'Leah, I hate to ask but I've got to get a portfolio to Huddersfield before two, so can you babysit Ben? I know it's Saturday but there's an art director up from London wanting to see my stuff. My mother was supposed to come over but my sister went into labour and she's had to take her to the maternity unit. Jake – that's Sally's husband – should have been around to do that but he's out on a rush site inspection and I don't know anyone else to ask but you. I'd take Ben with me but it's really important I get to talk business without having only half my mind on it.'

I watched the afternoon shred itself into little pieces.

Marcie didn't ask many favours and I liked her too much to say no – besides which, she wouldn't even have asked if it hadn't been too important not to.

I said, 'You want me to come down to your place or shall you bring Ben up?' She looked relieved enough to bust.

'Maybe if you came to Ben it'd be better. I can put him down early for his nap and with any luck he'll sleep a couple of hours.'

'Fine,' I said. 'I'll give him some juice when he wakes then we can play Lego and whatever until you're home. Give me two minutes to finish up here, OK?' She said thanks and went back down to Ben. I washed my hands, did a little cussing and followed her. She'd left the door open so I went on in and got comfy on the settee. From the exchanges coming out of the bedroom Ben wasn't too keen on buying the sleep-time idea. I didn't interfere; honorary aunts need to mind their own business. The protests grew less. Ten minutes later she was out of there and gone. I caught up on some reading until around two thirty when Ben decided enough was enough and started shouting out, 'Up! Up!' I don't know how Marcie copes – that kid has the energy of a horse and then some. She got home close on five looking pleased with herself and said it had gone great and it looked like she'd be getting a new contract. I was glad about that; it made the day seem less of a waste.

Maybe if I moved my ass I could still make it to Julie's before she and Eddie got started in on a Saturday night pub crawl. OK, I could have been misjudging the two of them, and maybe they planned to stay home and read the Bible, but somehow I didn't think that likely.

I collected my stuff from upstairs, got in the car, and drove across town to Westmoor. The Capri was still parked out by the kerb but the kids were missing. I took a look at the rear wing; Eddie hadn't got around to fixing it yet and it had decayed some. I didn't feel unhappy about that. When I crossed the pavement Julie's net curtain lifted a little so she could watch me come up the path, dropping back in place just before I reached the door. I knocked on it with gentle consideration. No sense getting the neighbours out when she already knew I was calling.

It took about thirty seconds to realise she wasn't going to open the damn thing without a lot more encouragement. Some people seem bent on making life difficult.

I pounded a little harder.

She popped the letterbox and shouted, 'Piss off!'

I gave the door a good thumping.

Eddie jerked it open, pink-eyed and sweaty. From the look of him he hadn't got around to shaving yet, his body odour wasn't too good and his temper hung at flash point. He jabbed an unclean hand and caught me mid-chest. I stumbled backwards off the concrete step, annoyed that I hadn't seen the move coming.

He gave me a neat lip-curl. 'Fuck off!'

Backing away from a bully just encourages the bad habit, besides which I just hate to be pushed around. I dusted off my shirt and snapped, 'Not without having a couple of questions answered.'

He came out of the house and repeated his cute jabbing trick, but this time I got a good grip on his outstretched arm and flipped him neatly on his back.

Julie shouted, 'You got no right to do that. Who asked you to come here anyway?' She squatted by Eddie, full of concern. He shoved her roughly off balance and got up rubbing at his shoulder and looking at me.

'What fucking questions?' he said.

'Who else came here asking about Jaz besides me?'

'Who said anybody did?'

'Somebody found out where he was living and who else could tell them that but you and Julie?'

'His twat.'

'They were two kids with lousy parents who looked out for each other and that's all. Who did you tell?'

Julie got back on her feet, 'I wasn't a lousy parent, it was him that was never grateful, always acting up, and you can't come here and say different.'

I didn't bother answering; we'd been down that road before. I kept my eyes on Eddie.

'Come on, Eddie,' I said. 'Who else has been around?'

He shrugged. 'Won't help you none, it was just a feller from the remand place, Gavin something or other.'

Julie said, 'Gavin Liddell. He said he needed to know where Jaz was for his records. What was I supposed to do? Tell him I didn't know?'

It would have been a real help if she had but it didn't seem like a good idea to tell her that. I said, 'Anybody else?'

'A woodentop yesterday.'

'Oh, yeah, you'd remember *him*,' sneered Eddie. 'Near as like had your knickers off ready, didn't you?'

'Piss off!' she yelled at him.

'I fucking will,' he bawled back.

I watched the Capri take off in a squeal of tyres and thud of a dodgy camshaft. 'He'll be back,' said Julie. I couldn't tell whether that was hope or resignation.

'Tell me about the police visit,' I said.

'It was just the one in plain clothes, nice blue eyes and a way with him.' *Nicholls! So he hadn't turned in all that early after all.* 'Said how sorry he was about Jaz and all that. Only person what has so far.'

I got a bad twinge of conscience.

'Everybody's sorry about Jaz,' I said. 'He was a nice kid and I guess you're going to miss him.'

Julie's eyes filled up, she got a pack of cigarettes out of her pocket and lit up, sucking in smoke deeply, letting it out again in a hard chimney. 'He came last night, latish, just before we went down the Grapes and he was all right ... You know what I mean? Like, I'd have been interested if *he* was, but what I get stuck with is the Eddies, isn't it?' She inhaled a couple more times and stared down at the weeds. I stayed silent. She sighed and the sigh turned into a cough; she dropped the cigarette on the path and stamped it out. 'He wanted the same as you – to know who'd been round asking where Jaz was. I told him just the two of you, you and Gavin.'

'I guess he was disappointed.'

She shrugged. 'He didn't look too happy, 'specially when he heard about you. Might get a visit yourself, see what I mean then, won't you? Anyway, what do you want to know for? What's it matter who's been?'

'The fire at Jaz's place could have been started deliberately,' I said. 'By somebody who meant to kill him.' Nicholls obviously hadn't mentioned that little fact – the shock on her face when she heard it from me was too real.

She said, 'Jesus,' very quietly. I stood around awkwardly for a couple of seconds and thought maybe I could have found a more tactful way to tell her.

'I'm sorry,' I said. 'I thought you knew already.'

'God, no. I thought it was his own stupid fault.' She got out the cigarette pack again. 'I'm going in now,' she said. 'I want to do some thinking.' She turned round and walked away and I watched her go back in the house. She didn't look at me again. I guess there was some kind of maternal feeling inside her after all and I wished Jaz could have known that too.

I drove out of the Westwood estate and past the Fox and Grapes. Eddie's car was there. I guessed it must be the kind of place where crusties were welcome – or maybe he'd got cleaned up in the men's room before the bartender got downwind of him.

I headed back to town with half my mind on the road and the rest of it occupying itself with other things. It isn't the best way to drive and I took a wrong turn and ended up on Lime Walk. Or maybe it was the right turn and I was getting to be psychic after all. Either way, it let me see Colin Stanton hopping out of a Merc and heading for the old Wilberforce place. I drove on by, then turned round and cruised back. He was waiting around in the little foyer and looking at the buttons. After a couple of minutes someone buzzed him in and he shoved through the door and disappeared. I wondered what kind of odds Ladbrooke would give on it being Drury who'd done the buzzing. And then I wondered what kind of business they could have to discuss at seven o'clock on a Saturday night.

That's the thing about Providence – every time it looks like I'm running out of steam it comes up with a peanut to keep me going.

23

It's really easy to get impatient and want to hustle things along, but it isn't always prudent to do that. Such knowledge would be useful if prudence were a part of my nature, which it is not. I reversed gently, cut the headlights and settled down to see how long it'd be before Stanton came out. I reckoned on an hour but I'd forgotten that I wasn't exactly having a good judgment day. I'd barely got comfy when he and Drury came out together and climbed into Stanton's Merc. I hunched down low while the sweep of lights went by and then went after them, bumping over the pavement in a fast U-turn. A couple of miles out of town they pulled into the parking area behind a Beefeater pub and went inside. I gave them a couple of minutes and went in after them; I wasn't exactly dressed for dinner but since when were Beefeaters ritzy?

It was one of those places where you select what you want to eat in the bar and then sit around increasing the alcohol profits until some waiter comes and moves you to the restaurant. Stanton and Drury were still at the first stage.

I took a spare stool on the dark side of a one-armed bandit and waited until they were through ordering.

The lighting left a lot to be desired, an intimate orangey-yellow that made everyone in sight look jaundiced. If they were trying for romantic it was definitely the wrong shade to go for. The barman tidied away the menus and put two lagers on the counter. Drury motioned to a table and Stanton nodded. I worked out that short of insinuating myself under it the chances of eavesdropping were nonexistent. Marking that particular setback down as just one more annoyance, I moved out from my hideaway, hitched up on a barstool and ordered a Pils, trying to pick up on male body language as I drank.

I wouldn't say Stanton and Drury looked like bosom buddies but then again they weren't arguing.

I watched them a while longer and got impatient. Damn it, why was I sitting around wasting my time like this?

They looked real surprised when I took my drink over and parked my butt on an empty stool. I smiled at them brightly. 'Hi,' I said. 'Isn't it amazing who you can meet up with in a place like this? Do you two come here often?'

Drury's nose got a pinched look; he threw a sideways glance at Stanton and said nastily, 'What kind of blackmail do you plan to try on me this time?'

'Depends what's on offer. Have you two just come out of the closet or are you working on a new variation in insurance fraud? Better be careful, Drury; keep playing with matches and you'll get burnt.'

Stanton said prissily, 'Miss Hunter, my advice is to leave now before you compromise yourself even further. Adding harassment to corruption won't exactly further your cause.'

'Whoo! That's nasty. But you see I'm going to be proved lily-white and clean at which point your friend here is going to have to do a lot of explaining.' I patted Drury's hand and he took it away as if I'd bitten it. 'Bet you wish you'd never left Loughborough now, don't you, Mr Drury? Why'd you give up a good and lucrative business like that to open up a carpet barn? I keep on trying to figure that out. Maybe you can explain it to me.'

'Why the hell should I? I don't have to explain anything; neither do I have to listen to a load of bullshit. If you don't get out of the place right now I'll telephone the police.'

I don't know why people think that's frightening.

'Go ahead,' I invited. 'Tell them I indecently assaulted your hand.' I took a look at Stanton. 'You want to call the police too? If so, ask for DC Fry or Detective Inspector Nicholls. I can guarantee they'll be over here really fast. They both find arson fascinating.'

Drury's lips thinned. 'You're looking for a lot of trouble. You should watch yourself.'

'I already have a lot of trouble,' I told him. 'Now I'm looking to get out of it.'

'This isn't a good way to do it,' said Stanton. 'Look around and count witnesses; several seem very interested in our table. Accept my advice, let things settle down of their own accord. You've a lot to gain by doing that and nothing to lose.'

It's amazing how some people seem to talk in clichés.

Stanton's problem was one of basic misunderstanding. He didn't know good advice was something I'd never got used to taking; if he had he might have phrased things differently. I ignored him, propped my elbows on the table and focused on Drury. 'Every tax inspector employed by Inland Revenue recognises long-firm fraud when they see it. You're still being investigated, Mr Drury, and you're not going to get away.'

Drury's face tightened. '*Crap.*'

'Go ahead,' I said politely, 'I won't watch, but while you're in there add three unlawful deaths to fraud and arson charges and take a good look at what you'll be facing.' I finished up my Pils, set the empty glass back neatly in its wet ring, and stood up. 'Gentlemen,' I said politely, 'it's been an enlightening experience talking to you both; hopefully I'll see you in court.' It seemed an enticing prospect to leave them with, and gave them something to fix their minds on over dinner.

It really annoyed me the way Drury thought laying false charges would leave him in the clear.

Long-firm fraud isn't a spur-of-the-moment crime. It has to be planned well ahead, and I knew in my bones that Drury had known exactly what was going to happen to Fast-Sell the moment he bought the place. The classic type of long-firm fraud is for an established company to be taken over with the intention of ordering in as many goods as can be got on credit. In the beginning the business is built up carefully and early orders paid for promptly, then, when suppliers think everything is above board, the bent operator places substantially larger orders, sells off the goods without paying for them and either decamps or arranges a fictitious burglary to mask the fraud.

I'd decided that Drury's scam was a variation on that. He'd bought in top-quality goods and then moved them out before the fire, replacing expensive carpets with cheap junk and claiming insurance for a warehouse full of good stuff. It was neat, and if I hadn't been poking around because of Billy it could have slipped right by me, *except it wasn't my account and it would have slipped right by Arnold.* The thought pleased me. I wondered if his chickenpox still itched.

I also wondered if the good stuff had found its way to Ed Bailey, and if so, how they were dividing the spoils.

When I got back to Palmer's Run and let myself into Dora's the place was quiet, no mewling, no scratching, no furry boa winding around my feet. I turned on the lights and called sweetly, 'Oscar! Here puss-puss, who's a good kitty then,' and a few other such idiot things while I played at hunt the cat. So help me, if he'd got out and been run over I'd kill him! I hunted through the sitting room, I hunted round the kitchen, and then I moved upstairs. No Oscar. Shit! I sat on the top stair and thought about how he could have got out. The answer was, he couldn't. The damn cat was playing games with me. I went back to the kitchen and emptied out a tin of Whiskas, mashing it up and rattling the fork in his pottery dish. Tail high, he wandered in through the door and began to trough. I told him exactly what I thought of both him and his antecedents but it didn't seem to spoil his appetite. I slammed down a saucer of milk and went home.

I expected Nicholls either to come round or call; he did neither which meant he had to be sulking again. I took a long soak in the tub then dined alone on frozen lasagne, after which I watched a television rerun of *Die Hard* and flopped into bed at eleven thirty hoping to dream of Bruce Willis. I didn't, of course.

24

It didn't matter that with no work to go to I could dump the usual routine and become even more slothful than was my natural bent. The way I saw it, to do that would legitimise the fact that I'd been suspended – moreover, it might even suggest such condition could become permanent – which of course I knew was impossible. Any day now Pete would be ringing up full of apologies and begging me to get back to collecting taxes. Bet your life he would. Meantime I got on with Sunday chores and made like such futile exercise was fun.

Around one, Marcie came up to tell me she was going to visit her mother, so her place would be empty for a couple of days. I asked if her sister had delivered OK. Marcie looked real happy and said twin girls and she couldn't wait to get a look at them. Which reminded me that I was an auntie too. Sometimes I can be very lax at family visiting.

My sister Emily and her stockbroker husband live thirty miles away at Ledford with two moppet daughters that I don't see enough of. Which is entirely my own fault. It isn't that I don't like visiting; it's that Em always insists on trying to fix me up with a husband, and I need one of those like a fish needs wheels. Convincing her of that isn't easy, but hey! it was Sunday, and who could she round up at such short notice?

The answer was Dermot who clamped a hand on my knee at the dinner table and had to be prised off with a fork. I swear I don't know where she finds them, but for once she had the grace to look shamefaced.

I arrived home again at nine thirty, garaged the car, fed a hungry Oscar and told him after the trick he played on me yesterday he was lucky I bothered. He rolled over and played kitten, which meant I had to stay around for a while and be nice to him.

133

Close on eleven I climbed into bed and went right to sleep. Catching up on family responsibilities really takes it out of a body.

Monday morning I did a three-mile run, breakfasted on scrambled eggs and coffee, then dressed in a black pants suit and milky-cream shirt. Halfway out the door the telephone rang in a neat rerun of Saturday. I went back and lifted the receiver. It didn't surprise me to hear Stanton's smooth voice. I guessed that both he and Drury were still a little upset and I got a glow of satisfaction from that. I said, 'Why, Mr Stanton, what a nice surprise. How'd the dinner go?' I could hear his pen tap-tapping at the other end; a dull sound like it was thumping on a blotter.

He said, 'Miss Hunter, it might be a good idea if we talked again.'

'Talk away,' I invited.

'Face to face.'

'The telephone suits me fine. I don't have time to run around having tête-à-têtes.'

'In your present unemployed circumstances that surprises me; I would have expected time to lie heavy on your hands.'

'Is that what you wanted to tell me?'

'No. What I wanted to tell you, Miss Hunter, is that it was a mistake to antagonise Drury so blatantly on Saturday night. I'm surprised you were that unprofessional; it gained you nothing and worsened your own situation. I hope you appreciate that.'

'Bet your boots I do. What's his arrangement with you then? Ten per cent off the top for speeding things up?'

The tapping stopped and turned to silence. 'Do you always tread such dangerous ground?' he said finally.

'What's dangerous about it? Look, Mr Stanton, I really am in a hurry; we've talked about Drury before and according to you there's no reason to think twice about his claim or to look further into the fire. Put that together with your cosy little dinner and to me it spells collusion. If I'm wrong, maybe I'll get round to apologising sometime, OK?'

'You know where my office is. I'll be in there until twelve thirty. It's entirely up to you whether we talk or not.' He hung up. I guess he didn't qualify as a perfect gentleman after all, but who was I to grumble? When he was around I had trouble being a lady.

I put the phone down and went to give Oscar a cream treat. I couldn't believe I was actually beginning to like the damn cat. I cleaned out his litter tray and sprayed some air freshener around. He trampled the new stuff to his liking and sauntered back to his saucer. I poured in the cream I'd brought, threw away the carton and left him to it.

When I parked in Charlie's yard he was clinching a deal on one of his recycled cars; a 1970s' VW Beetle in bright orange. The buyer looked to be in his forties with suede desert boots, a corduroy jacket and mid-length hair. I had a feeling part of the VW's attraction was a large dose of nostalgia.

I wandered over to the grimy lean-to office and sat on the step, waiting for Charlie to make his kill. By and by the punter reached out a loving hand and gave the motor a gentle pat, walking off with a spring in his step. Charlie patted it too. I wandered down to take a look. Nice paintwork, shiny chrome, the original bum-breaker seats.

'You give him a good deal?' I said.

'Depends whose side you're looking at it from. Got to make a profit to pay me taxes. You got your job back yet?'

'Imminent, Charlie, imminent. I hate to ask this, but does your sister still have all Billy's stuff?'

He delayed answering, moving off into the office and putting the kettle on. I stayed in the doorway where the air was fresher. The smell isn't all Charlie's fault but it has to be experienced to be appreciated. He got a couple of mugs down from off the top shelf and dumped in tea bags.

'What d'you want to know that for?'

'If she hasn't got rid of the stuff, I'd like to take a look through it.'

'The police done that once already.'

'Not for the same reason,' I said.

'Want me to ask her then?'

'I'd appreciate it.'

'Dunno what she'll think.' He came away from the kettle and picked up the phone.

I sat back down on the step, ears busy picking up his side of the conversation. His sister didn't seem too keen on having me go round, but Charlie's always great at wearing people down. After a couple of minutes' persuasion he said, 'No, 'course it won't take long, I'll come round with her if you want. – Yeah, I know I've a got a business to run but there's things what's more important. – Don't matter where they are, Viv. – Yeah, all right then, I'll tell her.' When he hung up I couldn't decide if he'd ended on a positive note or not. He got busy with the kettle again.

'Wasn't happy about it,' he said over his shoulder. 'Upsets her when she gets reminded. Anybody but you she'd have said no.' He took a sniff at the milk and shrugged. ''Ave a cuppa first an' then go on round.' He handed over a mug and I watched curds form. Charlie's tea can be something else.

I said, 'You sure it's not too much for her?'

'She'll be right; thing worrying her is she's boxed his stuff and shoved it in the garage 'til she feels like sorting proper. Said I had to tell you that in case it put you off.'

'It doesn't,' I said. 'Might make it more difficult to find what I'm looking for but that's all.' I took a drink of tea and swallowed it fast.

'If you know what you're looking for, Viv might be able to put her hand right on it.'

'Books, diaries, letters, scrap pads – that kind of stuff. I want to know what he was doing and thinking those last few weeks. I mean, there's a chance he's got something written somewhere, if I can just find it.'

'Police took a lot of stuff away,' he said. 'Dunno if it all came back.'

Brilliant. I took another mouthful of tea and grimaced. The stuff tasted like cat pee. Charlie reached for the mug.

'Milk's gone off a bit; shouldn't drink it if I was you.' I didn't argue. Like Gran used to say, small mercies are not to be coughed at. He wrote his sister's address on the back of a tatty envelope and gave it me. 'I'll tell her what you're after, love, then she can say which box is which.'

'Thanks, Charlie.'

'Makes a better cuppa than what I do,' he said.

I grinned at him. 'Hey, come on, Charlie, your tea's great; don't I keep coming back?'

'When you're after something,' he said. 'How's the motor. Still doing all right?'

'A bird on wheels.'

He nodded satisfaction and crossed the yard with me, inspecting the hybrid like it was a Rolls. 'Did a good one there, love,' he said.

'Want me to put a sticker on?'

He grinned, rubbing off a speck of grime with his sleeve. 'Couldn't cope with the rush if you was to do that.'

I started up the engine. ''Bye, Charlie.' He slapped the car's rump and went back to his office.

Charlie's sister lived in a box-shaped semi with Georgian windows and glass-panelled door, one of a dozen pairs built in a semicircle on a piece of land that had once been a playing field. The builders had thoughtfully planted a lilac tree in each front garden before naming the place Lilac Crescent.

I drove round to number sixteen, parked on the road, and walked up the short drive. When I rang the bell, Billy's mother came to answer it with flour-covered hands. I started to tell her who I was but she stopped me and said she remembered me from the funeral. 'The kitchen's back that way if you want to go through,' she said, sprinkling a little flour on the carpet as she motioned. I followed the warm pastry smell. 'Monday's baking day. It's a habit I picked up from my mother and I still haven't broken with it. Charlie said you wanted to look through Billy's stuff. Give me a minute to wash this off my hands and I'll show you where it is.' She moved to the sink and turned on the tap while she was talking. 'He said books and that sort of thing, is that right?'

'That's right. I appreciate you letting me do that, it can't be easy.'

She shook her head and didn't make eye contact.

'I'm just going in there to point out the box and leave you to it.' She dried her hands and led the way out of the back door. 'I'm not sure what it is you're hoping to find. Charlie tells me you still don't believe Billy caused the old woman's death. That's good to hear after what's been said about him, but the police went through all his things when it happened.'

'Charlie said they took some stuff away; did they get around to bringing it back?'

'They brought some back, I don't know if it was everything – I wasn't in any mood to check. What they did bring back is out in the garage with the rest of his stuff.' She raised the up-and-over door and frowned at the five-year-old red Fiesta taking up most of the space. 'I'd better move it,' she said and rubbed her head. 'Where'd I put the keys?' She left me and went back in the house. After a couple of minutes she came out, got in the car and moved it down the drive.

I said, 'I'm sorry about this, I should have picked a better time.'

'There aren't any better times,' she said bluntly. 'I put a face on things when Jenny and Mark are home, and that's it. Their father went off with a forecourt cashier five years ago and I've never missed him. He wasn't much use when he was around but it would be nice to have someone to shed tears with now.' She moved into the garage and put her hands on a pile of supermarket boxes. 'Billy's books and papers are in these two along with his video games and music tapes. I didn't go through the stuff the police brought back but it's in this top box over here.'

137

I said, 'Thanks, Mrs Tyler. I'll put everything back like it is; I just hope there's something in here.'

'It's Viv,' she said. 'I'll have the kettle on when you've done – not that you need to rush; I'm not going anywhere.' I watched her walk out through the door and wished I could think of some wise thing to say that would make her feel life was less of a shit. I pulled out the first box and started hunting. By and by a stronger smell of baking came out of the house and filled up the garage. I blocked out the urge to drool and kept on looking. I went through his schoolbooks, textbooks, notebooks, scrap pads and magazines. Nothing. Anything with writing on got read. I checked out his music tapes and video games, shaking out each box. Still nothing.

I piled everything back in the boxes then reached up for the third. Wouldn't you know it? The first thing I pulled out was Billy's diary. I turned it over in my hands, loth to open it up. Damn it, what was wrong with me? Wasn't this the kind of thing I'd been looking for?

I ran my mind back over the list of arson attacks Redding had given me. The first had been on the twelfth of January, at a kebab house on Charlotte Street. I turned to the diary entry for that day and found the fire described in detail; the time it started, the number of fire appliances in attendance, the time it took to get the fire out – it was all there. I lifted out the rest of the stuff. Scrapbooks filled with clipped newspaper reports of fires from way back to the present time, a collection of lighters – I flicked a couple and found they worked – one of them looked like an original Zippo – a small can of lighter fuel was in there with them. When the police found this stuff they must have thought it was Christmas. I unearthed a photograph of Billy and a group of firemen taken outside the front of the station with the big front doors open and the engines in clear view. He looked happy. Redding was there and so was Dan Bush. On the back an immaturely round hand had written, *Dan Bush, ace fire man*.

It looked like Dan had told me the truth about him being closer to Billy than Redding.

I flipped through a book on fire and fire-raisers that looked like he'd bought it in a library sale. It was well thumbed, as was a book on fire investigation that seemed to read like a fire-raisers' manual. I put everything back in the box and carried it out of the garage. Maybe the police had missed something and maybe they hadn't. I wouldn't know that until I'd spent some time turning pages, and I wanted to do that at my own pace. I set the box down outside the back door, dusted off my hands and went to find Billy's mother.

138

25

I stayed longer than I'd intended, sampling Viv's baking and letting her use me as a listening ear. When somebody dies the general reaction of friends and neighbours is not to talk about it, mostly because they're afraid of adding to the grief, but the truth is that when something bad happens everybody needs to unload. Talking about what's happened and how they feel is the only way to healing. That's something else Gran taught me a long time ago. What she omitted to mention was how hard the listening can be. Viv didn't try to make Billy out to have been a paragon; she'd had some tough times with him, but the picture I took away with me was of a basically good kid who'd got off to a bad start, and it was even harder to fit him into a fire-raising mould.

Instead of going right on home I dropped by the fire station to see if Redding was about. The big doors at the back were open and it looked like they were getting in some practice with the reels. I wandered across to take a look and stood idly watching the activity until Dan Bush turned round and saw me. He lifted a hand and patted his chest. I shook my head and pointed at Redding. Bush left what he was doing and came over with a macho, don't-I-look-good-in-my-uniform smile on his face. He did, but there was no way I was going to add to his vanity. He put an outstretched hand on the door at the side of my head and leaned his weight on it. The door shifted a little. 'Nice to see you, Leah, but it's not a good time to look for a chat with Redding.'

I moved myself out from between him and the door; I really hate to be confronted that way. 'Fine,' I said, 'I'll just wander over and tell him I've been around.' I stepped out across the yard without looking to see how he felt about that.

Redding spotted me midway over and halved the distance. 'Must be telepathy,' he said. 'I was thinking about you not five minutes since – come up with anything new about Billy?'

I shrugged. 'I don't know; right now I'm trying to dig in from the other end of things. I was hoping to talk with you about that when I dropped by on Friday, but when you weren't around I decided I'd try again today. Seems I've picked a bad time.'

'They can finish up without me,' he said. 'If they can't manage without a nanny yet they never will. I didn't know you'd been looking for me Friday. Who'd you see?'

I motioned back to Bush. 'He said you weren't around and tried to be helpful.'

'Fancies my job, I reckon,' said Redding. 'Want to talk in the office?'

'If it doesn't give you any trouble I'd appreciate that.'

He hollered, 'Finish up, lads,' and started back to the building. Dan Bush looked a bit peeved, maybe because Redding had found time to talk with me or maybe because he wasn't used to having his own sexual chemistry misfire. Either way the problem was his not mine.

Redding wasn't all that tall but he had a good fast stride. I had to step out to keep up with him. I said, 'Getting back to Billy, now you've had some time to think, has anything new come to mind?'

'Wish it had, but the truth is, if I hadn't got to like the kid I wouldn't even doubt he'd done it.' We climbed the concrete stairs. 'Except that some of the methods seemed a bit too sophisticated for Billy, but I said that before, didn't I? Know much about firebugs?'

'I know it's an alternative word for arsonist. Except for that, the file's empty.'

He held the office door open nicely and let me walk in ahead of him. 'Not outside a dictionary it isn't,' he said. 'I tell the recruits firebug is to arsonist what tomcat is to tiger. It stems from criminal intent; at the top end you get political arsonists, in the middle fire-raisers working for profit and down at the bottom a firebug starting a blaze for the hell of it. I can't see Billy being in it for money or politics can you?'

'Uh-uh.' I shook my head. 'I don't see him being in it at all; if I did I wouldn't be here.' I walked over to the window to take a look at the workers and they seemed to be doing just fine on their own. I said, 'Billy collected old lighters. He had more than a dozen that he'd cleaned up and got working again. The police searched his room and took them and a can of lighter fuel away as evidence. His mother has them back now; they handed them over when they didn't have anybody to prosecute any more.'

'How's she doing?'

I turned round and faced him. 'Not good.'

'Billy was always talking about her and the way she stood by him. Seems the pundits wanted to send him off to special school years back and she wouldn't hear of it. Went round raising a rumpus until the idea got dropped. It got a bit monotonous sometimes hearing him tell it.'

Viv hadn't mentioned that. 'Special school as in backward do you mean?'

'That's the impression I got, although as far as I could see there wasn't anything backward about him, except maybe emotionally, and having heard about his problems I could understand that.' He frowned. 'In different circumstances I'd have paid Mrs Tyler a visit and told her me and the boys miss him helping out.'

'She'd have appreciated it,' I said. 'The neighbours haven't given her an easy time since it happened, and the other two kids are too young to be much help.' Dan Bush looked up at the window, stopped what he was doing, and waved extravagantly. I kept my arms folded and moved away.

Redding said, 'Looks like a one-sided attraction blossoming there.'

'Uh-huh. No offence, but how about we stick to firebugs. You say you separate them out from professionals by the way they set fires?'

'Ninety-nine times out of a hundred, yes. A firebug is an opportunist who sees waste paper and puts a match to it, a pile of rubbish in a backyard gets the same treatment; it doesn't matter what burns so long as he gets to see the flames. What he doesn't do is go out tooled up with timing devices and accelerants – most firebugs don't even have the know-how.'

'Did Billy?'

He pulled a face. 'He could have read up on it, but I don't see how he'd have got a hold of the devices. I'm not saying he couldn't, I'm just saying it isn't likely.'

I said, 'You know, to an arsonist wanting to set up a scapegoat, finding somebody like Billy would be a godsend. Had you thought about that?'

'It crossed my mind.'

'Crossed mine too, which is why I need to ask some help following up a hunch. Do you have records of insurers? Can you tie an insurance company in to each fire?'

'Initially we collect that kind of information, but when our involvement's over it gets passed to Regional HQ at Birkenshaw.'

'That's what I was afraid of. Look, I need to get at it,' I said candidly, 'but if I ask Barlow for help he'll just give me a load of hassle.'

'Didn't seem to take to you much, did he?' said Redding. 'Doesn't like having mistakes pointed out, that's his trouble.'

'How did he come to make one anyway? I thought . . .'

I'd stopped there because pursuing the thought wasn't pleasant, but Redding didn't let me get away with it. He said, 'Thought what?'

'That the smell of roasting flesh is unmistakable.' I looked at him and shrugged. 'Somebody told me that; I thought it was you.'

'Probably was, but Turpin Street was a bit different. For one thing most of the inside had gone when the tenders got there and what was left of the body was down under the rubble; that'd cut down on smell. Couple that with the stink of cooking mutton from the kebab place up on the main road and it's easy to see why it was missed. By the time Barlow got there the place would be cooled down.'

I shrugged. 'Guess that has to be it then, in which case he should have been glad I put him right. How about the information I need? Can you get it for me?'

'If I bend a few regulations I can get it, yes. It won't be today though.' He looked through me and stared at some point inside his head. 'Give me until around this time tomorrow?'

'That isn't a problem.' I held out my hand. 'Thanks.' We shook, and I left him to get on with his work. I walked out of the building feeling I might be getting somewhere. I wasn't too sure how the insurance companies Redding came up with would feel about releasing information from their files, but the word fraud wafted around in the right places often works magic.

On the way home I did a little personal shopping and also picked up a can of salmon, telling myself I did that out of friendship for Dora and not because her damn tabby was getting to me.

I got back home a little after four and put Oscar's can of salmon on the kitchen table. Other things, tights, sanitary towels and a white silk blouse I'd been too weak to resist got tidied neatly away in the bedroom along with the clothes I'd been wearing. Keep this up and slut of the year title'd go to someone else. I shimmied into black leggings, topped them with a Greenpeace T-shirt and washed my hair. In the middle of drying it off the outside doorbell rang. I wrapped a towel round my head and wondered who was calling. I went to take a look out of the bedroom window and saw a white van with half a dozen daffodils and the word 'Florist' stencilled on its side.

How nice; somebody was sending me flowers. Maybe Nicholls was trying to get back into my good books. Such gestures were uncommon but not unheard of. Blithely I tripped downstairs and opened the door. A woman in a blue polyester florist's smock was holding a snappy arrangement of pink and white carnations brightened up by blue iris.

'For me?' I said.

'For a Miss Leah Hunter.'

'Guess they're mine then.' I took them from her and looked for a card. There wasn't one. The woman had got back down to the pavement. 'Hey,' I said. 'There isn't a card.'

'There is somewhere,' she said. 'No name on it, though. I looked. I think maybe he's shy.'

Nicholls shy? That was a new one. I carried the basket back upstairs and put it on the low table by the living-room window. After a little hunting I found a card tucked damply down between basket and foam. When I opened up the envelope and took a look I found she was right about the no name business; one fat cross in the middle of white pasteboard was all. How sentimental. When he rang – if he rang – I'd remember to say thank you nicely.

I went and finished drying off my hair. A kiss for God's sake. What kind of apology was that supposed to be?

I changed the bed linen and dumped the dirty sheets in the washer, picked up the phone to check it was working and put it down again. Then I took another look at the card; it hadn't magically sprouted any new words. I poked around at the green oasis and it didn't seem all that wet, so I took the whole thing into the kitchen and fed more water down between the flowers. When it felt good and soggy I set it back on the low table, propped the uncommunicative card up against it and told myself maybe it was romantic after all.

I should have remembered how wise it is to stick with first impressions.

26

Nicholls didn't telephone. So OK, if that was the way he wanted to play it, it was fine by me. Damn it, if he couldn't even put his name on the stupid card how was I supposed to know he'd sent me flowers? I could read him like a book. He'd sit around waiting for me to pick up the phone and tell him thanks, then he'd act dumb and make out he didn't know what I was talking about. I shoved bread into the toaster and heated up some beans, then I propped Billy's diary on the coffee pot and read through it while I ate.

He really seemed to have admired Dan Bush. It was Dan showed me this, and Dan showed me that, right the way through. I began to worry that I should have paid the man more attention; maybe if I'd chatted him up a little more carefully I'd have learned something. Billy had written about other fire crew too, but it was Dan who took up the most space. Redding he seemed to view differently. Redding was chief of the clan, the archetypal father figure to be respected and obeyed, and the wigging he'd given Billy about the way he turned up at fires had really gone home. The kid seemed to have remembered it word for word and it read like he'd been badly hurt by what was said. Obviously the boys in blue hadn't seen it that way. After he'd written it all down he'd added, *Asked Dan if he knew who'd been phoning me up but he said no so I must have been wrong*. I turned more pages.

Five weeks later he'd written, *Went to another fire. Suppose I didn't ought to have gone but I wanted to see the engines and it was* brill! A couple of weeks later Fast-Sell burned down. Just like always, Billy noted down all the details, number of fire appliances, how many crew, what time the blaze began, when it ended. He'd even counted the damn hoses! Right at the end he'd put, *Asked Dan what the smell was and he said that's a human body in there cooking that's what, and it made me throw up, hadn't ever thought about anybody being in there, thought about telling Mum but it'd worry her silly. Don't know what to do.*

There wasn't much else in the diary; just one more visit to the fire station written in without either detail or enthusiasm, and after that blank pages. I got another cup of coffee and thought about it. If I'd read it from Nicholls's starting point, would I vote innocent or guilty? The coffee was near cold. I gulped it down and stacked the pots. Some of the things Billy had written could be read either way, and if that was all I'd had to help me decide if he was a firebug or not I honestly didn't know which way I would have gone. I put the whole thing on hold and changed into sweats – black bottoms, white T-shirt, zipped and hooded red top – stowed the kit I needed into a holdall, and went to make peace with Jack.

The Tai Chi and Oriental Arts Centre on Pilkington Street shares a car park with the pub next door, an arrangement from which the pub gains the most benefit. There's nothing like an hour of nonstop physical effort to work up a good thirst. I parked tidily, hauled my kit off the rear seat and headed for Jack's back door. He's been teaching me karate for five years, owned the place for ten and I count myself real lucky that he's also a good friend. If I were in bad trouble he'd be right there helping out. The problem is that when I get into the kind of trouble he could best help with he's usually not within shouting distance.

I pushed through into the ladies' changing room and got into the cute white pyjama suit, hauling the sash good and firm before skipping along to Jack's office. I settled cross-legged on the floor behind the tall one-way mirror. It's real good fun to ogle beefcake without being seen.

The dozen or so males going through their paces in the practice room were near novices with a lot more enthusiasm than skill, but that didn't exactly detract from the enjoyment value! I sat there grinning for around ten minutes until Jack started winding up, then I got up and put the kettle on. Damn it – where had he put his Lapsang Souchong? I hunted around for the black tin caddy and came up blank. This was crazy. Jack without Lapsang was like Kojak without lollipop. I was still shifting things around when Jack drifted in the door. 'Hi,' I said, 'I can't find the tea.'

He said, 'Things change, monkey,' and picked up a Nescafé jar. I looked at it sadly.

'No Lapsang?'

He unscrewed the top and reached for the teapot. 'No tin,

love, that's what's missing. People aren't honest no more; it got nicked.'

'Why'd anybody want to take a tea caddy for Pete's sake?'

'Why'd anybody want to take a cash box? Maybe 'cos they was both black.'

'Uh-oh. You know who did it?'

'Got a good idea.'

I watched him brew up and wondered how much he'd lost. I said, 'I suppose you told the police?'

'Why'd I do that, Leah love? Jails is full enough as it is. Don't worry, I'm working on it. He'll give it back in his own good time.' He leaned his backside on the table and looked me over. 'I was beginning to think you'd given up for good.'

'Oh, come on, Jack, you know better than that. Didn't I say I'd be back when I was ready for it?'

'An' you're ready now?'

I shrugged. 'Who knows? A couple of falls on the mat and I might go into decline.'

'What you up to now then? Chasing villains again?'

'No.' I squinted at him. 'That tea ready yet?' I poured a little and tasted. It was fine. I took my mug over to the one-way window and stared out of it. I'd had this conversation with him before.

'Want me to mind me own business?'

'No! I mean ... Look I'm really trying not to get into that stuff again.'

'Tea's hot. Want to go try a few moves?'

I got rid of the mug and went meekly into the practice room. It looked bigger than I remembered. Jack whistled tunelessly and my hands started sweating. I wiped them off surreptitiously. Maybe I wasn't ready for this, maybe I never would be. My heart speeded up. I took in deep breaths and got started on the warm-up.

'Want some help with them stretches?'

'I'm fine,' I snapped curtly, cutting the routine short. 'So why don't we get on with it huh? The tea's going cold.'

'Right.' He bounced on the balls of his feet. 'Come on then, I'll be nice an' gentle, just like as if you was a virgin.' His voice teased much the same as always but not his face. That was watchful and still.

Maybe in a past life he'd been a lama in some high Tibetan monastery. He's got the right features for it – high cheekbones, round eyes and a squarish face – and a neat way of diffusing trouble. Of course, a lot of that could come from the fact that everybody knows if they pushed too hard he could take them to pieces.

He gave me a little bow.

I stepped on to the mat, exchanged courtesies and waited for him to make his move. When he did I was unready and totally failed to anticipate his speed. My legs swept out from under me. I fell hard and lay there winded. *Shit!* If that had been for real I'd be in deep trouble. I got back on my feet and felt my legs begin to tremble, knees slack as a badly strung puppet's. We faced each other and bowed again, then I sailed smartly over Jack's right hip pretty much the way Eddie had sailed over mine. This time when I landed, sweat broke out all over my body and when I sat up the shaking was so bad it rattled my teeth.

'Shit!' This time I said it out loud.

Jack squatted. 'Think yourself lucky you wasn't facing down some poxy mugger,' he said unhelpfully. 'Trouble with you is you can't let go of nothing; anybody'd think you didn't believe nobody ever got scared 'cept you.' He got to his feet and pulled me upright. I sank back down.

'Look, I just want to sit for a while, so leave me alone, Jack, OK?'

'Since you're asking, no, it isn't OK.' He hauled me up again. 'First you drink up your Lapsang like a good girl. Then we come out here and do it over again, only when we do, first off you get yourself centred, an' then you concentrate on putting me on me back. That'll be a thrill won't it? An' if you're lucky I won't tell the wife. Right?'

'Right.'

Teeth gritted, hands bunched to beat the shakes, I walked back to the office on legs that had to belong to someone else. This was great! I was going to spend the rest of my life like a fading daisy. OK, I'd dealt with Eddie but that was a fluke. I hadn't had time to think about what I was doing then, and if I had thought about it maybe I'd have turned tail and run. I dredged up all the bad words I could think of and strung them out in my head. It didn't help. I flopped on to a chair and felt angry enough to explode. What the hell was the matter with me, for God's sake? I wrapped both hands round the mug and gulped down the tea. Jack filled it up again.

'Didn't bother wasting time with a counsellor, I suppose?'

'What would I need with a counsellor?'

'Don't tell me you haven't never heard of post-traumatic shock syndrome.'

'Yes!' I snapped. 'I've heard of it.' Damn it, I couldn't have avoided hearing about it; Nicholls had yacked his stupid head off about nothing else for a month after I got out of hospital, and like I told him, the last thing I needed was to rehash what had happened to me. Once was enough.

Jack said, 'Suppose you thought it only counted if you fell out of the sky or something?'

'Yes! That's right! Look, Jack, I can handle my own head, so just back off.'

'Wouldn't do that, love; not while we're mates.'

I cocked an ear. The women's room was too quiet. By this time the rest of the class should be filtering through unless . . . ?

Jack said, 'No good expecting the rest of les girls; tonight you're on your own. They've gone off to an exhibition. Didn't know that, did you?'

'No,' I said hollowly.

'So, since we both know what the problem is, and with all this spare time on us hands, I reckon you should think about unloading all that angst on to my broad and manly shoulders. After which we go back to the mats so you can wallop the shit out of me.'

Grinning made me feel marginally better.

'Jack, love, I never *could* wallop the shit out of you.'

'Always a first time, monkey, always a first time,' he said, and came around behind me. His thumbs began to work on knots at the base of my neck and it felt good. I closed my eyes and took a look at that part of me where fear and guilt waited to be dragged up to the surface. I didn't want to do that, I wanted to blank it all out like I had for the past six months. I snapped my eyes open and stared at the wall. The alternative was telling Jack to mind his own damn business. And then what? Did I really want this sick thing festering for the rest of my life? I tilted my head and squinted up at him.

Jack looked back at me inscrutably.

I thought: What the hell! It was over . . . in the past . . . I couldn't change it. I hadn't picked the game, I hadn't made the rules and I'd near enough died. Kill or be killed. I took in a deep lungful of air and for the first time since it happened I let out the guilt of being the one to walk away, and it felt like I'd finally lanced a boil that should have been dealt with a long time ago.

Back when I was small and right up into my teens Gran was the one I confided in; she was my wise woman and the only adult I had complete faith in. When she died I decided the only way to handle things from then on was to rely on myself, and I'd forgotten how cathartic it can be to share the bad things with another person. It took me a while to work out why I couldn't do that with Nicholls, but then I knew. The truth was, if I opened up that much to him I'd be putting the relationship on a whole new level and I wasn't ready to do that. I liked things the way they were, uncomplicated and easy.

Jack brewed up again, after which, awash with tea, I needed to go pee before going back out to the mats so he could finish showing me how rusty I'd become. This time I didn't get the shakes and that had to be good. When we were through I helped him tidy away, pleased as little apples to have got back some concentration and timing. I skipped the shower and drove back to Dora's, tending to Oscar's needs and playing around with him for a while before heading home to my own little nest for a long hot soak. Around ten thirty I toasted a couple of tomato sandwiches, turned on the gas fire and picnicked on the settee while I read through the books I'd brought home from Billy's. It's just amazing how much knowledge can be picked up that way. Want to make a bomb? Visit your local library. Fancy playing at urban terrorist? Ditto.

Skimming through the slim volume on fire investigation let me pick up enough knowledge to hire out as a freelance arsonist. No use me pretending Billy couldn't have known about sophisticated methods – reading that one book alone would have given him that – but what it wouldn't have done is tell him where to get chemicals, fuses, timers and other such necessary devices.

I took a break there to get a can of Pils then got started on the second. It didn't offer the same amount of practical advice, but from my point of view it was a lot more interesting. Especially the chapter on a bunch of fire-raisers known as the Leopold Harris gang. I read that through twice and then leaned back comfortably to think about it.

Gran used to say there's no such thing as a new idea; they're all just old ones tarted up and sent out in fresh paint, and the Bramfield fires fitted in nicely with that theory.

A lot of people think fire assessors and loss adjusters are the same breed of animal – but they're not. Assessors put in claims for compensation to the insurance companies on behalf of clients whose premises have burned down; loss adjusters are employed by insurance companies to assess and investigate those claims independently. It wasn't always so.

Back in the late nineteen twenties, Leopold Harris and his gang set out to make a lot of money from arson, and until they got caught they were doing very nicely thank you. It was a very neat scam. Leopold himself was a fire assessor who made a habit of turning up promptly on the scene after commercial premises burned down, offering to get the owner maximum compensation from the insurance company in exchange for a percentage for himself. Such tactics built him up a large and profitable business and the fire-assessing side of it always stayed strictly legal.

What wasn't legal was the way he branched out into the Rent-a-Blaze business, hooking up with a chief fire officer and an arsonist to set up a new line in commercial fraud. It was so damn simple! First he sniffed out a business with cash-flow problems and then advised its owners to take out a good, big, fire policy. Not long after the policy came through, all the valuable stuff was secretly moved out and replaced by inexpensive rubbish. At which point the whole place burned down. *Zip!* Harris then walks in bold as brass to assess and inflate the insurance loss on behalf of the owner, taking off a nice percentage when the insurance company paid up. Even after paying the fire officer for falsifying the fire report and the arsonist for starting the blaze, he still managed to have a tidy little sum left for himself.

Of course, things couldn't work in quite that way now. For one thing insurance companies have tightened up their act enough to employ independent loss adjusters to check that claims aren't being inflated by the client or the client's assessor. And chief fire officers no longer determine a fire's cause – that's done by trained investigators. If he were operating these days Leopold would find life much less simple.

But the scam could still be done.

I put the book down, leaned back and drew myself a new picture. Instead of Leopold, I slid in Colin Stanton, fitted in an as-yet-unknown fire-raiser, plus, maybe, a couple of hired yobs to do the muscle work when Gavin slipped up, and . . . Who else? Would it be necessary to have a fire investigator on side? Someone like Barlow or his sidekick; or someone as senior as Redding to go in after a fire and mess with the evidence if that's what it needed? None of them seemed likely candidates for crooked dealings, but I'd made the mistake of thinking surface nice guys couldn't possibly have black hearts before. Such lessons are painfully learned and best not forgotten.

The room was sleepy warm. I blinked a couple of times and got the urge to rub my eyes; when the yawning started I checked my watch. Two a.m. How'd it get to that time? I turned off the fire, picked up the empty can and started for the kitchen. Over on the table the flowers were drooping already. I told myself it must be the heat – the room had really hotted up, a black mark in my ecologically careful copybook. I dumped the can, pulled the plug on the coffee-maker and went to drop the deadlock on the hall door. The noise when it came was a mixture of sounds. A whoosh, a splat, a fire-cracker. I turned round and ran for the sitting room.

Shit! Maybe Nicholls hadn't sent the flowers after all. The whole thing was flaming incandescently, the curtains already ablaze.

Mini bonfires burned on the carpet. I grabbed the rug, dumped it on the burning patches and stamped it up and down. While I did that the main fire got bigger and gnawed through the table.

I lugged the rug into the bath, turning on both taps and shower, getting it good and soaked before lugging it back again. Smoke was filling up the room. I held the rug out at arm's length and dropped it on the burning mess. It spluttered. Smoke poured both out of it and from under it, the wall behind was scorched and sooted, the curtains burned to the top, the wood frame charred and blistered; bits of burning curtain had dropped down and made more holes in the wool carpet. I got a bucket of water and poured it on the rug, got a second bucket and waited with it until smoke stopped puffing out. Then I set it down and tried to remember when I last paid the fire insurance.

Coughing fit to bust I hiked open the window, leaning out and taking in clean smokeless air, staying there alternately coughing and breathing until the paroxysms wore off and I could get myself into the bathroom and bathe my face in cool water. Adrenaline was still flowing fast, keeping me going, tipping the balance of emotion towards anger. I dried off my hands and face and went to telephone Nicholls.

The phone was dead.

I slumped down on the hall floor, leaned against the wall and cradled the receiver.

If I'd gone to bed at the usual time I'd be dead, too.

That kind of inner wisdom can be a pain.

27

When I got tired of wondering why the telephone didn't work I got the key Marcie had left me and went down to her place. It was a waste of time. Her phone was dead too. I locked up carefully and went back upstairs.

Coincidences like that I don't believe in.

The sharp smell of smoke and soot hung over the whole of my attic home. I looked at the mess and knew I couldn't face cleaning it up right then. Cleaning it up? I didn't intend to clean it up; it was staying right the way it was until I got to rub Nicholls's nose in it.

I shoved clean underwear and sweats into a holdall, added a nightshift in case anyone came calling and went to spend the rest of the night at Dora's.

Halfway there my brain finally caught up on the fact that I was wet. By the time I opened up Dora's door and turned on the lights I was also cold. Oscar came winding around my legs like he thought it was a good idea to have some company, then he picked out the smell of smoke and backed off, waving his tail and spitting. I knew just how he felt; smoke had pretty much the same effect on me.

I went up to Dora's bathroom and stripped off, then took a quick shower and washed my hair, towelling it vigorously to make up for the lack of a dryer. The cat sat around and watched. I guess when I put the nightshift on I must have smelled a little better because he came down to the kitchen with me and started on the best-friends routine again.

I poured him out a little milk and heated up some for myself, then I picked up the phone and started to punch in Nicholls's number. The hall clock struck three. I slid the receiver back in its cradle.

Let him rest; tomorrow was soon enough.

Tomorrow? Tomorrow was today already. I drank up my hot milk and went to bed. To tell the truth of it I'm scared of fire. I don't know why that should be, there's nothing logical to it, but I have this horror of finding myself slowly roasting and not being able to do a thing about it. Which is probably why I spent a lot of what was left of the night dreaming I was up to my nostrils in smoke.

I slept for almost five hours then snapped awake wondering where I was. Sitting bolt upright disturbed Oscar; he dug his claws through the sheet and got me up fast. That little habit he has of crawling under the duvet was something I'd forgotten about.

I went through the usual bathroom routine, pulled on the clean clothes I'd brought with me and ran downstairs. Nicholls picked up on the third ring. It was so good to hear his voice. I didn't tell him that. Instead I told him that if he had a little free time maybe he'd like to walk me home from Dora's. He took a little time to consider the implications of that, then asked cautiously why I wanted him to do it.

'Because my place near burned down last night, that's why, and you weren't damn well around to be any help,' I told him crabbily. 'See what happens when you get into a sulk.'

'I haven't been in a sulk. I've been busy.'

'Fine,' I said. 'Well, now you can get to be even busier; you can come and investigate a cosy case of arson – and I'll tell you right away – *Billy didn't do it.*' I enunciated that last bit very carefully and slowly so he shouldn't miss it.

He hung up.

I grinned at the phone and went to make some toast. I was still eating it when he arrived. Sometimes he drives too fast. I pointed out gently that if he kept it up he'd get a ticket, but that was something else he didn't appreciate. He turned down a slice of toast and a pot of tea, bundled me into his car and drove the two hundred yards to my place.

I really believe that right up to me opening the door and letting him walk in, he thought I'd been making the whole thing up. Then he saw the mess and swore nicely.

I got a lot of satisfaction from that.

He lifted the rug gingerly and peered underneath. It was near scorched through. 'I liked that rug,' he said plaintively. I knew what he meant; I had some fond memories of it myself. Then he got his mind back on to less pleasant things and demanded to know what I'd done.

'Done?' I said. 'I haven't done anything, except mistakenly think you'd sent me some flowers to make up, but I guess they must have been from someone else.'

'Why'd you think they were from me?' he said.

'I don't know. I guess I'm always crediting you with being nicer than you are.'

He sighed. 'How did you get them?'

'A woman in a white florist's van.'

'What did the card say?'

I shrugged. 'Nothing. All it had on was a Judas kiss. I thought maybe you hadn't put your name to it because you didn't like wasting that much ink.'

'Thanks,' he said.

'You're welcome,' I replied. He went out in the hall and picked up the telephone.

'It's disconnected,' he said.

'Not officially it isn't.'

He sighed again, walked into the bedroom and stuck his head out the window. I leaned on the door jamb and knew what he'd find. He ducked back in and dusted off his hands. 'It's been cut,' he said.

What a surprise.

I nodded sagely. 'Guess I wasn't meant to ring for the fire brigade. You realise if I'd gone to bed at the right time last night I'd have been cooked to a crisp?' The idea didn't seem to please him and I was glad about that.

'I'll use the car phone,' he said.

'Fine. You want to see the florist's card?' I moved back to the sitting room and made for the bookshelves.

'Don't touch it!' snapped Nicholls, shoving me aside. I watched him edge the card into an itsy plastic bag.

'I don't know why you're behaving like that,' I chided. 'I've been handling it on and off since it came. If you want the envelope it's in the waste basket.' He got out another itsy bag and repeated the process. I wondered how many he carried around with him. 'Guess I'd better start to clean up,' I said, looking around with a lack of enthusiasm.

'Go ahead,' said Nicholls sarcastically. 'Destroy the evidence. Since when did you pick up housewifely habits?'

'Since never,' I snapped back. 'But I do have to live in the damn place! Oh, hell! I need a new carpet, the table's burnt through, the curtains have gone ... You know what? The real punch line is I bet the insurance company send someone round to check I didn't start it myself.'

155

'Shouldn't think so. My bet is they'll take your word for it; the claim won't be big enough to worry them. Suppose you brew some coffee while I go and use the phone?'

Coffee! I swear in the middle of a riot he'd still be thinking of his stomach.

I squatted down and looked at the burnt patches of carpet. Maybe I could get someone clever in to repair it. Or maybe I should claim for the whole thing. After all, it wasn't *my* carpet. I'd just inherited it when I took over the flat, and the truth was until now I couldn't be bothered to change it. I poked at the underneath of the table and a piece of charred wood fell out. Dispiritedly I went to brew up.

By the time Nicholls got back I had all the windows open and a lot of the smoky stench had gone. The first thing he did was go around and close them all.

'Thanks,' I said. 'What did you do that for?'

'Were they closed when the fire started?'

'Of course they were closed.'

'So, when the scientific officers get here they'll want to find it just the way it was last night.'

'This morning,' I corrected.

'What?'

'This morning. Two a.m. to be precise.'

He sighed, eyed the dripping coffee and started rummaging for bread. 'You haven't asked if I know who did it yet,' I told him when he'd got it in the toaster. I could see his back freeze up. He turned round and looked at me. 'I have a theory,' I said, 'if you want to hear it. In fact, if you hadn't been in a megasulk you'd have heard about it before.'

'I haven't been in a sulk,' he yelled.

'So what are you shouting for?'

'I'm not.'

I shrugged. 'OK, you're not. I think Drury sent the flowers. Of course, he'd need a little help with the fire bomb part but I think the idea was his.'

'Drury!'

'That's a problem?'

He took out the toast, slapped it on a plate and smothered it in peanut butter. 'You want to tell me why you think it's Drury?' he mumbled.

'You want to tell me why you think it isn't?' I said.

'Did I say that?'

156

'You didn't have to. What did you think to Julie and Eddie? I hear you went out to see them.'

'They didn't have anything useful to tell me.'

'That so? And what about Gavin? Anything new there?'

'Leah, it's all being investigated and it's none of your business. Are you going to tell me about Drury?'

'You still think Billy started the fires?'

He struggled a while. I waited patiently. 'It's being looked into,' he said. 'Don't ask for more because you won't get it.'

'So look into Drury.'

'Give me a reason.'

I sighed. 'He threatened me. How's that? I ended up in the same restaurant bar and he said I was harassing him. That's the truth.'

'Were you?'

'Harassing him? Yes. What's that got to do with it?'

There were noisy feet on the stairs. Nicholls went over to the door, then turned. 'I was going to drop by and have a talk with him anyway. This gives me a better reason. Satisfied?'

I grinned at him.

'Not entirely,' I said, 'but it'll do for a start.'

28

I left Nicholls to look after his helpmeets and hiked down to Dora's to make a couple of phone calls. BT sounded like cut lines were two a penny and promised to get the line repaired pronto. The insurance company was less obliging. Suspicion oozed along the line and into my ear.

I didn't get it.

Torch a factory, claim a few hundred thousand, and heh! No problem! But mention how a basket of flowers near burned down a place and insurance fraudster of the year award arrives next post. I mentioned that politely. It didn't go down well. I suggested they send someone round to check the damage. Prissily I was informed they only did that *after* a claim form had been processed. I told Mr Know-it-all I'd be by to pick up a form and maybe meantime I should buy new curtains? He said fine, why not? Just so I remembered they didn't agree to pay for them. I hung up noisily.

Halfway home the forensic van passed me heading the other way. Good. That just left Nicholls and the mess. I climbed upstairs and found they'd taken a lot of it with them. Like the rug, the table, what was left of the curtains and a nice big piece they'd cut out of the carpet. I looked down at the gap. How foolish of me to have worried about a few little burnt bits when such an obvious solution had been staring me in the face!

Nicholls sounded uncomfortable.

'They did it when I wasn't looking.'

I grabbed his jacket up off the chair where he'd dumped it and laid it neatly over the hole. Then I went around opening up the windows. He looked at me aggrievedly, then picked up the jacket and shoved his arms in the sleeves. I moved around behind him. He spun on his heel defensively.

'Hey, no problem,' I said. 'If I want it I can get it. Since when did I have any trouble getting your clothes off?' He blinked a couple of times and made for the door.

'If I come up with anything conclusive from Drury I'll let you know,' he said. I pulled the vac savagely out of the hall closet.

'You mean I can clean up now?'

'Might be best to wait in case the insurers come.'

I said a couple of words I'd overlooked earlier. He looked surprised. 'Hey,' I said. 'I already talked to them. It could be Christmas before they get around to it.' I went over and opened the door. 'Don't let Drury sell you a sob story,' I said, and shoved him out.

I hauled the Hoover into the sitting room then took another look around and gave up on the idea. What was the point, for God's sake? The wall and ceiling were black, the window scorched and blistered. A fat lot of good vacuuming the carpet would do! I left the vac where it was and walked into town to pick up a claims form which I filled in on the spot. After which I demanded to see the claims manager. He looked a lot more interested in the idea of treating things with urgency when I gave him a card with Inland Revenue neatly embossed. I added my home number and told him I'd be taking some time off to get straight.

I didn't mention the fact that since I'd been suspended I was doing that already. There didn't seem any point in overtaxing his brain.

I crossed the street diagonally from Gold Star Incorporated to the Lamb and Goat, ate a ploughman's lunch washed down with a couple of Pils and then did some window shopping. When I got back home mid-afternoon BT had done a fast repair job. I knew that because the phone began ringing as I hit the top step.

It was Bethany again wanting to know how things were.

'Funny you should ask that. It's something of a burning question,' I said, and told her about the frazzled flat.

'Looks like you really got on the wrong side of somebody,' she observed. 'Any ideas?'

'Plenty. Drury for one. I guess he knows I'm about an inch away from proving what he's been up to.'

'Sounds like you've been busy.'

'And then some. Look, Bethany...' I let a couple of seconds' silence go by. If I asked about Stanton would her sense of loyalty make her repeat it all back to him? I took a chance. 'I wouldn't ask this if I didn't need to know,' I said, 'but how long has Stanton been based in Bramfield?'

'It's no secret,' she said. 'He's been with Saxby Associates around two years. Why?'

'Just curious.'

'And you're not going to tell me why, that's obvious. Have you talked to Drury again?'

'No. Have you?'

'I haven't needed to.'

'Best leave it to the police from now on in,' I said.

'It was a bad mistake,' she came back after a silence. 'Laying that kind of charge against you I mean. You'd probably have dropped the whole thing by now if he hadn't done that.'

'Probably I would, which makes Drury the weak link because when he panics he does stupid things, and that's fine by me. If I wait around long enough he's bound to make another.'

'Better go,' she said quickly. 'Stanton's watching.'

'Thanks for your help,' I said. She hung up and I replaced my own receiver, thinking how maybe I should have asked where Stanton had been before he hit Bramfield.

I put the vac away for a while and went down to the basement, toiling back up again with the step ladder. There are some things even a messy person like myself can't live with. I cleaned off as much soot and grime as I could and half the window paint came with it. Nice! Now I could start decorating all over again.

Or maybe Gold Star would pay for me to get in some hunky-looking painter. The idea was appealing. I put the steps out on the landing, took a long hot soak, heated up some soup and grilled a cheese sandwich, then relaxed with my feet up for a while. At seven I carried the steps back to the basement and went off to work out at the health club, telling myself what a goody-little-two-shoes I'd been that day.

Feeling that virtuous can't be good for the soul but, hey, who cared?

On the way back home I picked up a piece of cod from the chippy and fed it to Oscar. He danced around delightedly and looked like he could really get to like his new diet. I had a moment's guilt. If the damn cat could talk I'd be in real trouble with Dora. I got home at ten thirty and found Nicholls half-asleep in his car. He climbed out and did a bit of yawning and stretching.

'Drury?' I said.

'Drury.'

I waited to be told.

'Caffeine first; I'm brain dead. Where've you been?'

I shook the holdall at him. 'Health club.' Then I shoved my key in the lock and let him in.

He made for the stairs. 'You've never been home this late before from the health club,' he said querulously.

'How would you know?' I said impatiently. 'Anyway, I had to call in and feed Dora's cat.'

'Ahh. Right! The cat! I'd forgotten friendly little Oscar. When's she get home?'

I shrugged. 'Weekend maybe. Why?'

'Just seems a funny time for her to go away.'

'That so? What's wrong with April?'

He got to the top landing and turned round. 'I heard Jason Duncombe had a girlfriend.'

'Eddie told you?'

'Said she was a slag.'

'I heard that too. She wasn't.'

'Wasn't or isn't?'

'Huh?'

'You drove Dora and an unknown girl to the station. Fry saw, and followed. He watched them get on the Scarborough train. Want to tell me who the girl was?'

'Her grandniece,' I said.

'Sure about that?'

'Would I lie?'

'Yes. I'd like to talk to her.'

'Dora?'

'The girl.'

'What for? You've never met her.'

'I would have if you hadn't spirited her away.'

'How come a sudden interest in Dora's relations?'

'I haven't one, but I do have an interest in a girl who might have seen the Turpin Street fire start.'

'She didn't, so forget it.'

'You forget it, Leah. I want the girl back in Bramfield and I want to talk to her. If I think she can't help, you can hand her over to Dora again. That's fair.'

'A, It's her grandniece, and B, I don't even know where they are.'

'You want me to put out an alert in Scarborough? It wouldn't be that hard to pick them up.'

162

I shoved past him and went into the flat. 'Feel free. I don't even know if they're *in* Scarborough.'

He came in behind me and slammed the door. 'Why doesn't that sound like the truth?'

'Don't ask me. I guess you've just got a twisted mind. Forget about Dora and her family and tell me about Drury.' I loaded up the coffee machine and he sat at the table and sulked. I said, 'Hand on heart I don't know where Dora is. Until she rings me I don't even know when she's coming home. OK?'

'No,' he said, 'it isn't OK. I run around picking up after you and you whisk a witness away right from under my nose. What makes you think it's OK?'

I sighed and sat down with him. 'This is the truth,' I said. 'I knew about Jaz's girlfriend; I met them both and talked with them before the fire. I hoped Jaz could tell me something new about Billy, only they both ran out on me before we got that far. But I'd given the girl my address and she came looking for me. She was scared witless and didn't know who started the fire. She wasn't there – Jaz had sent her out to walk around for a while because he didn't want her to see who he talked to. When she got back the place was burning and she had to walk three streets to find a working telephone to call the brigade. She spent the rest of the night on my settee.'

'And you didn't think to tell me?'

'She'd gone before I got up next morning so what was the use?'

'You saw her again?'

'I saw her again because I went looking for her, and when I found her I took her for a burger and she told me about Gavin. If you remember, I passed on my little bit of knowledge to you.' I spread my hands. 'I don't know where she is now.' That was the truth, Jude could be any place. What I didn't mention was that wherever any place might be, Dora would be with her. Nicholls looked a little mollified. I pressed home my advantage. 'So!' I said. 'Now I've told you the truth about Jaz's girlfriend, how about filling me in on Drury?'

'I'm looking for him,' he said.

'Looking for him? Why? I already told you where he lives.'

'Maybe he didn't want you calling on him again. Either way he's cleaned the place out and gone.'

'Everything?'

'The lot. The caretaker let me take a look. Drury moved out yesterday in something of a hurry. Be interesting to know where he's gone. Are you going to let the coffee brew all night or do we get to drink it?'

I got down a couple of mugs, filled both and set one in front of Nicholls. I didn't like the idea of Drury running around like a wild card; it really worried me. For all I knew he could be scheming up something more foolproof than the fiery flowers he'd already sent.

That's what I thought at the time. The problem is, as I've said before, sometimes I get things wrong.

29

I hadn't expected Drury to move out so fast, and I wondered why he'd done that. Possibly I wasn't the only one who saw him as a weak link. Thinking that made me uncomfortable. Gavin had also been a weak link and look what happened to him. I mentioned that little piece of logic to Nicholls and, of course, he told me I was jumping to conclusions again. 'Fine,' I said. 'Silly of me to worry. Don't suppose you've heard anything more from Suzuki yet?' He went red, drank up his coffee and got ready to go. I walked him to the door. 'Still treating it as a simple traffic accident?' I said when he stepped outside.

He turned round, looked grumpy, and told me he'd call by tomorrow. I said that'd be really nice, and if he was lucky maybe the place wouldn't have burned down by then. When he opened up his mouth to impart some other piece of wisdom I shut the door smartish, turned off the lights and went to bed.

That's the nice thing about solo living; I usually get to have the last word.

Early Wednesday morning I went out to the Wilberforce place and leaned on the caretaker's bell. It wasn't that I didn't trust Nicholls – it's just that I couldn't help wondering if there might be some little thing he'd missed when he took a look around the empty apartment. I guess it's just the way my mind works, the way I have to check such things out for myself. It isn't a good way to win friends but at least if things go wrong I get to carry the blame instead of piling it on to somebody else.

The metal-faced speaker grid coughed a couple of times and a high-toned male voice told me to state my business. Obviously this was a person who didn't plan on running around after time-wasters.

I gave him my name, said I was from Inland Revenue, and told him there were things I needed to discuss. Things went silent. A couple of minutes later the door opened. I pasted on an encouraging smile.

According to the tab under his bell push the caretaker's name was Keith Squires, and I didn't know whether to class him as tubby or cuddly but either suited the way he looked more than just saying overweight. His skin was pink and soft as a child's with a soft down of hair on the backs of his hands, straw-coloured and coarse on his scalp where it was starting to recede. He wore navy trousers and a blue shirt with epaulettes and dark blue tabs. A bulky keyring hung from one side of a black leather belt and a mean-looking rubber-cased torch hung through a belt loop on the other. I guess what he really wanted to be was a security guard but he'd missed out on height.

His pale blue eyes fixed on me without giving away any of his thoughts. He said, 'I don't know what you want to talk to me for; only tax I pay is what gets deducted out of my wages and that's too much.'

I turned on a little charm, smiled at him sweetly and told him I was sure his taxes were just fine and what I wanted to talk about was the tenant who'd moved out in a hurry. The pucker went out of his forehead.

'Oh, right, well that's different then, isn't it?' he said. 'I mean I don't know nothing about his business but I do know he didn't give much notice before he went. Here one day and gone the next. I thought there had to be something fishy about it. Been doing a tax fiddle has he?'

'I didn't say that, Mr Squires, but I'd appreciate taking a look round his rooms.'

'Nothing left in there. Had some police inspector round yesterday and I told him the same thing. Waste of time you looking. Nothing in there now and there'll be less by dinner-time. Got to clean the place out properly so prospectives can look around.'

'It's a good thing I came early then; how about we go on up there now?' He looked doubtful. 'Look,' I said, 'if there's nothing left in there I can't be intending to rob the place, can I?' I took out another visiting card from my dwindling stock and stuck my finger on the name. 'See? Leah Hunter, that's my name, OK?' He tucked the card in his shirt pocket, stepped back and let me in.

He was right about Drury's place; except for fluff-balls sitting around on the carpets it would have been hard to say anybody had been living there. I sighed. 'The policeman who came yesterday – he took a good look around I suppose?'

'Didn't do him any good – went through the rooms, took a look in the built-ins, airing cupboard and suchlike, yes – he took a good look. Wouldn't have missed anything if it had been there.'

'Uh-huh. Did he ask about Drury's rubbish?'

'No.'

'So what happened to it? Drury didn't take it with him when he went?'

'Left it right outside his door in a black bin liner.'

'And you moved it?'

'Part of the job. Can't leave it there, can I?'

'Be a hazard,' I agreed. 'Where'd you move it to?'

'Down in the basement to wait for the compactor. Comes round Thursdays; ought to collect twice a week by rights.'

'You sure the police didn't go through it?'

'Never even asked about it.'

I felt a little smug. 'I'd like to do that right now if it's OK with you.'

Squires's fleshy shoulders waggled more than shrugged. 'Whatever you say.' I followed him down a second, narrower set of stairs into the basement. He had a three-quarter-sized pool table down there, balls neatly stacked in the triangle and waiting to go. Over in one corner a pile of filled black bin liners took up space and I wondered how he'd remember which was Drury's. He strolled across and heaved one out.

'You sure that's it?' I said.

'Hey, I stack them, all right? I know which is which. How many times d'you think somebody comes banging on my door and says they threw out something they want to get back again? I'll tell you. Too many. So now I remember which is which and it saves me a lot of trouble. That's Drury's bag.'

I untied the string. A smell of rancid food rushed out and said there was kitchen waste in there. Maybe Nicholls hadn't been so dumb after all. I rolled the bag sides down to get a better look.

The white liner from a pedal bin took up most space, crammed full with messy take-away containers spilling out of the top. Three-day-old curry is not a good thing to handle. I lifted Drury's garbage out with care and looked at what was left. Newspapers and carrier bags I put on one side, torn and screwed up envelopes and pieces of paper I kept separate. When I was through, I put the first pile back where I'd found it with the garbage and gathered the rest of the papers into a neat but small stack.

'I guess this is what I want,' I said. 'Thanks for your help. Maybe there'll be something here to tell me why he's gone and where he's gone.' I scrabbled around in my shoulder-bag, fished out a folded-down Marks and Sparks carrier and shoved the little pile of papers inside.

'Don't think I can let you do that,' he said, shaking his head. 'It might be rubbish but it's still the tenant's property.'

'What tenant? He moved out; that means the rubbish isn't your responsibility any more.' He still looked dubious. 'Look,' I said, 'suppose I give you a receipt for the stuff I take; will that make you feel better? If you get any complaints just refer them to me and I'll deal with it.'

He shook his head. I shrugged. I have been known to lie when the occasion demands, and it demanded it right then. One way or another I was taking part of Drury's trash home with me.

'OK,' I said. 'Have it your way, just don't blame me when the ceiling falls in. Inland Revenue have the right to impound any documents they believe might relate to a tax fraud, so if you won't cooperate I'll just have to get a warrant and do it the hard way. Of course, that means I'll probably have to go through your stuff too and disturb the other tenants, but if that's what you want . . . ?' I shrugged again. 'I appreciate the loyal way you look after your tenants' interests but in this case the loyalty is misplaced. Maybe you'd take good care of this while I get a warrant and some backup?' I held out the carrier bag. He eyed it like it had horns.

'If you want it that bad, just give me a receipt.'

'You sure?'

'I wouldn't want you to have to go to so much extra trouble just to get the same result,' he said. 'Wouldn't be worth either your time or mine.'

I did some more fishing in my bag. 'Of course a receipt makes it official and if it ever comes to court Drury'll know you helped me get his stuff, whereas if I just take it away no one need ever know you had any part in it.'

He tied the string back around the neck of the black liner and carried it over to the rest of the pile. 'What stuff?' he said. 'I don't even remember you coming here.'

I shook hands with him. 'We appreciate your cooperation,' I said in my best official tone. 'I promise Mr Drury won't get to hear about it.'

'Or the landlord,' Squires said. 'He wouldn't like me to break the rules and I like this job.'

'Not even the whisper of a whisper will get back to him. We like to keep this kind of thing confidential.' I gave his hand an extra shake and when I left him his soft pink face was creased in a conspiratorial smile. I felt bad about all that deceit but I'd have felt worse if I'd come away empty-handed. I fast-footed it back up the basement stairs and out to the hybrid. When I drove home the idea that I might have nothing in my little carrier bag but genuine rubbish didn't even enter my head. But two hours spent squatting on the sitting-room carpet fitting little pieces back together again changed my views. Of course, when I'd finished I had a greater insight into Drury's lifestyle. I knew he visited the Regal car wash, had pizzas delivered by Mr Antonio's Pizza Parlour and sent his shirts out to Ritzi Cleaners. None of which did me any good at all.

I pieced together a letter from Susie telling him no thanks she didn't want to go out to dinner with him and talk it all over, he could take a bimbo out instead. Nice one, Susie, I thought.

There was a final notice for his telephone bill but the calls weren't itemised. Little things like that really irritate me sometimes; Philip Marlowe and Sam Spade never got hung up over that kind of thing. Oh no, they'd just ring up a friend at the telephone company who owed them a favour. Five minutes, no sweat, and they'd know all about who called who and when. I added the bill to the discard pile and eased my position. A screwed-up circular letter invited him to subscribe to *Reader's Digest*; curry sauce had trickled between the creases. *Yukk!*

I spent some time on a letter from Drury's bank manager, the inch-size pieces sticking to my fingers like I was playing Peter and Paul. It invited Drury to drop by for a chat about investments.

Investments?

I set the letter aside and pressed on. Does anybody actually read junk mail? I found a rent reminder and a torn-up cheque for the same amount. I guess Drury thought that since he was leaving he'd hold on to his money. I noted down the number of his bank account, smoothed out an offer to replace his double-glazing, peered into three empty envelopes and then shoved the whole lot back into the carrier bag.

I really hate wasting my time that way – or maybe on reflection it hadn't been a complete waste. Still thinking about that, I dumped the bag in the hall closet then skipped into the kitchen to fix a snack; I didn't bother to think of it as lunch – the time for that was long gone. I put some spaghetti to boil, heated up tomato and basil sauce and brewed coffee. I'd just got the whole thing dished up when Nicholls came to call. He trailed after me into the kitchen, looked at the plate and said, 'Don't suppose there's enough for two.'

Bet his ass there wasn't!

'No,' I said shortly. 'And I thought it was tonight you were coming round?'

He sighed and sat down with a mug of coffee, his eyes on my plate.

Shit! He knew damn well I couldn't eat when he did that. I snatched a clean plate out of the cupboard and shared out the spaghetti.

He wolfed it down like there was no tomorrow and started looking in the fridge. 'How about a couple of fried eggs and some toast?' he said.

'Fine if you're doing the cooking. I like mine dippy.'

He grinned at me. 'I know.'

'You know too damn much, and especially when I'm just about to eat. How do you do that, Nicholls? Are you psychic or something?'

He shrugged. 'Just luck.'

I said, 'Why aren't you working?'

'I have been; this is the first break I've had.'

'Likewise.' I watched him expertly cracking eggs and put my feet up. I've learned not to look a good cook in the mouth. 'What have you been up to?'

He said, 'Eat first and I'll tell you what I've been up to later.'

The words had a familiar ring. Usually when I hear them it means I won't like what's coming next. I mused over what might have gone wrong with his day. Maybe he'd tripped over a real arsonist in the street. That really would have upset him. Such pipe dreams seldom come true and that day was no exception.

We ate our way amicably through Nicholls's culinary treat and by and by I remembered the bag of trash in the hall closet and asked if he'd found Drury yet. He picked up the empty coffee jug, rinsed it out, dumped the old filter paper and started another brew, all without answering. I said, 'Does that mean yes or no?'

He cleared his throat and shifted his weight, not quite looking at me. 'It doesn't mean either. Look, I'm sorry, you're not going to be happy with this but I'm going to be tied up most of the night.'

'That so?' I said coolly. 'You mean the date's off and I don't get to eat out at McDonald's? You shouldn't lay so much disappointment on me – it's almost too great to bear.'

'I already said I'm sorry,' he came back stiffly. 'It's unfortunate I can't pick and choose when and where bodies turn up.'

He had my full attention. 'Bodies?'

'As in playing with fire, and since I have a vested interest I get to go to the p-m.' He dropped his voice a notch. 'I'd rather be with you.'

Wow! That was nice! I made better company than a corpse? After a compliment like that it'd be a real shame to mention I was just the tiniest bit pleased he wouldn't be coming around. I still had a lot of thinking to do and thinking is a solitary pursuit. Right then a hot tub, a long soak and a solo pigging session seemed every bit as attractive as trying to be a fun dinner date. I debated whether to tell him about that, then looked in his soulful blue eyes and toned it down a little.

'That's really tough,' I said patting his hand consolingly. 'But I appreciate the job has to come first.' He got a suspicious look in his eyes; I could tell he was trying to work out if I was really serious or just yanking his chain. 'It's OK,' I said. 'Honest. Give me a ring when you're not busy.'

'Tomorrow,' he said rashly.

'Fine. Meantime do I get to know who the body belongs to or are you going to make me wait?'

The coffee dripped its last and burbled. He brought the jug over, filled up both our mugs and sat down. Then he looked me in the eyes and wasted my day.

30

Some things are just too unlikely to be true and that was the way I felt about Nicholls's news, mainly because on a one-to-ten scale of improbability it measured around nine point nine.

For the first few seconds after he stopped talking all I could do was stare. After that I kind of exploded.

'*Shit!*' I said. 'I don't believe it! Drury wouldn't be that stupid. Nicholls, what are you trying to tell me here? How did it happen?'

He shrugged and got on his uncomfortable look. 'Indications so far are that he intended to destroy evidence and it went wrong.'

'Oh, come on. Drury wouldn't be that stupid; he'd know damn well he couldn't get away with it.'

'Yes, well, that's what I'd have thought too, except it fits in with your theory of insurance fraud. The lockup was his and jammed full of top-quality carpets. It looks as if he did move the good stuff out before the Fast-Sell fire. What do you want me to say, Leah? Arson is a risky business even for experts and I don't think Drury was that. Maybe he got caught in a blow-back, or the stuff ignited too soon. Either way, he's dead.' His forehead puckered up. 'Damn it, I don't know what you're looking like that for. You've been crying insurance fraud all along and this proves you right.'

'That so? Well, I can think of better ways to do it, and how come if the lockup was in Leeds you got to know so fast? Don't tell me Bramfield's finest have to police Leeds city too.'

'We'd put out a general query on Drury's whereabouts,' he said stiffly. 'And don't knock it, Leah. At least this means you'll get your job back.'

'I'd have got it back anyway,' I snapped. 'This thing smells. It has to be a setup, it's too neat. The way I see it somebody got worried about all the new interest in Billy and this is supposed to shift the whole thing neatly on to Drury's back. It's a con trick, Nicholls.' He looked

173

at me like I'd just grown two heads. 'I'm not paranoid,' I said. 'I just know a lie when I see one.'

'Sure,' he said. 'Somebody set up Drury to torch his own lockup and then persuaded him to stay inside and fry. How do you suppose they did that? It's a good scenario, Leah, but I can't quite see it.'

'Hey! How many movies have you sat through where some nogoodnik puts a gun in a dead man's hand?'

'Fiction,' he snapped.

'You mean it couldn't work in fact?'

'I didn't say that.'

'OK, so you're admitting it could.'

'If he was dead before the fire it'll show up at post-mortem,' he growled. 'Unless you think the pathologist is in on it too.'

We killed each other with criminal looks.

'Lung damage,' I snapped. 'I know about it, in fact I should think any fourth former knows about it.'

He finished off his coffee and lined his chair up neatly with the table edge. 'I have to get back.'

'So soon? You haven't heard my conspiracy theory yet.'

He got all bristly and walked to the door.

'OK,' I said, 'but when I'm proved right, don't bother coming round apologising because it'll be too late.'

Nicholls turned back. 'Too late for what?'

'For it to look like you thought it up unaided.'

'Huh!' he said, and stepped out on to the landing.

'But just in case you want to try working it out for yourself,' I told him sweetly, 'look up the Leopold Harris gang. Want me to write it down for you?'

He started off down the stairs. When he got to Marcie's landing I leaned over the banister. 'Nicholls?'

He looked up.

'*What!*'

'Thanks for driving back to tell me.'

'I don't know why I bother.'

I leered at him. 'Maybe it's something to do with cocoa.'

His face lightened up. 'Tomorrow we hit the town,' he said, and started off downstairs again. I called after him.

'McDonald's?'

He waved a hand. 'Too expensive.'

I went back into my scorched nest and measured up the window. Some more burnt paint dropped off. I wondered how the insurance was coming along. Then I sat cross-legged on the carpet and did some thinking about colour schemes. At four o'clock the telephone rang. Pete didn't go for any preamble. 'Leah, the investigators want you here tomorrow morning. Nine thirty all right?'

'Depends on the reason,' I said. 'Have they found something I added up wrong or do they want to apologise?'

'Nine thirty,' he said.

'Make it ten o'clock,' I told him. 'Being unemployed is really tiring. I have to sleep late.' It sounded like he'd covered the mouthpiece but I could hear a low-grade muttering going on. After a couple of seconds he came back on.

'Leah, the meeting will be in conference room one, at er . . . ten o'clock. I'll be there too.'

'That's nice,' I said. 'We can catch up on gossip like who sent me a firebomb.'

'*What?*'

'Tell you about it tomorrow,' I cooed, and hung up.

Face to face it's usually easy to read people, something in the eyes or set of expression will give away the thoughts behind the voice, but talking on the telephone is different.

I wasted a little time trying to analyse Pete's tone; it'd have been really handy to know what they had lined up for me tomorrow, but in the end I had to give up. The trouble with Pete is he's been at his job too long and he's good at that neutral, noncommittal approach that gives not one whit of information away. I told myself it had to be apology time, that he and the investigators were going to have to eat crow and like it, but that didn't dispel the worry. OK, so I was sure they couldn't find anything wrong in my case load, but with Drury dead it was going to be hard to persuade him to drop the complaint.

I messed around until eight o'clock when Dora rang to find out how things were going. I told her fine, it looked like being cleared up in no time and asked about Jude. Dora's voice took on the affectionate note it gets when she talks about Oscar, so I guessed they were getting on pretty well. She promised me that when they got back home I wouldn't recognise the kid, she was really getting herself together. I felt glad about that. I didn't remind Dora that Jude would be whipped away into another council home when the authorities found out where she was. The idea made me uncomfortable – there had to be some way of keeping her out of those places?

At ten, having tended to Oscar's needs, I went to bed but not to sleep. I lay there with doggie ears that picked up every sound. At ten thirty I got up, checked the locks and took a look out of the windows. The back yard was full of shadows but the street was empty and quiet; most of the houses had downstairs lights on. No one lurked. I crawled back under the duvet. A couple of times I almost fell asleep, then jerked awake, visions of Drury crowding into my brain.

I tossed and turned for a while longer then padded out into the kitchen, heated up some milk, added a spoonful of honey and took the sweet stuff back to bed with me, sipping it slowly, hoping the honey's soporific effect would work. My little radio played soothing night music soft and low. I snuggled back into the duvet's warmth, alternately dozing and waking, watching time slip by until almost two in the morning when I finally admitted what was keeping me awake. *I was worried someone might drop by and have another go at me, that's what*. I thumped the pillow some, really annoyed with myself.

What did I expect to happen, for God's sake? Some hit man to swing in through the window like an SAS macho man?

It'd have to be a window because they sure as blazes couldn't get in through the front door.

Lights swept the bedroom window. I leapt up with little hairs atrembling and peered out. Across the road a late-night neighbour and his wife climbed out of their car and went in home to bed. I envied them the warmth of each other's bodies; a pair of friendly arms would be a real comfort right now.

A night breeze wove treetops into intricate patterns. Wide awake, I leaned on the windowsill and watched them shift and change. Two cats crossed the road and disappeared; maybe a minute later a happy yowling started up. I closed the curtains, turned on the lights and climbed into sweats and running shoes, splashing water on my face and giving my mouth a quick rinse before letting myself silently out of the house. Whatever I was afraid of was out here in the night and I could either face that fear or carry it around and let it grow bigger. Neither appealed to me overmuch but I've always hated excess baggage. I took a quick look around, turned left, picked up a good running speed and did a three-mile circuit around the empty streets. On Maybush Road a cruising Panda car caught me in its lights and stopped to ask what I was doing. I did little sideways running steps to keep the muscles going and said I couldn't sleep. The nosy police driver demanded name and address. 'Hey!' I said. 'I'm an honest citizen out for a run, no burglary kit, no swag bag.' I put my arms in the air and did a fast turn. 'See?' He cut the engine and got out, about eight inches taller than me and unamused.

'Name and address,' he said, 'and quit jigging up and down.'

'Uh-uh. Got to keep the circulation going,' I said, then meekly gave him the information he'd asked for. He checked it out on his radio, climbed back in his car and drove off. I thought what a nice courtesy it would have been for him to say good night, but I guess we can't have everything. How was he to know I wasn't a six-foot terrorist made up to look like some frail female?

I got home around three, drank a pint of juice, took a fast shower, fell into bed and slept like a stone, waking at eight thirty and thinking what an amazing forethought it had been to get Pete to reschedule his meeting for ten o'clock.

31

Pete was looking smug, up on his feet as soon as I walked in the door and waving at a chair directly across the table from him and his two buddies. I hadn't bothered to knock; it seemed more fun to interrupt the chitchat they'd been having. The way I figured it they were going to do one of two things, reinstate or fire me, and either way I was too damned angry about the whole process to care too much about being polite. I arranged myself neatly on the hotspot and smoothed my skirt.

Pete said, 'Leah, this is Ben Nesbitt and Allan Bridges from Internal Audit.' I nodded without smiling. I'd seen Nesbitt a couple of times before, once when he led a training seminar and once just wandering about the building. I checked him out critically. He'd gone to seed in the last year and a few good work-out sessions would work magic for his blossoming belly. Maybe I should tell him that? He shuffled papers around and avoided looking at me. Bridges had no such inhibitions and his eyes didn't miss a trick. He'd watched me eyeing up Nesbitt and didn't intend me to play the same game with him. We fenced a couple of glances.

I sat back and relaxed, making sure they got the right body language; I'd have hated them to think they had me all wired up. 'OK,' I said sweetly. 'Who's going to start? Am I fired or rehired?'

Nesbitt brought his head up and eyed me. 'Miss Hunter, you're about the last person I expected to be running an audit check on, but a complaint has been made and such things have to be followed through. You appreciate that?' I nodded and he hunched forward. 'Mr Innes here tells me you like to get right to the point, so let's do that. I'll tell you frankly that when we started out, I didn't see how you could extricate yourself without a long-drawn-out process of hearings unless the complainant withdrew, and I didn't expect him to do that since it would invite us to take a closer look into his affairs –

179

something I understand you were doing already?' I flashed a look at Pete but he was busy watching the ceiling.

'I wasn't too happy about an insurance claim Drury made,' I said.

'Not strictly a matter for Inland Revenue though, was it, Miss Hunter?'

'It was very much a matter for Inland Revenue,' I defended. 'Drury was practising long-firm fraud. That means we miss out on tax revenue when he ships out good quality stuff to be sold elsewhere and doesn't declare the profits, on top of which he makes a fraudulent insurance claim. Investigating his affairs seemed to me to be a priority.'

Bridges leaned over and mumbled in Nesbitt's ear. Nesbitt nodded. 'My colleague wonders why you didn't discuss the idea with Drury's insurers.'

'Did you check on that?'

Nesbitt looked at his sidekick. Bridges started leafing through papers, stopping at one and stabbing with a pointy finger.

'We talked with a Miss Mills at Saxby Associates. I gather they were acting as loss adjusters. Your first contact with her was to seek confirmation of Drury's address. Fraud wasn't mentioned,' Nesbitt said. 'Would you agree with that?'

'I guess so at that point. I needed something a little more substantial before I could start wheels moving to block his claim. I'm sure she told you I tried to do that a little later.'

'At which point you were already suspended.'

'It didn't stop me trying to do my duty,' I said brightly. 'And the complaint was false; Drury got in a panic and that was all he could think of.'

'Miss Mills did say you'd been something of a thorn in her boss's side since then.' Nesbitt eased up and did some staring at the table. 'Your client files are in excellent order and Mr Innes has been strong in your support.' I gave Pete another glance and this time caught his eye. I gave him a warm look and he coloured up a little.

'Thanks, Pete,' I said. 'I really appreciate that.'

Nesbitt said, 'Despite which you'd still be in deep trouble if Mr Drury could pursue his claim. Understood?'

'Understood,' I said. 'I guess we both heard the same news.'

'His death doesn't clear the complaint but with no corroborating evidence I don't intend to pursue the investigation any further.' He sat back and waited for me to look grateful. I was real sorry to disappoint him but the way I saw it I was due an apology, not a suggestion of maybe I was guilty but they couldn't prove it.

I pointed that out to them ungently then rubbed the message home. 'I suppose you know Drury died trying to torch a lockup full of carpets,' I said. 'And if that doesn't prove which of us was lying then I guess I'm wasting my time here.'

Nesbitt straightened up his papers, flipped the folder shut and sat back. 'Accept the investigation's ended and leave it at that,' he said.

I could feel myself heating up. 'No!' I snapped. 'No, damn it, I don't intend to leave it that way at all. I intend to have the record set straight. I won't settle for a suspension on my staff file with the complaint marked unresolved. That just isn't good enough; I want a clear record.'

'Then maybe we'll look at it again when the police investigations are over. Meantime I'll recommend you be allowed back to work.'

Wow! How'd he ever get to be so generous?

'Balls!' I said rudely.

'That kind of reaction doesn't help,' Nesbitt said.

'Help who?' I said tartly. 'Me? I've got news for you. That kind of thing helps me a lot!' Pete had sat there with his eyes moving from one to the other of us and looking white and tight. I recognised the signs. He shifted around in his seat and iced up Nesbitt's ear.

'This – is – my – department,' he enunciated carefully. 'And what I don't like is to be misled. Before this meeting you told me Miss Hunter's name was cleared. Now you've told her the opposite. When she lodges a complaint about the outcome of her interview, my name will be alongside hers.'

Nesbitt shrugged. 'Your neck,' he said. 'Stick it out if you feel like it, but as far as I'm concerned Miss Hunter has an attitude and it's time she dealt with it. If she's cleared by the police inquiry the personnel file will be scrubbed. Otherwise it stays as is.' He got to his feet and picked up his papers. Bridges did likewise. I'd have loved to slap the grin from off his freckled face but it'd be a shame to make him cry.

I pushed back my chair and got ready to walk out on them. Pete said, 'Don't go, Leah, I want to talk with you.' I settled back down and watched him follow the other two out of the room. When they got outside he really went to town. I grinned. Pete doesn't normally lose his cool but when he flips the performance is worth listening to. The trouble with Internal Audit, of course, is they all have a God complex. A couple of minutes went by before the argument wound up and Pete came back.

He said, 'I'd like to have you back, Leah, but it's up to you. As far as I'm concerned this whole thing's been a farce.'

'Maybe I'll take a few days' leave,' I said. 'I'd kind of like to see the Drury business over with before I get back to work. I tell you, Pete, I'm disillusioned with the whole process. When did Nesbitt get to be such an asshole?'

He shook his head. 'Always has been. Take my advice and file a complaint now while you're still angry enough. I'll back you on this one, Leah. He was supposed to tell you you were in the clear.'

'His decision,' I said. 'Look, Pete, let's face it, it could be months before the police inquiry winds up. What am I supposed to do until then? By the time it's over, Nesbitt'll say he's too busy to change things.' I sighed. 'OK, you're right; I should go for broke. Get me an official form and I'll fill it in while I'm here.' He trotted off and I thought things over. Maybe I was due a career change. Maybe nothing! I wasn't going to be hustled out by a cheeseball like Nesbitt.

When Pete came back I wrote out my grievance in ladylike prose and Pete countersigned it. He looked happy. I said, 'Why are you grinning?'

'Because he didn't think you'd do it, that's why. He thought you'd just come on back to work and keep your head down.'

'Guess he doesn't know much. Arnold back yet?'

'He's got a sick note for another fortnight.' He shrugged. 'We need you back and that's a fact.'

'Thanks, Pete,' I said. 'That near enough makes up for Nesbitt but I need a couple more days; the insurance company still have to send someone round to my place and check the damage.' He blinked and said he didn't think I'd been serious about the firebomb. I told him what had happened and he clucked his tongue and said take what extra time I needed and come back to work when I'd got it all sorted. Then he got hauled away to his office and I went home.

Which was when Bethany rang to say could I call by the office. Naturally I asked what for but she was being cagey. I told her I'd drop by around two and headed for the kitchen to fix myself a cheese sandwich and a bowl of tomato soup. I guessed Nesbitt would have been really upset to know he hadn't spoiled my appetite. I virtuously rinsed off the pots, then took a shower and washed my hair, wondering as I did that what it was that Bethany had come up with that she thought I ought to know.

I swear if I'd known she was just fronting for Stanton I never would have gone, but my little crystal ball let me down again.

32

A short-cropped redhead on reception set me to cool my heels in a Lilliput-sized office. I sipped the vending-machine coffee she'd given me and ran through the reasons Bethany might have had for inviting me to be there. A tête-à-tête with Stanton wasn't among them but that's what I got.

When he came in the door I hauled up from the chair and headed out, but he snapped the door shut and parked himself in front. Anger sparked. I measured him up and worked on the best move to shift him without wrecking the place, busying my brain with possibilities. I checked out the furniture again. Wrecking what, for Pete's sake? A desk and two chairs?

'Look!' I snapped. 'We've nothing to talk about. I came in to see Bethany, not you.'

'Miss Hunter, I asked Bethany to arrange it that way. Examine the alternative; if you'd been asked to come and talk with me, what would you have said?'

'A fast no.'

'Exactly. And yet we do need to talk. I, um, never have liked making apologies, but you appear to be owed one.' I eyed him uneasily, wondering what kind of new angle he'd thought up to shake me loose. He came away from the door and gestured with his hand. 'If you don't want to hear it feel free to leave.'

I shrugged. 'Go ahead, I'm listening. I grew up on fairy tales.'

'If you were less abrasive . . .' He swallowed the rest and got his voice back down to polite. 'We made a mistake in accepting the Fast-Sell fire as a random arson attack.'

'None of them were random,' I cut in.

His right hand went in his pants' pocket to jiggle small change melodiously. My, but he looked uncomfortable. I felt really guilty for getting pleasure out of that.

He said tightly, 'The point is, Miss Hunter, recent developments seem to confirm that a fraudulent insurance claim was made, very much as you suggested. I apologise for having added difficulties to an already stressful situation by dismissing the idea out of hand.'

'That's it?' I said. 'We've kissed and made up and now I can go home and forget about it? Just where did *you* fit into Drury's scam? Quiet little dinners, threatening telephone calls? Whose idea was it to send me a firebomb, yours or his?'

He pasted a puzzled look on his face. If I hadn't known better I'd have said it was genuine.

'I don't know anything about a firebomb. When was this?'

'A couple of days ago, but now Drury's dead let's blame it all on him. If you're lucky you might even get away with it.'

'Miss Hunter I know nothing about this.'

I moved to the door and yanked it open. 'Bet your boots you don't, but Bramfield police do, and that's what counts. Hope you've got a good story fixed up when they come calling.' He picked up a worried look; I was pretty sure that at least was genuine. 'It's been really nice talking to you, Mr Stanton, but please, don't send me any more flowers,' I said, and walked out on him.

You'd think by now I'd have learned not to push so hard, but not so; I'd gone rushing in again with both feet. Maybe I should visit an analyst. I stepped out of the place briskly. An apology from Stanton was like a slap on the back from Brutus.

I stepped out briskly, turned right at the top of the street and called in on Gold Star to find out who'd been sitting on my own little fire claim. According to them no one had, I just hadn't been home when they phoned. I fixed up for someone to call around later that afternoon, got back to the car fast and drove home. I'd been there all of twenty minutes when a thirtyish roly-poly in a blue-striped shirt came and spent all of thirty seconds checking out the damage. I guess that could be termed efficiency at its best.

I changed street clothes for leggings and a long shirt and put my feet up for a while. Just before five, Nicholls telephoned and said he'd be round at seven thirty. I told him fine and not to be late because we had a whole lot of things to talk about. He said like what? I said that was for me to know and him to worry about. He did one of his pitiful sighs and said he'd see me later. I put the phone down and got back into relax mode.

Around seven I took a shower, fixed my hair, and put on some glad rags. Nicholls was five minutes late. He eyed the little black dress with grinning approval and hustled me down to his car, pulling out from the kerb before I could get myself properly arranged. I buckled on the seat belt and tugged the dress hem to a more decorous level. 'It looked better the other way,' he said.

'Just keep your eyes on the road, Nicholls. How'd the post-mortem go?'

'Like char-grilled steak,' he said. 'And do you mind if we don't talk about it until we've eaten?'

'Not at all,' I said politely. 'Where are we doing that? The Bar-B-Que?' He sighed and looked at me glumly, then drove through town and out along the A636 to Denby Dale.

Nicholls isn't exactly keen on Italian food so when he parked outside the Bella Napoli I guessed his experience had really upset him. I told myself it would be really unkind to take advantage of that and didn't mention Drury again until we'd finished eating. When we were drinking near black espresso, I said, 'If the fire was that bad, how do you know it was Drury?'

'Who else would it be? It was his lockup and his car was parked over the other side of the road, so it's a pretty fair assumption. What made you ask?'

I shrugged. 'Just an idea. Forget it.' He set his cup down and regarded me intently. 'Damn it, Nicholls,' I said crossly. 'Why is it you always pay attention to the wrong things?'

'Where'd the idea come from?'

'Oh, I don't know. They always do that kind of thing in old movies – switch bodies to confuse PC Plod.' I leaned on the table and stared right back at him. 'Couldn't get away with that sort of cheating now, could they? Not with Supercop on the trail.' I waved at the waiter. 'Do you want more coffee? Yes, of course you do. Two more espressos,' I said without waiting for him to decide.

He hates to be hustled that way and I hoped it would take his mind off other things, the truth being I hadn't yet worked out a way to tell Nicholls about the thugs who'd called on Jaz without bringing Jude back into it; and that was something I still shied away from.

'Nice try,' he said. 'Now suppose we talk about who might have got crisped instead of Drury.'

'Nicholls. You're a pain. How would I know?'

'I don't know how you'd know,' he said argumentatively.

The waiter came back, emptied his tray fast and beat a smart retreat. 'Did you get around to looking up Leopold Harris yet?' I said.

'I looked it up.'

'Neat scam, huh?'

'Not applicable.'

'OK,' I said. 'Have it your way. I give in. Billy started every fire except Fast-Sell, then conveniently killed himself. Jaz played around with matches and got burned, Gavin had a freak accident. Just a string of coincidences and I also believe in fairies. What did the Suzuki expert say?'

'Leah, just go back to work and leave it to me now, will you? You've been reinstated, you've part cleared Billy and I don't see what else you want.'

'How did you know about that?' I said. 'Who said I'd been reinstated? Not me, I haven't said a thing about it.' He looked guilty. 'You talked to Nesbitt, didn't you? Well, thanks very much but it didn't do me a lot of good. You want to know what happened? The corruption charge stays on my file, that's what,' I said heatedly. 'Goodbye to any ideas of promotion.'

'I'll talk to him again.'

'Don't bother – I already filed a complaint.' I drank off the second espresso and pushed the cup away. 'Just do one thing for me will you?' I said. 'Check on Drury's bank account. Let's see how much money he arrived with and how much is in there now.'

'Thirty-five thousand,' he said. 'That's the current balance. And before you ask, he sold the business in Loughborough for ninety thousand and bought Fast-Sell for a hundred and thirty thousand. Fifty thousand of the purchase price was his own money, the balance came from a bank loan.'

I said, 'You've been busy.'

He looked at me solemnly. 'I'm good at my job too, Leah,' he said. 'How about this time you let me get on with it?'

'Nicholls,' I said. 'Anybody'd think I spent my life running around trying to mess up your day.'

'You could try looking the other way occasionally.'

'Tell me that when you're getting your head kicked in,' I said unkindly. 'Anyway, I tried doing that already and look what happened to Billy. Debts like that can't be walked away from.' He grabbed a hold of my hand and started peering at the palm. I snatched it back. 'Damn it! My lifeline is my own affair. If Drury's dead and you're right, why should it get any shorter?' His face closed up.

We split the bill, then he drove me home and said goodnight, the both of us subdued and needing to do some solitary thinking. The trouble is, Nicholls worries too much about the wrong things. If he spent less time trying to keep me out of trouble he'd maybe see the holes in his own argument, especially the way it fell to pieces when he tried to fit the blame for Billy, Gavin and Jaz on to Drury's back. Whichever way I looked at it, that idea wouldn't fit. If the carpet-barn fire had been a one-off, an opportunistic hopping on to the coat tails of another arsonist, then how would a panicking Drury know who to hire for a little human elimination work? Arson is one thing but murder is in a different league.

Or maybe Nicholls knew all of that already and just didn't want me to guess. I climbed the stairs and felt weary, wanting to do nothing more than fall into bed.

About a minute away from doing that came remembrance that I still had to feed the damn cat.

33

I got up around seven, took a shower, scrambled some eggs and made a neat pile of toast. The phone rang as I buttered the last piece. I sighed a little and went out to the hall.

Dora with another progress report or Nicholls offering more discouragement? That early it just had to be one or the other.

Redding said cheerfully, 'Hope I didn't get you up. I have that information you were after if you want to call by. Better make it today, otherwise it'll have to wait until Monday.'

'Nine thirty all right?'

'Nine would be better.'

We settled for that.

I breakfasted fast, dressed at speed and went to tend to Oscar. Was it imagination or had fat-cat put on weight? Stricken with guilt I scratched his favourite spots and told him Dora would be home soon. He gave me a squinty look and arched his back. Felines can spot a lie a mile away.

I backed the car out of the garage and drove across town to see Redding, pushing in through the side door a couple of minutes before nine and getting the same swivel-eyed response from the busy-bee workers that I'd had before. I gave out my best smile and went on up the steps to Redding's office, knocking politely before I went in. When we'd exchanged greetings and a couple of comments on the good weather, he picked up a manila folder and wagged it in the air. 'Hope you appreciate how much soft soap I had to use to get this. I hope it's worth the effort.'

'Has to be, otherwise the bad guys get to win.' I reached out and took it from him, doing a quick flip through the contents, then going through them more slowly. 'This is great,' I said. 'OK if I copy out a few things?'

'Those are photocopies. Take it with you, just so long as you let me have it back when you're through.' He came round the desk and plucked it from my hands, shoving it in a larger blue file with *Duty Rosters* stamped on its front. 'I'll walk you out,' he said. 'What the eye doesn't see the heart doesn't grieve for.'

'Hey, I don't want you to get in trouble.'

He patted the blue cover. 'Who's to know?'

Fewer eyes watched me leave. Dan Bush raised a hand. I gave him a finger wave and kept on going. He stopped what he was doing and started to come over. I dropped back a pace and waited.

'Fancy a drink sometime?'

'Might be fun. Not right now, though; I'm kind of busy.'

'Just say when.'

'Maybe next week. Want me to give you a call here?'

'Yeah, OK. If I'm not here, leave a message. I'm – er, sorry about last time. I didn't think Redding would want to break off.'

'I've forgotten about it already,' I told him. 'Better go now; can't keep the boss waiting.'

He glanced at Redding. 'Nothing I can help with?'

I made up a fast lie. 'Uh-uh. Official business, like Inland Revenue stuff.' He didn't look all that convinced, but since when did I need to explain what I was about? 'I'll speak to you next week,' I said. 'OK?'

'OK.' He half turned, then spun back. 'Anything new about Billy?'

'What could be new about Billy?' I said. 'Besides which, I've been too busy to think about it much, you know how it is?'

He glanced at Redding and shrugged. 'Probably best to let it lie.'

'Can't bring him back,' I agreed sombrely and edged away. 'Got to go now; work just piles up.' He conjured a serious kind of smile and said he'd see me. This time when he turned away he kept on going.

I caught up with Redding outside and got the file back, then told him thanks again and climbed into the hybrid. He hung around watching me reverse off the forecourt then raised a hand. I waved back and felt good. It was nice that Providence had got around to helping out.

I took a short cut back to the town centre and parked in the multistorey, sitting in the car for a while sorting through the fire reports and feeling like a kid who's been handed a lollipop. Playing detective isn't all that easy, although watching Spenser run around righting wrongs in forty-five minutes flat might give the impression it is. Television has a lot to answer for. The truth is that without a police warrant card to flash, prising out information is about as easy as running up a hill backwards.

Nicholls, of course, could have dug out the dirt in no time flat if he ever took it into his head to do a little lateral thinking. It really riled me the way he always has to do things his way.

I shoved the reports back in the folder, locked up and went to put my freshly garnered information to good use. It's kind of odd the way firms in the same line of business tend to cluster together in one part of town; it's all to do with competition but I've never quite been able to work out the logic of it. Take insurance companies; except for the odd straggler and Johnnie-come-lately the whole lot of them are bunched up around Cheapside. A neat arrangement that saved me a lot in time and shoe leather.

Knowing what I did about Fast-Sell, there didn't seem much point in calling in on Northern Alliance, so I crossed over the street and visited the Pilgrim offices instead. Pilgrim had been unlucky, paying out on three arson claims, which seemed a little unfair when the rest of the companies had got away with one each. Luckily for Pilgrim the claims had been small.

The nineteen-twenties-style façade hid a modern preoccupation with security. A long oak counter with high glass safety screen protected an open-plan office from all comers. I doubted that it would stop a heavy mob with shotguns but I guess the prime idea was to keep the staff happy. I dredged up a cagily professional smile, flashed my little plastic-covered ID that said I was with Inland Revenue and asked for the name of their loss adjusters. Having a file full of fire reports on my side of the counter helped. Official-looking documents tend to loosen tongues.

By and by an efficient soul did a little searching and came back with the name Bickerstaffe & Tenby of Leeds. I checked that that firm had dealt with all three fires, noted down the name neatly, said thank you nicely, and trotted off to put the same question to Triton General. Triton were a little more cagey. I got passed on up the hierarchy a couple of times before the third pretty-please got me the name Saxby Associates. A tingle hit the back of my neck. Triton, like Northern Alliance, had faced a big claim; if Stanton's firm hadn't acted as loss adjusters it would have shoved my ideas way off line.

I bestowed a warm smile on the bespectacled man behind the counter. 'Tell me,' I said. 'Do you flip around from one loss adjuster to another when claims come in, or do you contract with one firm?'

'Triton give contracts,' he said, 'but it doesn't work that way with all insurers. Some companies like to alternate between three or four firms.'

'Which is best?'

'Can't see it makes much difference if the job gets done,' he said. I told him I appreciated his help and walked out of there on light feet.

It took me until a little after noon to cajole the rest of the companies into parting with the same piece of information; some people are so tight-lipped it worries me what they might be trying to hide.

I did a little shopping on the way back to the car, then drove home thinking what fun it'd be to see Nicholls's face when he heard what a neat piece of detection work I'd done. He'd said give him proof not speculation and proof was exactly what I was going to hand him. No way could he walk away from the fact that Stanton's firm had acted as loss adjusters on three major fires that between them had collected more than a million pounds in insurance payouts. I wondered what percentage of that had gone to the arson ring. Ten per cent? Fifteen? I also wondered if Saxby Associates would weather the trauma of having employed a crook.

I stopped by Dora's, told Oscar I hoped all that fawning around wasn't just make-believe, then foolishly unbolted the back door and let him out in the garden. He strutted over the threshold like a furry Mick Jagger, tail up and nose twitching.

I sat out on the garden seat, ate a Marks & Spencer sandwich and watched him play around. By and by I offered a little titbit of salmon and brown bread which he took with delicacy. I fondled his ears. 'Just don't get any big ideas, huh? Outside the garden is off limits.' Maybe it was the wrong thing to say. He blinked his eyes like he was real sleepy, took an easy, rubbing walk around my legs then showed me how fast he could move.

Shit but that damn cat could go!

I left the bench like a real athlete, but not fast enough. When I made the fence he was three gardens away, gallumphing along like a kid out of school. I dragged out Dora's deckchair and settled in the sun, cursing felines in general and Oscar in particular.

Falling asleep wasn't supposed to enter into the scheme of things, but the bright light, warmly aromatic garden smells and gossiping birds sent me off into a slumber from which I woke cross and heavy-eyed at three thirty. Oscar was still on walkabout.

I called his name and added a few blandishments. If he heard them he was playing coy. I folded up the deckchair, stacked it in the shed and thought what a lot of fun I'd got out of swapping one guilt trip for another. It's the truth; I really don't know what people see in cats; they just can't be relied on. I put a saucer of milk down on the kitchen floor, left the catflap open, locked up the house and went home.

Jude was sitting hunched up on the top landing, knees up to her chin and arms hugging them. I could hear the telephone going frantic. She looked at me warily and said, 'Hi, Leah.'

I opened up the door and snapped, 'Inside.'

She got up jauntily and stepped into the hall. I slammed the door and grabbed the phone. Dora said, 'Leah, Jude's gone off somewhere and I can't find her. I'm worrying myself sick wondering what she's up to.'

I scowled at the kid. 'It's OK, Dora; I just got back and she was waiting for me. I'll put her on the next train back.' Jude started out the door. I grabbed an arm and hauled her in again. 'Ring you later,' I said, and hung up, then I eyed Jude tetchily. 'OK,' I snapped. 'Explain.'

34

I eyed Jude's new outfit – blue Levis, white shirt and denim jacket – and saw Dora's hand. The pinched little waif in a ra-ra skirt had turned into a nice-looking kid, hair loose and shiny and a bloom back on her skin. Regular food and breathable air had done her good and I told her so. She kept on staring down at her feet and didn't say anything. 'Look,' I said, 'suppose we start by you explaining how you got here. But break it to me gently; I'm getting too old to be traumatised.'

She squinted up at me. 'Hitched.'

I stared at the ceiling. 'Uh-huh. Hope you didn't feel obliged to pay for the ride?' A pretty shade of red came up her neck and went over her ears. Hair shook out in a halo.

'I didn't have to do that.' I guess the relief I felt must have shown. 'Didn't think it'd worry nobody,' she mumbled. ''Cept for Jaz it . . .' She struggled for a bit. 'I mean . . .'

'You mean before you and he got together nobody much noticed if you were there or not,' I finished up for her. She nodded. 'Things have changed,' I said. 'Dora sounded like she was about ready to wet her pants. Guess that shows she cares about you.'

'Didn't think about it, did I?'

'You told me you didn't run out on friends.'

'Got to do it sometime, haven't I, 'cos I'm not getting banged back in a home, not ever. I'd rather . . .' She clamped her mouth shut.

I viewed the alternatives thrown up by that word *rather* and didn't like any of them. 'Jude,' I said, 'you've got to learn a little trust. Suppose we fix something to eat while you think about that.' She eased up off the wall and followed me into the kitchen, standing with hands shoved into her jacket pockets while I hunted through the freezer. 'How about moussaka? Like the stuff?'

''S'all right. I need the bathroom.'

195

'Help yourself. You remember where it is?'

'Yeh.'

She pulled the door shut behind her. Great! Now I couldn't see which way she was headed. I waited to hear the front door latch and told myself it wasn't paranoia – Jude had run out on me before but if she did it again and got a good head start maybe I'd lose her for good. The idea of her back on the streets picking up punters was nauseous. The bathroom door closed. I put the moussaka in the microwave and started throwing together a salad. The lavatory cistern emptied; a couple of minutes later I heard slow, soft footfalls. Ears close to jumping off my head with all the listening, I sliced cucumber and tried to look cool, counting off seconds of hesitation as she hung around outside the kitchen door. When the count passed ten I quit slicing and got ready to run. On eighteen she pushed open the door and I got back into a nice, even action and asked how she liked French dressing.

She hitched up one shoulder.

'Depends. Don't like that crappy stuff in bottles.' I watched her home in on a slender-necked gourmet mix I'd parked on the worktop and pull a face. 'Dora's is nice 'cos she doesn't put no mustard in. Want me to do some? She showed me how.'

'You bet! I really appreciate the home-made stuff, but me – I just don't have the time.' I waved a hand. 'Utensils bottom left, food top right, anything you can't find, just ask.'

'Fancy vinegar,' she said. 'You got any?'

'Red wine. Over to the right . . . yes, in there; oil underneath. OK?'

I watched her hunt around for the stuff she needed and then get to work with it. I wondered what else she'd picked up from Dora and hoped maybe a little common sense. She said chattily, 'Went out on a boat; never done that before. Thought I'd be seasick.'

'You weren't?'

'It was great – dead bouncy. Dora said we'd go back and do it again.'

'Can't do that if you walk out on her,' I said.

'Yeh, well, I haven't done that. I know I said I would but I wasn't doing it. I come back to find out what's been happening, that's all. I'd have hitched me way back again. Honest.'

'Uh-huh. So why'd you try to run off when I was talking to Dora?'

She scowled down at the bowl. ''Cos I didn't want sending back, that's why. It'd have been a right waste of time, wouldn't it? Wouldn't have found out nothing about nothing, an' Dora won't tell.'

'Maybe that's because there's nothing *to* tell.' I dumped all the salad stuff in a bowl and cleared the offcuts. 'Jude, the police are still investigating the fire and there are other complications too. There's no such thing as an instant answer.'

'What complications?'

One was there hadn't been enough of Jaz left to identify without dental records and he didn't seem to have any. That wasn't the kind of nightmare I wanted to pass on to Jude.

'Gavin at the secure unit – remember him? Well, he got himself killed, and it's hard for the police to question a dead man.'

'Yeh, well, I'm not sorry; serve him right.' She stopped mixing. ''S'not all I come back for. Thing is I don't want Jaz buried or something and me not there. I mean I don't believe in all that heaven stuff but there ought to be somebody what knew him and that's me, isn't it? Who else'd be there for him?'

Nobody except Julie and any other neglectful relative who turned up to take in a little whiff of publicity. One hint of a media camera and they'd be out of the woodwork fast, tears and all.

'Jude, I promise that won't happen without you being told, but it isn't happening yet and I want you back with Dora pronto. And this time on the train, not hitching,' I added.

'Can I stop here tonight then?' She dredged up a semblance of the lost waif from someplace. 'I won't run off. Honest.'

I took two cans of coke out of the fridge and dished up the moussaka. 'What's wrong with going back tonight?'

Her shoulders jerked raggedly.

'Don't know.'

I forked in a mouthful of salad and chewed a little. 'The dressing's good,' I said. 'You'll have to sleep on the sofa – and don't give me any arguments about getting an early train.'

'Ta. Think Dora'd mind if I go see Oscar?'

'Not if he's around,' I said. 'He went walkabout. I'll need to go down there and check if he's back when we're through eating. Come if you like.'

'Dora said he's streetwise.'

'Hope he is; I don't know how many lives he has left.'

We cleaned up our plates and shared what was left of the toffee-pecan, then Jude got started on washing up while I checked train times and talked to Dora. When I was through doing that I phoned Nicholls and told him he couldn't come around because a girlfriend had dropped by. He said why didn't he come round and meet her. I told him because I didn't want her falling for his baby-blue eyes. He really likes to think I get jealous.

We chitchatted a while until I worked around to telling him the latest newsflash on Stanton. When I did he went quiet for a bit, then came back and said he'd known it all along and it still didn't prove anything. I yelled at him for not telling me that sooner so I didn't waste a whole morning finding out. He snapped back huffily that he'd been trying to keep my nose out of it, not give me something else to poke into. I told him thanks a bundle and next time I got to know anything I'd take good care not to let him in on it. He said I should maybe look at what happened last time I did that.

I hung up.

By then Jude had moved into the sitting room and got a good look at the bubble-charred paint and neatly holed carpet. Her face had lost some colour and she was scowling. 'Don't worry about it,' I said. 'It isn't as bad as it looks. I'll end up with a new carpet and the place redecorated.'

'Yeah, an' you could have ended up like Jaz. 'S'my fault isn't it?'

'Hey, it was a fast blaze. I put it out in no time flat and it was meant to make a mess – not kill me,' I lied. 'I promise it had nothing to do with you or Jaz. This was done because I'd been asking questions about Billy.'

'If I hung around a bit I could help you do it up.'

'Nice offer, Jude, but maybe in a couple of weeks when the insurance comes through.'

'S'pose me an' Dora'll be back here then.'

There was an awkward gap while we both gave some thought to what might happen when she did get back. Dora knew a lot of people and had useful contacts. I hoped she might want to call in some favours and keep Jude from getting slammed back into care. I didn't at that point think too closely about what alternatives were available.

Dora's place was still catless. Jude took a good look around the garden and said, 'He's got a friend lives down the bottom, Dora told me; a ginger what got doctored like him. He'll have gone visiting.'

'Great! I'd better go get him before they hit the town,' I said.

'Don't think they do that when they've been chopped,' she said knowledgeably. 'I'll go get him if you like.'

'Might as well see where he hangs out,' I said. 'That way I can head him off.' Except I didn't need to. Jude homed right in on him.

The sun was medium-high and plenty warm enough to keep sleeping cats happy. I stared at them sourly, one ginger, one tabby.

Jude leaned her elbows on the brick wall and turned mushy. 'Aw, look at them, aren't they nice?'

'Depends on your point of view,' I said. 'You going to call him?' Instead of that she went in the gate and scooped him up. I waited for the claws to come out, but I guess there was some kind of love affair between them after all – he just lay in her arms like a baby and let her whisper sweet nothings.

We hiked back up the alley to Dora's and I bolted the catflap again, telling Oscar baby exactly what I thought about his unprincipled behaviour. He eyed me disdainfully, throwing temporary cupboard love overboard in favour of something a little more lasting. I poured him out some milk and slammed the saucer down.

Damn cat.

35

Unasked questions can be worrisome. Before we turned in Friday night I told Jude I needed to go out early and talk with someone, asking how she felt about having the place to herself for an hour. She said I should quit worrying, a promise was a promise and she'd still be around when I got back. I hoped I was doing the right thing believing that.

Waking early is a habit, performing my toilette in near silence is not, but Jude was still sleeping when I tippytoed out of the place next morning. I picked up the car from Dora's and drove out to Susie's place, hoping I'd chosen a good time to do that. One of the things I hadn't got around to asking when we talked was what time she got home from work mornings. Such snippets of information can be useful.

I just hoped I'd catch her up and about before she hit the sack; I felt bad dropping in that early to ask petty questions.

Petty? What was petty about them? With four people dead, checking up on things like whether or not Drury knew Stanton before they came to Bramfield seemed worth a little hassle. Susie had said that Drury ran an insurance agency as part of his financial consultancy business in Loughborough. If he'd known Stanton then ... Damn it, why didn't I ask Bethany where he'd moved from?

I turned left, skewed around a milk float, thought some more about Drury selling insurance and wondered how much arson there'd been in and around Loughborough.

When I turned into Susie's street it looked like most of the houses belonged to two and three car families, with single garage overflow taking up most of the kerbside parking. I eased into a gap four houses down and walked back. Susie's place was quiet; curtains closed and no sounds coming out. Maybe this wasn't such a good idea after all.

Even night-stackers get time off. I went round the back and found the same silence, debated whether to knock and thought better of it. If she'd been home all night, maybe she wouldn't sleep late. I gambled on that and went back to the car, telling myself if there was no movement by eight I'd give up and call back later when I'd put Jude on the train. I turned the radio on low, got comfy and caught up with the morning music.

If there's anything more boring than waiting around I don't want to know about it. I swear I only closed my eyes for a second but when I opened them it was a quarter past eight and the car in front was revving its engine and moving out.

I jerked upright, angry that I'd been so lax, opening the door and checking the mirror as I started to climb out. At which point Susie's front door opened and Stanton came out, followed a couple of seconds later by Susie herself. For a second I froze, then slid back into the driver's seat and angled the rear-view mirror so I could see them at the side of a black Mondeo acting like a loving pair. By and by, Susie shook her head then shrugged her shoulders. Stanton kissed her like he meant it and got in the car. I slid right down. A minute later he passed me by. When I checked the mirror again Susie was back in the house and I had a whole new slant on things. Facts I'd struggled with before bent themselves into interesting shapes; plots and plotters changed places in a macabre double-cross.

Susie and Stanton.

My, but my old school chum had spun me a fancy tale and I'd believed every word of it – or maybe part of it was true. Maybe Drury really had been a two-timing louse and Stanton's shoulder had been handy to cry on.

A lesson in how to get rid of a husband and make a fast profit at the same time. I wondered how they'd pulled everything together and what they'd felt like when it started to get out of hand. I tried telling myself that maybe Susie hadn't known about Billy or Jaz or Gavin, but deep down inside I knew I was struggling to hold on to an old image. Things change and people change and not always for the better. Thinking that made me sad.

I drove home filled up with anger, gathered up the milk from the doorstep and carried it upstairs, letting myself into my attic home and seeing the vac out of the closet and standing in the hall. The place was silent.

I'd been gone almost two hours and during that time Jude had been up and busy, her sofa nest dismantled and tidied away, the pile of used pots left in the sink after last night's late takeaway washed and dried, the kitchen table set for two and bread in the toaster ready to cook. The only thing missing from all the domesticity was Jude herself.

Shit!

My stomach ached with hunger and worry. I couldn't think how I'd suddenly grown so stupid or how I'd explain it all to Dora. I put the kettle to boil and turned on the toaster, then trawled the flat for a note or somesuch to tell me where she'd gone. The way I figured it she at least owed me that much.

After ten unfruitful minutes I gave up and brewed a mug of tea, buttering cold toast and chewing on it without enthusiasm. I couldn't believe she'd walked out on me again. Coming on top of Susie it was too much. Even the damn cat had dropped me from his list of friends.

Oscar!

I grabbed my bag and fished out Dora's keys, convinced I'd find Jude and the tabby together, completely forgetting how easy it is to make mistakes out of wishful thinking. I made good time to Dora's, turned in the gate, and saw Oscar on the windowsill keeping a solitary vigil. I stood quite still and looked at him, and knew that wherever Jude had gone it wasn't there.

I dealt with Oscar's needs, then went back for the car and trawled the town's streets and hideaways looking for Jude, moving the search out in a widening circle that took in the burned-out house on Turpin Street, now boarded up so solidly it'd take a wrecking crew to get in. Bramfield isn't all that big and despite picking up the same amount of aggro as Leeds on Saturday nights, it's less than half the size. After a couple of hours' fruitless searching I knew I was wasting my time. A worrisome conviction grew that this was more than just a simple disappearing trick.

The thought brought sweat back pricking my palms. Thinking of her as a runaway was bad enough; real trouble was something I didn't want to contemplate – not that I had any choice. The notion grew that something had happened while Jude was alone in the flat, something that had made her break off from what she was doing and vanish.

I don't know why it is that when things go wrong the *if* factor comes into play, like *if* I hadn't been so keen to visit Susie that morning, none of this would have happened. I guess it's a conscience ploy to induce a fast guilt trip. I closed my eyes, leaned back and looked blindly at the car roof.

I'd missed something. Events don't happen without cause. I turned the hybrid round and headed home, zipping through amber lights to get there fast and systematically search through every damn room to come up with zilch!

Failure makes a picky kind of friend.

I recited a few choice words my ladylike mother would be ashamed to hear me say, then hunkered down in the hall to phone Dora. It took her maybe a half-second to say she was coming home. I said I'd meet her at the station. She told me sharply to never mind the station, just keep on looking for Jude.

I put the phone down and wished I knew where to start doing that, staring obliquely at the vac and hauling up off my haunches to do what I should have done a long time ago.

Sometimes I can be slow!

An honest-to-god shamus like Spenser would have had the nous to take a look in the damn closet right away, but me – what do I do? I run around town wasting time, that's what.

Anger at my own stupidity engulfed me.

I'd left the box with Billy's stuff in it at the back balanced on a couple of paint tins; now it was neatly lined up at the front. I knew what had happened. Jude had tugged out the cleaner and the box had fallen over. I could picture her on her knees on the hall carpet piling everything back in and seeing something I hadn't, then hunting for a pen to leave a message I'd been too dumb to find.

I picked up the photograph of Billy standing with the fire crews and turned it over. *Dan Bush ace fire man.* Billy's hero.

Right up until then I'd thought 'fire man' was a misspelling but Jude had underlined the fire part three times and printed underneath, *This is the sod what had the carrier bag. Get it?* The pit of my stomach knotted up as I worked out where Jude had gone. It hadn't been a case of Lord deliver me up from mine enemies, but more deliver me up from mine friends. I was supposed to be the one keeping her safe, instead of which I'd provided her with the means to follow Jaz and Gavin.

I snatched up bag and jacket, left a message for Nicholls on his answering machine and went downstairs two at a time, slamming into the hybrid and leaving rubber on the road as I took off, stomach knotted with apprehension and guilt, ignoring traffic laws as I road-hogged a fast track to the fire station.

Social niceties weren't at the front of my mind as I barged in and grabbed the first body I came on. His little name badge said that he

204

was Brian Hind, and I demanded to be told where Dan Bush was. From the expression on the guy's face I guess I must have looked a little wild. He backed off. 'Not here.'

'Where then?'

'I wouldn't know, love; he's been in but you missed him.'

'How long since he left?'

'Couple of hours.' He looked at his watch. 'No, closer on four. Said he wasn't feeling too good and went off shift.' He cocked his head and measured me up. 'Don't think he'd fancy company right now if that's what you're thinking.'

It amazes me the way men have one-track minds; like this one thought I was chasing up Bush to jump his bones.

Four hours? I blanked out images I didn't want to see.

I said, 'Before he went did you see a kid hanging around. Blonde girl, white shirt, blue jeans and jacket?'

'Yeah. Yeah, I did. She came in looking for him.'

'She talked to him?'

He shrugged. 'Couldn't tell you. I had work to do.'

'Anybody else see her?'

'Look, who are you after, the kid or Dan?'

'Both. Did they go off together?'

'Hey, come on! She's too young.'

'I know that, but I'm supposed to be looking after her and . . .' I improvised rapidly, why waste a perfectly good fixation? 'Look, she's heard me talk about Dan – you know what I mean? I'm a little worried about what she might tell him.'

He winked at me broadly. 'Got it. Want me to ask the lads?'

'I'd appreciate that.'

I watched him move around asking questions. Eyes swivelled in my direction, a couple of laughs went up. I started getting impatient. *Come on!* I needed to get out of there and find her! By and by he came back with a curly-headed blond guy who stuck out his hand and said, 'Hi, I'm Kevin. You're looking for the pretty kid in jeans?'

I shook hands politely as my first confidant wandered up the stairs to Redding's empty office. I'd have taken bets he was going to get on the telephone to Bush. I turned my attention to Kevin. 'Do you know what happened to her?'

'I know she wasn't around when Dan went home. She'd been gone a while then.'

'Uh-huh. Know what she came in for?'

'Sounded like she wanted to talk about Billy – you know, the kid

205

who got put away for the arson fires?' I nodded. 'She knew he used to come down here and learn about things, then she fixed on Dan and said Billy had told her all about how good he was with fires. Dan told her we were busy and she shouldn't be there.'

'That's when she left?'

'No, he started hustling her away, but I thought he was being hard on her so I showed her the engines, told her what Billy used to do down here and talked about the routine.'

'How long did all that take?'

He shrugged. 'Half an hour, no more, then I took a tender out.'

'Bush go too?'

He shook his head. 'Not on the same crew. Anyway, it was a hoax, waste of time and energy, and when I got back he was here but the kid had gone. So wherever she is it's not with him.'

'And no one saw her go?'

'Gets pretty busy in here; I guess she either wandered off or someone turfed her out.'

'You think Bush might have done that?' He shrugged. I said, 'How many people would still be around after you took the tender out?'

'Eight or nine.' He shifted his weight. 'I've seen you here before – talking to Redding? I didn't notice you being all that friendly with Dan. You really worried what she might say to him?'

'No. I'm worried where she might be – the rest of it was a conclusion your friend jumped to.' Out of the corner of my eye I saw Brian come back down the stairs and walk away. I said, 'Look, Jude has problems and she could easily get into all kinds of trouble. I need to find her.'

He raised his voice. 'Hey, Stu – over here a minute.'

Stu reluctantly quit leaning on the engine and came over. Kevin said, 'Tell her when the kid left.'

'What for? Wasn't with Dan, that's for sure.'

I sighed. 'Believe me, I'm not interested in Dan.'

Stu looked at Kevin. Kevin said, 'It's right, she's not.'

'And I'd really appreciate hearing what happened,' I said.

'Nothing happened – except Dan got sick and tired of having her follow him round and hustled her out.'

'Which way?'

'Out the side door.'

'Did he go with her?'

'I dunno, I didn't look round. Shouldn't think so though, he was having a coffee in the canteen five or ten minutes later. Said he felt a bit off it – something he'd eaten. Be about half an hour later when he went home.'

'Either of you know where Bush lives?' They exchanged glances. I could see them closing up, protecting one of their own.

'Can't give out his address,' said Stu. 'Not allowed.'

'OK, then how can I get in touch with Redding?'

'You can't until Monday.'

This was getting me nowhere fast.

'But *you* could get him on the phone and ask if he'll talk with me,' I suggested. Stu started to shake his head. 'Come on,' I pleaded nicely, 'I'm in a real bind here. Picking up the telephone isn't going to cause a walkout.'

Kevin said, 'I don't see harm in that,' and Stu agreed grudgingly that he supposed he could ask, and moved off. I told Kevin thanks and tagged after Stu up the concrete stairs. He had his hand on the phone when all the bells in Hades went off and he ran out on me. I took a look around and wondered how to pass the time. Maybe a poke around the personnel files wouldn't go amiss, said my bad fairy. I closed the door carefully and sped over to the cabinets. It was really careless for them to be left open that way. Engines revved and started to move. I speeded up and found what I was looking for, memorising Bush's address before I closed up the drawer.

When I peeked out the door there was just one tender left behind in the big open space and Stu was on his way back to the stairs. I met him at the bottom. 'Look,' I said. 'I didn't know you'd be this busy. Don't worry about the phone call.' His face lightened up.

'I hope you find the kid,' he said.

'Oh, I will,' I told him. 'You can bet your best boots on that.' I went on out and I wished I felt as confident as I sounded.

36

When I walked out of the place there were eight crew left, apart from Stu, closing up the big red doors and looking like they'd missed out on being picked for the team. Maybe they'd get lucky and some careless nut with a chip pan would let them have a turn. Nationwide, eighty per cent of brigade call-outs are to domestic fires and twenty per cent of those start in chip pans, which tends to prove chip butties carry other hazards than a cholesterol overload.

The last of the big doors slammed. I checked the time and found I'd just lost another forty minutes. A precise little brain monitor let me know it had taken Billy no more than five minutes to dic and Jaz maybe less. I didn't even want to think what might have happened to Jude while I'd been wasting time. I stepped inside the glass BT box on the corner and punched in Nicholls's number. This time he picked up. I said, 'Ni . . .' and he cut me off impolitely.

'Leah! Whcre the hell are you?'

'If you playcd the message tape already you know that. I'm at the fire staaa . . .' I couldn't stop the word going up in a little shriek. Bush's arm draped grippingly across my shoulders and something hard shoved hurtfully into my ribs. Mouth up close to my ear he crowded in the box and said pleasantly, 'I heard you were looking for me. Put the phone down.'

Nausea swept through me. Whatever object he had in his hand it was pressing into the spot where I'd taken a bullet last year. I heard tape sounds down the phone and knew Nicholls was recording. He said quietly, 'What's happening, Leah?'

I said, 'Hi, Dan; guess one of your buddies must have rung you up. Isn't it lucky you were home?' He shoved me up against the metal box and jammed the rest down. Maybe I should mention how I bruise easily.

'Hang up,' he said.

I shrugged and did as I was told; what use was a disengaged line? 'Now what? You going to kill me on the spot or wait a while?' 'Now we walk out to your car. Passenger side. And let's take it nice and easy.' He backed out of the booth, pulling me with him, ramming me into his side with both arms neatly pinned. To a casual observer we must have looked like a couple of real lovebirds, all close and cosied up.

'Maybe you should think about this,' I said. 'If I disappear you'll be top of the question list.'

'That so?'

'That's so. One of your good buddies might be watching us right now. Stu, for example. He was on his way up to the office when I came out.'

He took a look at the window then bent his head so it nuzzled mine. 'I don't have a real lot to lose,' he said. 'So look happy.' I stretched back my lips in a skeleton smile. He swore at me and grabbed the keys, jerking back the door and shoving me in so I banged up painfully on the gear lever and half fell across the driving seat. *Shit* but that hurt. I hitched over behind the wheel as he climbed in after me, fastening up his seat belt like a good little citizen and handing over the keys. Then he let me see what was in his other hand.

I looked at the neat little snub-nosed revolver and clamped down on the urge to fall apart. 'Hard to tell a replica from the real thing these days,' I said, hearing Gran's voice telling my eight-year-old self not to let the school bully know I was scared. Things had been easier then.

'Drive.'

'Sure, where to? Disneyland? The police station? I kind of like that last idea best.'

He sat quite still and showed he wasn't the kind of man to let himself be provoked into rash moves. I was sorry about that; provoking people is about the only advantage I have. 'Drive,' he repeated.

Where we went was a disused grain warehouse on the south side of town, the whole place gaunt and windowless, bricks blackened and crumbling. On the town redevelopment plan it was scheduled like a lot of other things for demolition, the problem being that the council never seemed to get around to such insignificant body traps. The front wall peaked up into a point beneath which a rusting pulley wheel flaked away. I knew just how it felt. It wasn't the kind of building I ever got an urge to explore. I already knew what was in

210

there – rotting floorboards, spiders and rats. All of them things I'd live better without. I drove around the back the way Bush said, out of sight of everything except crumbling ruins and wasteland.

'Out!'

'I don't like these kind of places,' I said reasonably. 'How about we go somewhere a little more upbeat to talk.'

'Out.' He waved his little toy. 'And leave the keys where they are. You won't be needing them.'

'You planning on driving it back into town or is Stanton dropping by to pick you up?'

He grinned at that.

I said, 'You don't intend me getting out of this place do you?' He gave me a slow and measured shake of his head. The worms came back in my stomach. I eased out of the car and closed the door, looking at him across the roof. 'You, Stanton and Drury. Drury sniffs out the businesses that are heading for trouble – easy when he's in the Chamber of Commerce – Stanton offers them a way out and you take care of the arson. Clever. Set a whole mess of fires to cover up the real ones. Whose idea was that – yours or Stanton's?'

He grinned again and waved the gun some more. 'Better be careful,' I said. 'A bullet hole would be hard to explain.'

'What makes you think it'd be found,' he jeered. 'This place is just waiting for a match; it'll go up like a . . .'

'Pyromaniac's dream,' I cut in. 'Neat trick to set Billy up that way.'

'He set himself up hanging around and telling his history. I'm grateful to him; it saved a lot of bother.' He gave me a push. 'Inside. There's someone waiting for you.'

I said, 'Jude?'

'Who else were you looking for?'

'A psychopath, but I guess I've found him. What's it like – burning people? Gives you a high does it?' I waited for him to slap me. His hand moved in reflex but he didn't tip over the edge. I turned round and walked in front of him, up two steps to a doorless opening and on to shrunken floorboards. The place was a wreck, refuse and leaves competing with debris and bird droppings, the whole mingling into the kind of smell nobody wants to bottle. I stopped walking and looked around. 'Where is she?'

'Next floor. Keep over on the left; the stairboards are rotten.'

'And you'd just hate me to break a leg, is that it? That's really nice. Everybody has some good in them. Or maybe it's just you don't want to have to carry me.' I climbed, trying each tread cautiously, making sure it would bear weight before I moved on up. It didn't take a genius to work out I had a better chance of getting out of this alive if I stayed mobile. I got to the top and breathed in hard. *'Jude!'*

The word billowed and eddied in empty spaces, rising and echoing in the silence. The kid lifted her head; streaky dirt on her face showed she'd been crying. The sight of her tore me apart.

A vicious push sent me flying off balance, banging painfully down on to one knee and cursing. Adrenaline rose up in a surge. For a second I balanced like a sprinter, taking a fast look behind for an opportunity that wasn't there.

'End it here and now if you want,' he invited coldly. 'Far as I'm concerned timing doesn't matter.'

I got up and faced him, giving provocation one more try. 'That so?' I said rashly. 'Well, you've got problems buddy-boy. Too many people know about you, including the detective inspector I was talking to when you cut me off. Didn't think about that, did you? But why should you? You're not the brains, you're just the matches.' I held my breath. If I'd guessed wrong it was over; I was banking on a need to get physical and not just shoot. I watched his eyes fill up with anger, telegraphing his move a second before it came. His hand lifted and swung for my face. I turned as it came, deflecting some of the force but still feeling pain enough for the yell I let out to be real. I let myself collapse in an untidy little heap and whimpered, eyes smarting sufficiently to make it easy to coax up some tears.

He pointed the gun, voice thick with rage. 'Up,' he yelled. *'Get up!* Over there.'

Over there was where Jude sat on the floor, back to an upright, hands tied behind her and the rope looped around the beam. Uttering little cries I crossed the space between us and dropped to my knees, wrapping her in my arms and whispering that a few noisy tears would be a help right then. She gave out a couple of loud sniffs and started to wail. My eardrum near burst. Bush yelled for her to cut it out and I started up a few little noises of my own. Just beyond the edge of it all I heard a car engine. Shit! If that was Stanton I didn't have time to mess about.

I quit making noises and began to fiddle with the knots. Bush grabbed a handful of hair and pulled me upright. That really hurt. I'd been mad enough before but the pain from that little exercise pushed adrenaline out in a tide. He spun me round and raised his fist, gun hand down for balance, pulling back on his elbow to get more force. As his shoulder tilted back I kicked him hard on the kneecap, hearing it crack as he dropped. Howling hard enough to override the noise Jude was making, he grabbed at his knee, the gun skittering over to her feet. I got it in my hand and listened to a new set of feet coming towards the stairs. Bush sat on the floor rocking from side to side still clasping his knee, letting out little moans as he swayed. I hoped I'd broken the damn thing. I set the gun down and got to work on Jude's tether, breaking nails and cursing, setting her hands free as Stanton's head came slowly up through the rectangular stairwell. He looked at the three of us with a blank face.

Bush screamed, 'She's broke my fucking kneecap. Do something with the bitch.'

Statistically firearm offences are increasing year by year, criminals are really getting to like playing with guns, so I should have expected Stanton to have one of his own. He brought it up out of his pocket and aimed in my direction. I shoved Jude over and rolled as he fired. The bullet hit the floor right where I'd been. I skittered behind another upright.

That was close.

I looked at the thing in my hand. The only time in my life I'd ever fired a gun was down at the fairground, shooting clay pipes, but, hey, I'd seen Cagney and Lacey do it every week. I heard the hybrid start up and guessed what part Susie was supposed to play. I got the gun butt comfy in my hand and squinted round the post. 'Where's Susie supposed to leave it?' I yelled. 'Loughborough?' Stanton chipped splinters off the upright then turned the gun on Jude. Still half-hidden, I held Bush's gun in both hands and loosed off two shots.

One of them spun Stanton round and knocked him back down the stairs. From the noise I guess he forgot to keep to the left. His revolver formed a neat parabolic arc and landed six feet in front of Bush. He took a hand off his knee and threw himself forward. I could have shot him easy as apples. Instead I used one of Jack's neat little tricks, launching my bodyweight at him feet first, heels snapping into the side of his face as he touched the metal. He rolled over and lay still. I got to my knees and felt his pulse, pleased I hadn't killed him. By then Jude had got her ankles untied and between us we trussed Bush up in his own ropes and left him to sweat.

Getting back downstairs was harder than coming up. Stanton had taken most of the treads with him. I eased down carefully, stepping wide over gaps, waiting at each rest for Jude, both of us hyper-ventilating a little by the time we got to the bottom.

I took a look at Stanton and decided he wasn't going anywhere. A scarlet rose spread across his right shoulder and his left leg bent out at a freakish angle. I checked his pulse and the fast, thready beat and shallow breathing worried me; I didn't want to be responsible for another death.

I got Jude outside and went to find a phone, after which we both sat on the pavement edge and waited patiently for what was to come.

Sometimes Nicholls goes in for overkill – I tell him it'd be a good idea if he brought an ambulance and he turns up with half the riot squad. Men just have no sense of proportion. On noise alone you'd have thought he was heading for a major incident. We watched all the blue lights heading down the road towards us and shared the same thought. When Nicholls bounced over the rubble we were round the back leaning on Stanton's car and trying to look nonchalant – no sense at all in having him think we'd been having a worrying time. He squealed his wheels a little and got out on the trot. Right after him came two uniforms from a squad car and six heavies from a police van. The ambulance pulled in more sedately.

He eyed me up and down, didn't find any holes and looked a little less pinched. The paramedics opened the ambulance doors. Nicholls said, 'What happened?'

I put an arm around Jude.

'Stanton tried to kill us,' I said evenly, 'and I shot him. He isn't looking too good I think they'd better hurry.'

He said, '*Christ!* How the *hell* do you get into these things?' and set off to see for himself. I told Jude to go wait in Nicholls's car and went after him. Stanton didn't look in any better shape. The paramedics did a bit of low-voiced conferring; one went to fetch a splint.

Flat-voiced, Nicholls asked, 'Where'd you get the gun?'

'I took it off Dan Bush. He was waving it around too much.' I looked up the broken and splintered stairs. 'If you want it, it's up there – and so's he.'

'What!'

'Stanton's gun is up there too.'

He started up gingerly. I said, 'Even if you make it to the top, you won't be able to get him back down without help. Might as well wait for a ladder.' He balanced on the third tread and looked back at me.

'He need an ambulance too?'

'Might need some help. I think he broke his kneecap.' Nicholls cussed prettily and went a step higher. 'He can't get at the guns,' I told him reassuringly, 'he's sort of tied up with other things.'

214

'Any other way up there?'

I shrugged and spread my hands – did he really think I'd had time to spend looking? Tight-lipped, he went back to climbing; a third of the way up a tread gave. Putting his weight on the rail near brought the whole thing down.

I bit on an urge to say, 'I told you so,' and watched him turn round.

When he got back down he went into a huddle with one of his buddies. After a couple of seconds the buddy walked out. 'Where's he going?' I asked interestedly.

'We need a ladder.'

I'd told him that once already!

Stanton groaned as he got moved on to the neat little wheeled stretcher. I tried to feel sorry for him but it was too hard. Nicholls said ungently, 'Suppose you go sit in the car so you're not in the way?'

'Fine,' I said meekly, 'I'll just go and do that.' I started walking. He caught up and turned me around.

'Leah, did you get hurt?'

'I near got my hair wrenched out and if I hadn't ducked, Bush would have broken my jaw; apart from that and being shot at I guess I'm all right.' His eyes went all mushy on me. I said, 'Save it for tonight, huh?' and he close to bear-hugged my breath out.

It wasn't until he walked me back to his car that I remembered Susie and the hybrid. I listened to him call it in over the radio. 'Nicholls,' I reminded him mildly as he finished up. 'I'm really fond of that car – and I'd kind of like to get it back in one piece. Just tell them no high-speed chases. OK?' Then I patted his arm, got in beside Jude and thought what fun it would be to make another statement.

37

It took a while for Stanton to be in a fit state to talk and when Nicholls finally did get to question him, he tried to bluff it all out. Unfortunately, by then Bush had done his best to load everything on to Stanton's back and such tactics did no good at all.

That's the trouble with villains they've got no sense of loyalty.

Stanton and Bush had been in the arson business for the last eight years, moving around and picking up fat commissions. While they'd been operating around Loughborough, Drury gravitated towards them. He'd supplied them with potential clients and business had boomed. Then Stanton fell for Susie and between them they worked out the Fast-Sell scam. Drury had never been meant to live long enough to enjoy the profits – they were Susie's nest egg.

Things change and people change; a big part of me felt sad for the Susie I'd once known.

Nicholls found it really hard to tell me about Billy. I guess he felt partly responsible; he'd been so sure that Billy and the firebug were one and the same. For once I didn't gloat over his mistake.

Bush admitted that the kid had seemed a perfect scapegoat, but Billy had been smarter than anyone had guessed. He'd recognised Bush's voice – knew the telephone calls were coming from him – and he'd confided in Jaz, naming Bush as the real arsonist. He probably would never have told anyone else – Bush was his hero. But uncaring care assistant Gavin overheard and next day tried to blackmail Bush.

Gavin's big mistake.

Mistake number two was letting Bush in to see Billy when no one else was around. After that, Gavin Liddell was in up to his nasty neck; he couldn't go to the police without incriminating himself so he just took the money and kept quiet. Then Bush asked for a little help with Jaz and he did that too – a real sleazeball. He got just what he deserved when Bush messed with his motorbike. I guess he never realised he was swimming with sharks.

After that Bush must have thought he was home and dry and Jude's turning up had given him a nasty shock. He'd been really rattled – enough so to risk bundling her into the back of his van, using the same kind of encouragement he'd used with me. The big difference was, she'd been tied, gagged and terrified.

When Nicholls let Dora take her home, Dora pulled all the strings she could. Luckily, Social Services turned out to be not anywhere near as difficult as we'd expected. I guess Jude had run away so many times from so many places they were only too glad for Dora to take a turn, and the new fostering arrangement is working out great for the both of them.

The biggest surprise turned out to be Bethany.

I'd wondered where Nicholls had picked up his titbits on Stanton and now I knew. She'd given them to him. Undercover insurance investigator Bethany had been scared sick that my butting in was going to foul things up before she got the goods on Stanton. It's a pity she isn't staying around – we could have got to be good friends.

That just about tidies everything up except Billy's family, and they've come through it all fine. John Redding is spending an awful lot of time round there, and from the way Charlie tells it, romance is blooming. I hope that wherever Billy is, he's happy about that.

Yesterday I finally got the apology I was due from Nesbitt. It really killed him to make it, but with the BIG BOSS standing right behind him he didn't have much choice. I suggested to him politely that he put it in writing – just in case any doubts about it came up in the future. *He* said over his dead body. BIG BOSS said it'd be on my desk next morning.

Maybe I'll get it framed.